1

DREAM

by Don West

DREAM

A Dancing Bear Book by Don West

© 2019 Don West
Photos: Barbara West
Cover design: Robert Aulicino/Don West
Interior design: Mylinda Butterworth/Don West

ISBN: 978-1-59778-092-6 EBOOK
ISBN: 978-1-59778-091-9 TRADE PAPERBACK

Printed in the United States of America.
10 9 8 7 6 5 4 3 2

This book is a work of fiction. Although some of the locations in this novel are real, the characters are figments of the author's imagination and exist only between the pages of this book. Any resemblance to persons living or dead is entirely coincidental.

dancing bear books, Tucson AZ

3

for Barbara,

who not only read these words more times than should be humanly possible but was instrumental in the book's conception. For this, keeping me honest, and our incredible life together, I owe a debt of gratitude and love impossible to repay.

Coming . . .

It's the aromatic memory of the Pacific that beckons Jack and Maggie Lawrence across the dunes of the Mohave—the anticipation of the moment when that special fragrance first becomes a perceivable event, heralding a week of true escape and pure indulgence. It isn't until they make the turnoff on Interstate 5, heading for the Grand/Garnet exit several miles north, that they actually see the source of their excitation, making one of their recurrent dreams in life a recurrent reality. Usually, the smell of the ocean arrives on the wind at a different time and place along the route, as they hurtle over Interstate 8 at eighty-five miles an hour, somewhere between the coastal mountains of San Diego County and the car dealerships, movie-plexes and strip-malls of El Cajon. Led by their noses, they breeze past Ralph's Market, Fatburger and the Cold Stone Creamery heading up Mission Boulevard, towards Pacific Beach, where they'll reside in a new but familiar world—the Seaview Apartments on the cliffs overlooking the water—for an eternity that will last precisely seven glorious days.

Thursday

Chapter One

The Brightons' house was a two-story Spanish-colonial stucco, nicely situated on Callé Solar in the fashionable Palm Grove section of L.A. Unlike some of its neighbors, it sat alone up in a culde-sac, facing west, with a mission-tile roof and twin widow-walk balconies festooning its façade. Although Emma found the perfectly matched Queen Anne's palms that lined the serpentine streets of the surrounding vicinity visually tedious, as she did the houses repetitively embedded in similarly lush landscaping, the house had seemed familiar and welcoming, like a secret refuge out of one of her childhood storybooks.

Aside from those of the gardeners, painters and plumbers who arrived to work in the area every day, only a few vehicles were to be seen meandering about at any given time—mothers, mostly, taking the kids to a tennis or piano lesson. Other children rode their bikes and romped safely at the park, nestled in the center of the neighborhood, where Emma had taken the girls to play when they were young. On rare days, when the breeze blew inland hard enough to carry away the smog, she could smell the ocean, though she couldn't see it from the balcony where she stood.

Like today, storm clouds were threatening overhead on another misty May morning, seven years earlier when she and Bob first saw this house. Even before they'd come inside, she knew they were going to live here. Bob had been late to meet her then as well. He was already a half hour behind, and this was pushing it. It was just like him to twist their time into a tailspin, rushing them around in a state of panic trying to make a plane at the last minute. "Damn," Emma said and looked up at the sky, as if in supplication, when she couldn't see Bob's car coming up the street. The disappointment cut deep; it always did. No doubt, he'd blame it on the weather.

The palm fronds moved in a sudden gust of heavy air. Emma caught a fleeting scent of the sea and stepped back into the bedroom. She drew the sheers behind her and went to the mirror in the changing room to remove a mote from her eye. She wiped the tears from her lid. "Don't rub it, Emma," she whispered. "It'll just get worse if you rub it." She headed to the bathroom for the drops. Those shiny glacial-blue eyes, that she'd always considered her most striking feature, struck her today as troubled. And although the sterile solution faded the redness, it did nothing to soothe her growing irritation.

In the bedroom, she removed her robe, brushed a solitary black collar-length hair from it and packed it into one of two large Gucci cases on the bed. She was looking forward to this trip, even though it looked as if she might be doing all the packing herself. It occurred to her that she seemed to be evermore on her own lately. Well, if she was more alone, she was also more territorial.

This room had become her domain except for the bed that she and Bob shared less frequently of late; he often slept cradling the remote in front of the big-screen Sony in the entertainment room. Nevertheless, as much as she loved her house, she knew it would do them both good to

9

get away. Emma went back to the changing room for her Johnny Was, Georgette rayon and Fitigues.

It would be good to be on their own, away from the kids. Beth had become somewhat listless and uncommunicative recently. It was getting under Emma's skin. Beth found the onset of her menses embarrassing to discuss with her mother who was more than content to let Heather handle things. Unfortunately, Heather was in Europe studying art—a well-earned graduation present. Yes, indeed, two weeks' time out with Aunt Colleen and her cousins in Arizona was exactly what Beth needed right now.

Emma returned several times to Bob's closet to select suits and ties to lay out for him to consider taking with them. She also pulled from his dresser some casual wear, slacks and shirts she thought he wore well. Her cellphone startled her with its ring.

"Hi, Sweets," Bob said, before Emma had a chance to say hello.

"Where are you? We have a plane to catch in three hours, and I need you here."

"I know. Look, Hon, something's come up, and I won't be able to go with you today. Bill Collins broke his ankle and can't make the presentations in L.A. John asked me to cover, since I'm the only one scheduled with free time just now."

"But I planned the week just for us, without Beth."

"These are Bill's big hospital and HMO accounts and they've got to be serviced. We'll do the B & B another time. We still have the week of the conference."

"You promised."

"I know, Hon, but it can't be helped, sorry. Gotta go, call you later."

"Don't do this to me, Bob," she said, but he'd already switched off.

Emma floated out of the bedroom. She encountered the fiery little impasto painting called Heat, hanging at the end of the hall. Deep red, it mirrored Emma's mood precisely. She could feel the warmth rising up the back of her neck. She grit her teeth, shook her head to stop the coming tears, and fled downstairs to stand in the calming presence of her most recent acquisition, a big beautiful painting titled, Dream of the Great Blue.

Six by ten feet, Great Blue took the better part of the living room wall. She'd known that it was destined to be hers when she first saw it. It gave her an indelible sense of peace whenever she stopped long enough to look at it thoughtfully. She'd surprised Bob by removing a sofa and two end tables from the room to give the painting space to breathe. It was a new and satisfying experience.

She further surprised him when she'd told him that with her 50% gallery discount, it only cost $18,000. She'd had to give him credit—he'd been smart enough to close his mouth and keep his comments to himself at the time. It must've been the shock that struck him dumb, however, because he didn't have the good sense to leave it that way, unfortunately. He recovered a week later, in the kitchen, when Emma was preparing dinner.

"You know damn well we can't afford this painting. You think I'm made of money?" he said, opening the fridge for a Bud longneck.

"Oh, and we can afford to have that '65 Mustang of yours sitting out in the garage with the Expedition and the Porsche and the Jeep and the Harley and the canoe that you never use?" She stopped dicing the jalapeño on the black-granite countertop at the kitchen island long enough to look up at him and point the knife over her shoulder at the garage. "How many sets of wheels can two people drive at once?"

"Three people. Heather drives, and she loves the Jeep."

"Heather's in Europe, remember?"

"You know I need the Porsche for business; I have a certain image to maintain with my clients. I got the Expedition for you and Beth, the groceries and whatever else you do all day long."

She put the hot pepper in a bowl and rinsed her hands. "You're in my way," she said and waited while he moved away from the fridge. She reached in and removed the cilantro, onions and tomatoes.

"If you think I'm gonna sell the Mustang, you need to think again. You know how I feel about that car."

"Oh yes. I know you'd sell me before you'd sell that car."

"Don't be ridiculous."

"You just don't get it, or you just don't care. You never talk to me first about what I want."

"You didn't talk to me before you spent all that money last week on that monstrosity in the living room."

"You buy things you want all the time, when and wherever the mood strikes you. New golf clubs, smartphones. That monster TV in the entertainment room wasn't something that I needed." She started chopping the onions.

"What nobody needs is an $18,000 painting." He retreated a few steps beyond the range of her gestures, which seemed to be getting more emphatic with the moment, and leaned against the counter by the sink.

"That's your opinion. I need this painting. But it's interesting how we can afford the things that you want. You never deny yourself anything. Although when it comes to something I need, like this painting or season tickets to the theater or the opera, well . . ."

"You can buy all the damned tickets you want. And I don't care if you have to buy a painting, now and again, but $18,000 is a little much, don't you think?" He finished his Bud and set the empty bottle on the counter.

"Obviously not, or we wouldn't be having this conversation."

"If I could just see something in it, a landscape or a picture of something recognizable, that might be different." He took a Bud and a Stella Artois from the fridge, flipped the caps and handed the Stella to Emma. "Maybe I could understand it. But this, this . . . this abstract shit is totally incomprehensible. A three-year-old could do it. They've got monkeys and elephants doing it for Christ's sake."

She put the knife down, sipped foam from the top of the bottle and turned to face him. "You'd understand it better if you'd just come to the openings more often, learn the visual language. You'd begin to see what the artist was saying."

"Look Emma, I really don't give a fuck what most of those self-indulgent little peacocks that you and Gen show down at the Gallery have to say, much less the kind of art they make. I don't mind the symphony now and again as long as they do the 'pops' thing, but the opera? . . . might as well be cats screeching on a fence, as far as I'm concerned."

"But you should give a fuck. Those are the things that I love to do. They're inspiring."

"I get all the inspiration I need on the golf course. If I ever need more inspiration than that, I'll go to church; and you know how I feel about church."

"What about your clients, the pharmacists and doctors that you see every day? They like and support cultural events."

"Most of them don't like that crap any better than I do. It's political. They go to be seen, impress the boss, whatever. They support it for the wives, mainly, but not because they like it. You should hear what they say about it the next day, on the tee." He finished off the beer, put the empty bottle down on the counter beside her—rather more loudly than necessary, she thought—then turned his back on her and walked out of the room.

There it was, finally. He wouldn't even do it for her. She hadn't realized it at the time, but Emma began collecting art when she first sensed Bob pulling away from her, the marriage and the girls. The decision to fill the gaps in her life with paintings had not been a conscious one. It had just happened, and this was the result.

Her eyes watered, irritated more by her memories than by her mascara. In the bathroom, a tissue simply couldn't straighten out the mess she'd made of her lashes. She took a clean washcloth, held it under the hot water and then lightly cleansed her face. She reminded herself to pack some hankies. She freshened her makeup, fluffed the hair about her head, tossed several toilet articles into her vanity case on the sink, and brushed her teeth. That was as good as it was likely to get.

In the bedroom, she put Bob's clothes away—returning them, along with his bag and shoes, to the closet; let him get his own things to pack, she thought. Then, for absolutely no reason that she could think of, she paused to look at a framed snapshot of her and Bob on the day of their wedding, sitting on the dresser.

It had rained the day before, but the sun was sharp and intense, burning off the mist. The air had had an unusual clarity to it, she remembered. Although the day was bright and things appeared hopeful, it didn't show, now, in their expressions. Hers looked stunned; his, pained. There was a certain sort of resolution about them that she'd never noticed before. Staring straight at the camera and not touching, they stood alone on the church steps where she, in her lacy white veil and cocktail-length bridal dress, held a bouquet of tiny white roses with ribbons streaming down over her mid-section, as if to hide the baby—growing there at a phenomenal rate—threatening to expose their secret and embarrass their families.

Standing square-shouldered beneath his high-and-tight hoo-rah haircut, with his black pin-striped suit hanging on his tall, skinny frame, Bob held the white satin-backed folder containing the paperwork given to them by the minister—their license signed by the witnesses and a small chapbook done in calligraphy on the joys of maintaining one's marriage vows—over his crotch, a badge of honor to show the world that he would always do the right thing.

Heather's birth had prematurely curtailed their college days. Emma had dropped out, and Bob had become a legitimate drug dealer as the marijuana and cocaine of his college career became the mood elevators and Viagra of his daily grind. At the time, she'd had the oddest sensation of being numb throughout the day. She'd thought that it was just her mind playing tricks, her body's reaction to all of the premarital tension.

If only she felt as numb right now. As she looked back in time through the prism of experience, at this particular moment of her past, she could see that although they were standing next to each other, they'd been as far apart on their wedding day as any two people could possibly have been, in ways only now becoming apparent to her, eighteen years later. It was like waking from a dream.

"Emma," she said to the empty room, "this wool-gathering won't solve your problems or get your packing done." She put the photo back and went to collect some underwear from the laundry room downstairs. On the way, she stopped to give Beth a hand with her suitcase. Back in the living room, she poured herself a scotch, neat— something she didn't do very often—and sat a few minutes with her feet up, languishing in the smoky essence of the twelve-year-old liquor and gazing deeply into Great Blue.

She knew it was the last chance for them. It made her angry all over again to think about it. She slapped her thigh, sipped her drink and closed her eyes. She'd gone to some lengths—plane tickets, a reservation at the Mountain Shadows in Tucson where she'd hoped to generate some real and lasting passion between them before it was too late, dinner reservations at the Hacienda del Sol and a Crown Vic to get them around. Well, she was going anyway. This had to work. Flushed by the scotch, she felt her spirit lifting, unexpectedly, as she returned to the bedroom to finish packing. She simply would not let this gray, drizzly day get her down.

She dressed in her linen travel suit—the natural off-white color of the fabric accentuated the soft sable highlights of her hair—and called a taxi. With their luggage and an impatient Beth stowed in the cab, she walked through the house one final time to see if she'd forgotten anything. Oddly, she was heartened by her small collection of paintings; they were more empowering than ever. She stood again in front of Dream of the Great Blue, remembering the fight they'd had over the money. Yes, I paid a lot for that beauty, she thought. But when it comes to love, I've paid a lot more for a lot less.

Chapter Two

Alex Koury stepped back from the wall, cleared a space with his elbow and put his paint and brushes on the worktable. "Just look at this room," he said. Paint pots, boxes full of plastic tubes, pint jars of acrylic paints, brushes, sponges and paint buckets—in short, the entire paraphernalia of a working muralist—filled the bedroom, threatening to engulf him where he stood.

"God, I love it. Now where did I put that thermos?" He sifted through the stuff on the table. He found his cup with the blue whale on it. Dried coffee rings dropped to the stale, cold coffee at the bottom, like floors in a skyscraper— successive levels down to the basement. Not worth the effort it took to clear the door and pour it out in the bathroom, he drank down the dregs just before he uncovered the thermos beneath the table. It didn't get any better than this.

He sat on the stepladder to listen to the Gypsy Kings playing in the living room where Mary O'Brien, one of the owners of the Mountain Shadows Bed and Breakfast in Tucson, had turned up the CD player. He'd come to like their music, just as he'd come to like Mary and her husband, even though his own taste ran toward the jazz of Miles Davis and Ornette Coleman. Sipping his coffee as he listened, he realized that he'd finished the job.

Always astonished when he reached this point, miraculously back among the earthlings, he couldn't figure out where his time went. There was a sense of otherness and dissociation. He experienced the work as if he'd never seen it before. Until that very moment, it had been just a series of problems to solve—which line here, which color there—until now, when the dream became reality. He couldn't imagine he'd done it, against all evidence to the contrary. Something had taken over his body and worked this magic while he was under its spell. From the looks of the room, it must have been some kind of demon.

"It's awful quiet in here," Mary said as she poked her head through the door. She stopped there, since that was as far as it would open with a five-gallon paint bucket sitting in front of it.

"Coffee break," he said.

"I'm leaving. There's black bean soup in the crockpot, shredded cheese, onions, salsa and raspberry tea in the fridge, and a fruit compote with whipped cream. Tortillas are under the dishtowel on the counter. Warm them up in the microwave."

"Off to work, then?"

"Yep."

"Is Steve coming back today?"

"Five, five-thirty, so lock up and go out the front. Okay?"

"You got it."

"Just look at this room. He's going to be knocked out when he sees this. These murals are incredible." She paused. "By the way, I had a call from Emma Brighton, the woman Steve and I met in Hawaii. She's checking in tonight around eight, and she'll want this room. So, that means we have to get the furniture back in by no later than seven."

"I thought they were staying in the Pueblo."

"Nope. I promised her the Hacienda. Her husband won't be coming with her."

Alex sensed the anxiety she was concealing at the thought of having her first paying guests at the B & B. After a moment, he said, "Guests, that's what it's all about, right?" Then he added, "I'm done."

"I know. It's marvelous!"

"I'll be back in the morning for a final walk-through and my check. After that, I'll be out of your hair for good, okay?"

"You bet."

They enjoyed a thoughtful moment with each other, looking around the room.

"Gotta run," she said.

"Try not to kill anybody."

"Just you, if you don't get back to work and get this stuff out of here." She smiled, again, and popped out of the room as quickly as she popped in, pulling at the door that wouldn't close now with a drop cloth wedged beneath it.

Alex felt a tug of regret when she left. She shared his height, his sense of humor, his dark eyes. She had the relaxed lanky stance and self-assurance of an experienced horsewoman. He'd grown fond of watching her from the window every morning, doing her chores. She exhibited such grace and efficiency of motion while mucking out the corral and feeding the horses that, sometimes, Alex found himself just standing entranced and had to force himself back to work. Looking about, Alex understood that his time here was over now that guests were, in fact, scheduled to arrive. He put his coffee down and started to clean up, getting ready to leave another finished job and the people with whom he'd developed professional, but affectionate, working relationships. This was particularly true of the O'Briens. Intelligent, open and interested people, they'd fostered an incredible artistic experience in Alex. Mary trusted Alex's vision and backed it with her own money, armed as she was with only the vague notions of what she wanted. Foolhearted, he thought. She'd just assumed that he knew what he was doing, without so much as asking to see evidence of his previous work. When he told her his dream, she opened her mind to his vision and dared to dream it with him. For Alex, it was the first time his patron became a true collaborator. Although he had many clients for his work, the O'Briens were his first true patrons. Mary thrilled at every change; every day's accomplishment was a marvel to her.

As he gathered his tools, the customary depression of re-entry from flights of such fantasy descended upon him. Thinking about her now, he realized that he could've fallen in love with her. In fact, if he didn't know better, he could almost believe that he had. Kind, playful, joking easily about his seriousness, but never his work, Mary was attentive and relaxed in his company. He was in awe of her willingness to create her own dream and the determination she'd shown to make a go of it. For the first time in her life, she was working part-time, but she was also teaching herself to cook gourmet cuisine with recipes handed down from her grandmother. It had been Alex's good fortune that she agreed to provide his mid-day meal as part of his fee, saving him the hassle of brown-bagging every day, joking that she needed the practice before the real people got there.

Alex removed the five-gallon paint bucket from in front of the door and took his water buckets to the bathroom to pour them out. Back in the bedroom, thinking about how Mary had moved to Tucson from the East Coast with only her nursing skills, ambition and desire—how she had embraced her chosen city and taught herself to speak the local Spanish—he couldn't help but feel awe at her accomplishments. He admired her ability to change course in the middle of her life without crumbling under the fear of failure. These were qualities that Alex found attractive and desirable in a woman. Getting to know her made his longing for someone to share his life with that much more apparent and, thus, that much harder to bear. He had to admit that he envied Steve, and he wasn't comfortable envying anyone.

Alex packed the remaining paints and consolidated his tools. He finished clearing a way through the door and went out to his truck for more boxes. On the way back, he stopped to study the bronze sculpture on the porch. He had seen it every day for a month and never tired of looking at it—a desert hare with ears cocked, nostrils flaring, standing at full height, frozen in place by the blood call of the coyote. The hare was so life-like, it quivered on the cusp, poised between the unassailable paralysis of fear and its absolute imperative to run. He knew the feeling. He sometimes felt that way, staring at the blank wall on which he was supposed to begin a mural.

Susan McCarthy, the artist who'd sculpted the hare, had told him about Mary and her desire to have some wall painting done. "A few pictures," she'd said, "nothing extensive, but tasteful, to decorate a couple of the rooms that lack a certain appeal." It was just the kind of thing he hated. At least he knew someone he could recommend, if he didn't take it. Back in the room, Alex organized everything before he started hauling stuff to the truck.

Mary's directions off the highway into the surrounding chaparral had led him right to the front yard where he sat waiting, the door of his Ford pick-up open in the heat. She'd told him that she might be several minutes late and, in fact, he wasn't upset that she wasn't there. He was just dreading the whole charade. He'd done this kind of thing too many times before and would have begged off when he first talked to her on the phone, but something in her voice wouldn't let him.

The heat that day made him irritable. That, and the fact that his financial light was pretty dim at the moment, niggled at him to take a job he would have, in other straights, disdained. He slammed the door of the truck and drove away. He noticed by the clock on the dash that he'd waited just four minutes. Hoping to get out to the highway before she returned, he was a bit chagrined when her van approached slowly, giving room on the narrow gravel road. In passing, their eyes met through the glass, and he was sure that she knew who he was. He knew her. Hesitating, she flashed her taillights but didn't stop. When he got back, she was standing in the drive, keys in one hand, arms akimbo. She was dressed in jeans, boots, a western shirt with silver points on the collar and a bolo tie around her neck. Not his style at all, but it suited her. He suspected that she was as much as six years older than he, something that he didn't guess when first seeing her in the van.

"I told you I'd be late."

"Yeah, I know," he said, looking at his feet as he followed her into the house.

The meeting went as he'd assumed it would except for one thing. She showed him two bedrooms that she called the Mexican and the Anasazi rooms. He quoted her a price that he knew she'd consider excessive and probably wouldn't accept. He told her that it was not really his favorite kind of work but knew someone who might be interested. He hinted that she'd probably need to talk it over with her husband anyway, then said he'd call back in the morning to find out what she'd decided.

When he got home, he had intended to call his friend who specialized in this kind of wall decoration, but he didn't. Maybe it was because of the long ride; maybe he was unwilling to let go of the chance to make some money. Or, maybe it was the fire he'd seen in her eyes when she told him that, as the primary owner of the Mountain Shadows, she made all of the decisions and didn't need to talk to anybody, about anything. He admired the smooth passion with which she'd corrected his unwarranted assumptions.

Alex heard Mary's van, starting up outside, in the silence between the changing CDs. Looking around the room, he saw that he hadn't gotten very far in his clean up and renewed his efforts. Funny thing, that night after his first meeting with Mary, he dreamed the murals in black and white right down to the last complete detail— something that had never happened before.

He was an Anasazi boy of thirteen who was apprenticed to an aging shaman. He often traveled with his mentor to tribal gatherings; and, at one particular corn festival, he fell in love with a beautiful young girl. Because she'd been promised to an elder member of his own tribe when the man lost his wife, she would never be allowed to marry the young shaman.

As the man was an important tribal official, her parents were given the appropriate gifts, and she was given to the official; the young boy and girl were forbidden to see each other. But because the young couple couldn't be kept apart, her husband eventually took her and his children north to a distant pueblo.

The young man realized that she would never return and set off after her. Believing that she'd gone south, he traveled in that direction many days, living as he could off the meager provision that he carried. To be driven by such passion liberated him from the constraints of his reason. When he encountered others along the way, they were content—out of fear or compassion, who could say?—to offer him food, water and shelter or leave him to his reveries. In either event, he traveled unmolested through New Mexico and Arizona, into Sonora, Old Mexico.

One day, exhausted and near starved, he stumbled onto one of the largest ranches in Mexico. A great caballero on a huge Appaloosa stallion rode up behind him, followed by his entourage. The man reached down and lifted him up by the arm onto the back of the horse. They rode at full gallop into the hacienda. The man set him down in the niche of the adobe wall enclosing the courtyard, where he was told to wait. The caballero rode off, leaving behind three of his men and three of the women.

The dream didn't happen the way that Alex wrote it down and read it to Mary the next morning. In the real dream, he never saw the girl again, and she didn't fall in love with him, even though she liked him. She was much more interested in the powerful man who'd lost his wife and feared losing him to a prettier and younger girl of her tribe. The dream was unusual because it was colorless. The Pueblo and the Hacienda were so vivid in his mind, in the stark contrast of black and white, that they gave rise to the story. His usual dreams were in color, much less coherent, and disjointedly rife with incomprehensible images and bizarre happenings.

For instance, in the dream itself, the fact that shamans as a group were notoriously hermetic—not the marrying kind—didn't occur to him. But upon waking, it popped perfectly realized into his head—the answer to the problem of Mary's bedrooms. Alex knew the pueblos in northern Arizona and New Mexico, and his experience of them had given flesh and bone to his vision. It was just what Mary O'Brien needed, although she didn't know it at the time. But the thing Alex didn't tell her was that he had dreamed that she was the young girl with whom he fell in love, and it had left him bereft when he woke in the morning. Dreaming answers wasn't uncommon behavior for Alex. He'd long since learned to trust his instincts. Casting his problems into the sea of his subconscious before he drifted off to sleep at night usually hooked him some answers by morning. It was a simple matter to reel them in the following day. What Alex found unusual was the fact that he didn't set out to solve her problems.

It was only the following morning, when he woke with his visions, that he considered for the first time the actual possibility of doing the murals. Alex knew that the B & B didn't need decoration depicting romantic locales adorning its walls. It needed accommodations that would give the visitor a true sense of place, the same vivid sense of being there that Alex had experienced in his dream. It begged for something so unique that the environments, as he now conceived of them, would lure the people back and draw others for the first time. He also knew that people needed to feel a sense of their own humanity—something these murals expressed in abundance. If he painted them convincingly enough, he knew the guests would be transported beyond themselves into participating in the dream-like world that he'd created.

He remembered showing up to work that first day. There were no drawings. He worked from the dream images in his head. Just before he began, he thought, What if I've gotten in too deep? What if I blow it?

Chapter Three

Late Thursday afternoon, Jack and Maggie stand on the sloping sands of Pacific beach tossing the last of their bread heels to a flock of squawking gulls. The birds, of which there are three or four different species fluttering about them—impossible to tell at a glance how many in all the commotion—go about their evolutionary imperative to determine some sort of pecking order while fighting

for the bread. Jack and Maggie have long ago worked out a pecking order of their own. To their chagrin, when the bread is gone, so are the birds.

"Ingrates," Jack says and bends to grab the back of his legs.

Maggie, already bent double and patting the sand with both palms, scrambles sideways, like a crab, to get out of Jack's way and give him more room to stretch his hamstrings. "Need the whole beach, or mind if I stretch out here next to you?" she grouses.

"Oh, sorry," he says and scoots sideways, until it almost looks as if they are not together.

The stretching commences in earnest; minutes later, they stand jaws agape, tapping their toes on the sand, exercising their shin muscles, trying to absorb as much of the sunny ocean ambiance as possible. Totally ecstatic, Jack and Maggie are transfixed by the heady atmosphere of rotting kelp, the music of rocks tumbling about in underwater tidal depressions and the soothing mist of ceaseless rolling boomers thundering on the beach. They finish their warm-up with arms akimbo in a flourish of torso twisting.

Starting a brisk pace south along the crest of the shingle, Jack takes the waterside so he can talk to her good ear without having to shout. For some reason, walking cliff-side, as he will on their return, he finds much more uncomfortable. They glide up and down, following the vagaries of the shoreline. Occasionally they split apart, sidestepping piles of seaweed and the fated half-eaten carcasses from the sundry mix of unfortunate creatures inevitably washed up on the tide. They walk where the surf retreats—where the clear green water disappears into the glassy beach and blotches the variegated sand with foam.

"You want to know what would make me happier?" Maggie asks after a quarter mile of steady exertion.

"Ah, let's see—the full moon, a blanket of stars, a bottle of Pinot Noir and Tom Hardy," he says.

"Ha-ha. You want to know or not?" She gives him the look.

"I know what you want—the same thing I want—to come here whenever the mood strikes."

"That's it—to have enough money to be able to come here on a whim."

"We always get this way. We've had this conversation how many times now?"

"Too many."

"Right. And how long have we been coming here?"

"Fifteen years or so, I suppose. One year we came over three times, remember?"

"Yes, it was great. But the point is that things never change. Unless we can scare up a way to make more moolah, my little woman, we can't come here whenever we want, no matter how much we like it."

They pass a teenage couple going in the opposite direction, embracing each other, unmindful of the world around them. Maggie smiles, then frowns, remembering how it felt to be young and in love. She misses the feeling, being married so long to one man.

"Get on you loafers," Jack says as he flaps his arms, shooing a flock of resting gulls into the air. At one point farther along, they slow down and wander around an uncommonly rich bed of seashells, pausing periodically to examine some individual jewel or other.

"So what are we going to do?" she continues.

"Head for that bathroom," he says and begins to walk in that direction, indicating the lifeguard station clustered among the shops along this part of Mission Beach.

The shops sell everything from sunscreen to designer beachwear, from sno-cones and cotton candy to boogie boards and frogman flippers. There are restaurants, bars and grills, and even a guy with purple hair in a little shack, specializing in fish tacos. One year, there was an artist painting beach scenes in a tiny studio shop, too small to live in, who was gone the following year. Would Jack fare any better? He'd have to paint by the numbers. On the other hand, maybe he's getting too cynical. Maybe there's just no market here for art of any kind, good, bad or otherwise.

Standing at the urinal, he hates that the muscles of his prostate won't shut down his urethra as easy as they once did. Seepage in the pipes, dampening his boxers after putting his boy away, gets damned irritating—though not, he admits, as irritating as the hemorrhoids. Squeezing and shaking, he's reminded of the Chink—a character in a Tom Robbins novel who would whip out his wanger and shake it vigorously at some unsuspecting young woman, whenever he got the chance. It's a gesture not as graceful as some, but one that expresses certain of Jack's feelings with concision. Somehow, if he could just shake his wanger at it, the world might become a somewhat better place than it had been before—he thinks.

True or not, ever since Jack read the Robbins book, he shakes his at Maggie at every opportunity, appropriate or otherwise. He likes to shake it at her in the morning, especially if she's distracted or in a hurry and on her way out the door. Sometimes she calls in late and comes back to bed. At other times, she says, "Don't even start that with me, Horndog, I'm already late." Still, he catches her attention, slows her tempo down for just the moment. If nothing else, it always makes her smile. Yeah, right. She just thinks it's funny to look at. He's fooling himself and has been all these years. Well, maybe.

Waiting outside on the boardwalk, watching a group of sexy young women go by in their spicy thong bikinis, he'd like to shake his wanger at them, but he knows it wouldn't elicit the same response that it does from Maggie. This must be what it's like, he thinks, turning into a dirty old man.

Maggie is sitting in the ladies' room, doing her Kegel exercises to keep the muscles down there tight for Jack. She reads about such things in the women's fitness-zines that she finds in the rack at Barnes and Noble. It helps her hold her water as well. She can walk much farther along the beach without having to stop and pee every ten minutes, and she can practice these movements anytime, anywhere, and nobody knows but her. She hates exertion in general. Jack's always pestering her to exercise, to do upper body training with weights or aerobics, which she does under protest.

"You don't want those old lady turkey wattles hanging from your deltoids, do you?" But she knows what he's saying, even if he doesn't; he just can't stand to see her getting older. The thought of growing older makes him crazy. He has mentioned that they should stockpile some pills for when they can't take care of themselves any longer. She doesn't like it any more than he does; but what can she do? She exercises, although she'd never tell him that she does these exercises; she'd never hear the end of it.

Of course, there are other benefits, looks of admiration, fitting into her suit without all of the flab hanging over. Since she and Jack have been working out, they feel so much stronger. The seven-hour drive from Tucson is not as hard on them. Without last year's excess fat, they have more energy and their sex life has improved. She would never have thought that it would get better with the years. She even has more interest in checking out men's bodies on the beach. Jack's always telling her, "Now don't look at those muscles over there; I don't want you to be disappointed," or "Did you see the muscles on that guy? I'll bet his dick's about as big as my little finger," as he holds it up to show her just how big his little finger is.

When she leaves the restroom, she spies Jack ogling the girls. It no longer bothers her, though she'd never show him even if it did. Over the past few years, Jack has begun to open up about his desires and thoughts regarding the sexual nature of humans, males in particular, trying to deal with the feelings he has by sharing them with her. Sometimes, she wishes he wouldn't, but she knows it's one of his ways of growing closer and never discourages him.

"What took you so long?" he asks. "Twiddling your twinkie?"

"I was just thinking we could stop at The Sundowner one day this week and have oysters for dinner."

"Sounds good to me."

Dodging the skaters and cyclists, they make their way down the concrete boardwalk and pass through an opening in the surf wall, resuming their trek south along the beach. Jack recognizes that they've walked two and a half miles from the Seaview Apartments and, in a somewhat contemplative mood, appropriates the moment to inspect a shell that he's taken from his pocket. "You could do something with your photographs, you know—postcards, magazines, maybe book covers." He knows better than to say it in the first place but doesn't feel quite right about changing the script on Maggie at this late date.

"Have to sell a boatload of cards. Besides, I don't like the idea of doing my photography for money. I've told you that before."

"I know. You're a dilettante."

"I do what makes me happy."

They walk at a more leisurely gait, now that time seems to have been suspended. Jack flicks a broken sand dollar into the surf.

"Oh hell, I don't know what to do," he says. "There's no market for my work unless I decide to devote my life to painting romantic pictures of the San Xavier Mission. Spare me, O Lord; show mercy upon my soul. I need something to really inspire me. Maybe I should go back to mural painting. Why did I ever give it up in the first place?"

"You missed me too much. Besides, to hear you tell it, it's a younger man's game."

"Oh yeah. I forgot. So, what then? How about we collaborate on some kind of beach book project—you know, photo-collage or a coffee-table book with your photos and my paintings or drawings. At least it's something we can do for the money."

"I'm not sure I like that idea."

"Hey, look at this."

"What?" She turns back to see why he's lagging behind.

"I don't know. Looks like a shark's tooth." The asymmetrical triangular shape registers in Jack's eye, marked by its incongruity within the field of identically round, jet-black stones that litter the beach in this particular spot. He stoops, picks it up and hands it to her.

"You know," she says after several moments of close examination, "I think it's going to rain again this week."

"You may be right," he says, spying a bank of ominous-looking clouds passing inland from the northwest. "By the way, you can return that now—if you don't mind."

He looks back up the beach, gauging the distance they've come.

"But I want to keep it," she wheedles.

He turns back to her for the tooth, but she's already taken off for the Jetty at a much faster clip—with the tooth dropped safely into her pocket.

Friday

Chapter Four

For the first time in years, Emma awoke feeling like a child on Saturday morning with no school ahead of her. Though it was only Friday, she had the beautiful spring day before her and an uncommon sense of freedom. She could just lie here alone in this huge bed. She had no kids to keep up with, no gallery to think about, no husband to get off to work and, best of all, no guilt about any of it.

Her visit with Colleen and her brother the night before was unplanned, uninhibited and long overdue. It's funny how other people can see things in one's life that one didn't even suspect about oneself. How could she have lived nineteen years with one man and not known that she didn't love him?—that she never truly did. In the end, there was no one to blame but herself. What did she expect when she went through life asleep?—letting the world lead her around in her routines, doing just what others thought was the right thing for her to do.

She and Bob had a lot to talk about when they returned to L.A., but not today. For now, she'd left the rain behind. Beth had slipped right into the family as if she'd been living there her whole life. There was a truce between them; Emma was grateful and hoped it would last. She spread her arms and legs and made an angel in the snowy white sheets of the giant California king. She smiled; it just felt too good to indulge herself in a bad mood.

An hour later, Emma woke again—this time to the sound of a truck pulling up outside. As she listened to the vehicle's motor shutting off, she studied the murals around her. She'd looked at them last night, of course, but had seen them through a veil of exhaustion. Emma had arrived two-and-a-half-hours late. By the time she'd checked in, made her apologies to Mary and Steve and went to bed, it was past midnight.

But when she'd switched out the lights, the starry sky blazed to life on the ceiling, overhead. Strangely enough, it took her breath away and gave her a sense of her own smallness in the immensity of the universe—the same sensation she'd had as a little girl when her father would point out the Big Dipper, the Pleides, Orion or any one of those easy to find constellations that made her fall in love with the sky. Who would've thought phosphorescent paint stippled to the ceiling could be so beautiful?

Although the stars had stopped blazing overhead, the midmorning light of a beautiful Sonoran spring day filtered through the curtains of the window. She had slept surrounded by murals: The courtyard was enclosed by an adobe wall that joined the house. Beyond the wall were the village casitas, the church, the cornfield and the corrals where the vaqueros put away the horses. On the other side of the room, in the well yard and the outdoor kitchen, were the women, dressed in their colorful skirts and flounce blouses—all painted in vibrant color.

It was an astounding illusion, so enigmatic and evocative—a night scene of trees moving softly in the breeze beneath a pale red glow, silhouetting the mountains. The intriguing vision propelled Emma out of bed, her heart beating to the rhythms of the composition of the paintings. The brilliance of the forms, lines and colors excited her passions. But without warning, something ambiguous, something she had not felt for years transformed those prosaic images before her into a sad but profound commentary on the complexities and inadequacies of her life. Struck by the marvelous simplicity of the rendition, she realized that her own life was not as straightforward, as simple, or as happy as the lives of the women depicted in the murals appeared to be.

The man knew what he was doing, she thought. Oh, the painter was a man all right. She knew by the muscularity of the style, the robust sensuality and desire expressed so clearly and economically. He was a man with a vision, a man who could see beneath the surface into the hearts of things—a man who wouldn't lie or hide his feelings. He loved and respected women. He probably knew more about the hearts of women than many of them knew about themselves. It was all there in front of her. The women in these murals were strong and enduring, capable of great passion and tenderness. He had seen it all, and now he had shown it to her.

Mary O'Brien was the woman holding the cat—the only creature in the mural that was looking directly at her— not a portrait of Mary, but her profiled essence. Emma walked over and touched the cat as if to pet it. Across the room, men were at work: A man coiled ropes; a man stood head down in contemplation; the last intently watched the horizon as if he searched for someone or something beyond his perceptions. They were projections from the heart, soul and mind of the painter.

The images swirled through her consciousness—an awakening of sorts—making her tingle with the mystery and improbability of it all: a young boy sleeping in the niche of the adobe wall, the field of tasseled corn bordering the road leading to a pass in the mountains. Was that an escape? What was he waiting for? Who would come down that road? How long had he slept? How long would he wait, asleep in the twilight? How long had Emma slept? She shook herself loose, feeling flush and wanting, but what? She grabbed her long flannel robe, stepped into her slippers and headed for the bathroom.

On her way back from the kitchen, passing through the dining room with her coffee, she stopped at the table to peel an orange and look out the French doors. Down by the corrals, a thin dark-haired man was speaking to Mary. Emma assumed that he was the man who painted the murals. Something in his posture was familiar—the way he leaned so casually with his arms across the fence and one foot upon the bottom rail. He was tall, wide-shouldered with long chestnut hair hanging over the collar of his shirt. Emma felt the throbbing of her heart, as it pushed blood up through her neck. Not an unpleasant sensation, she thought, touching the pulse at the base of her throat.

She ate the last segment of her orange, wiped the sweet, sticky juice from her chin and licked her fingers. Emma had to meet this man. She grabbed her vanity case, took it into the bathroom and began to fill the tub. She slipped out of her robe. But on an impulse, before taking off her nightgown, she headed back to the kitchen to freshen her coffee.

Stepping around the corner, she was surprised by the man from the corral standing there with a thermos in one hand, filling his cup in the other. Her first thought was that he looked like Keanu Reeves. Now she thought that he was rather more handsome than Keanu Reeves. She realized that he was admiring her form through the clingy silk of her nightgown.

"You must be Emma, Mary's first guest," he said, smiling down at her as she covered her breasts with her arms, holding the cup out in front of her without realizing. He leaned in close and slowly poured coffee into her cup.

"Cream and sugar?" he asked.

"Just cream," she said, looking up, trying to decipher the look on his face. He had large white teeth and a slender gold ring piercing his right nostril. "Oh, the water," she cried, setting her cup down on the table and running from the room."

Emma was flushed by the steam rising from the tub, or was it by the appreciative look in his eye? She patted her face with a cool damp facecloth, slipped back into her robe and went out to the dining room. He was setting out a dish of pastries and a bowl of fruit on the table. He pulled out a chair as she approached.

"You must be the man who painted those wonderful murals in my bedroom."

"The clothes give me away, I'm afraid. Alex Koury." He reached over and shook her hand.

"Emma Brighton, Mary's first guest. You're quite an artist." She was surprised at her own reluctance to let go of his hand. "So, where'd you get the ideas for those murals, if you don't mind my asking?"

"Not at all. Now, let me see—Mary had some thoughts about what she wanted, of course, but then I had a dream."

"Easy as that?" Emma sensed his interest in her and was flattered. She could feel her cheeks flushing again. What's with all this cheek flushing? she wondered. It's not as if she wasn't used to speaking to strange men, working in an art gallery as she did.

"Well, not quite, but in a way, yes."

She wondered if he could sense her excitement. His attention seemed focused on her, and only her. They stood silent for a moment.

"Hey, how about that coffee?" he said.

Emma retrieved the cup that he had poured, took a Danish, then sat at the table across from him. He was pouring cream into his cup. She couldn't stop looking at him, even though she didn't want to appear too interested. He appeared to be at ease, and it made her feel comfortable to be in his presence. He smiled at her; the warmth of it spread across her like the sunrise.

"Do I amuse you?" she asked.

"It's just this image I had of us meeting here just now."

"Are you going to tell me?"

"Maybe, when I get to know you better."

"What makes you think you'll get to know me at all? I doubt that I'll be here that long."

"Yes, you do have a point there, I see. Then again, who really knows where and how things come about?—or where they will lead?"

"Okay. But for the sake of convenience, why not just assume that you already know me better, and we can go from there?" She thought, My, oh my, what's got into me?—a tad too forward, maybe? She felt a blush rise and tried to ignore it.

"Well, all right, if you insist. It was just an image—you know—a couple of coyotes and how they greet each other, like all canines."

A bit impertinent, a little crude, Emma thought, especially when meeting someone for the first time. But then, it was an apt image—she had to admit—the two of them sniffing around each other like a couple of dogs. Apparently he was comfortable with her, and that made her feel just fine. She laughed. "You're right," she said. "It is kind of like that, isn't it? So, what happens now?"

"Why don't you tell me about yourself?"

"Really? Just like that? I don't want to bore you to death." His grin was infectious. "Well, okay," she said and laughed again. "What would you like to know? There's not a whole lot to tell."

"In that case, you must tell me everything."

"You first," she said and smiled.

Later, as Emma cleared the table and put their cups in the sink, Alex sketched a map for her.

"Alex, I thought you were leaving an hour ago," Mary said as she came in through the dining room doors.

"I was. I guess I was waylaid. Has it been that long? I'd better run." He turned to Emma. "I'll see you at the studio at one, then." He stood, pushed in his chair, and felt for the keys in his pocket.

"I'll be there, if I don't get lost," she said.

"The number's on that map; just call me if you do."

"Don't forget this," Mary said, rinsing his blue whale cup in the sink.

"Let me know what you and Steve decide about your opening. Send me some invitations that I can mail to friends. I'm not sure I can be here with my Seattle gig coming up so soon, but I'll try."

"You have your check?" she asked, handing him the cup.

Alex tapped his shirt pocket and smiled. "Adios ladies," he said. He crossed to the door and closed it behind him on his way out.

"He doesn't like talking about his work, does he?" Emma said. "An interesting man, but then I've met interesting men before, and a good many of them were dogs. And an artist, besides. You know the kind of reputation that some artists have—they move around a lot. I've seen his kind before, a wolf in sheep's clothing. He's quite the flirt, you know. Have you known him long?"

"Well, actually no; we just met him a couple of months ago. But I feel like I've known him for years, and he doesn't strike me as wolfish. Although, I do think he's a hotty who likes to let his work speak for itself." Mary grabbed a cup from the rack over the counter and joined Emma, who pushed the thermos across the table. "And yes, he is an interesting man. There's more to him than that handsome face and scrumptious tush." She poured the last of the coffee into her cup.

"Mary!" Emma gave Mary a penetrating, wide-eyed look.

"Well, it is scrumptious. So there. Now, never mind and tell me—What did you two have to talk about all that time?"

"Let's see . . . pleasantries mostly. He told me about growing up on the Atlantic and how much he loved to sail. His father taught him, and he hoped to teach his son, Josh. We talked about his mural project in Seattle and how much he looked forward to getting back on the water. Of course, his art, the murals. It went by so fast. I felt like I was prying when I asked about his painting. I finally got him to invite me to look at his studio work. I thought I would go. Maybe he'd be a good fit for the gallery. We can always use another good painter. Think I'll need a chaperone? He doesn't seem old enough to be able to paint so well, does he?"

Simultaneously, they both looked out the French doors. The sun was still rising over the Catalinas.

"He's thirty-five . . . just a babe," Mary said. "And if you ask me, I think he's the one who might need the chaperone." They looked back at each other and laughed right out loud.

All the way back from the Mountain Shadows, Alex's anxiety was giving him the fits; it was something he wasn't used to and didn't like. He'd been in these situations before. A dealer was coming to look at his paintings, and a good-looking one at that. He couldn't get the image of her standing there, trying to cover her voluptuous body, out of his head.

Some dealer, he thought. They should all smell so good. Maybe if they did, he'd be more inclined to pursue that end of the business. "Nah!" He liked his mural work too much to start into hassling with galleries again. He caught himself speeding. He had a straight shot downtown, so it was easy to let his mind wander and his foot get heavy. It was even easier this morning.

"God, she's gorgeous," he said off the top of his head to the guy who went speeding by in a red truck, singing at the top of his lungs. Yeah, well, maybe her nose was too big, if she was thinking about becoming a fashion model. Besides, she wasn't the true model type. Classic beauty or otherwise, he must admit, he'd like to see more. There were some serious curves in that terrain.

"Get your mind back on business. She's a dealer and married at that." Alex had had too much coffee. He felt the caffeine buzzing in his brain. With the excitement of the morning, he couldn't hold on to his serenity. He was just too damned elated.

It must have been the coffee doing all that talking back at the B & B. It had been a long time since he'd found anyone he could just sit and talk to like that except for Mary; and she didn't count because she was already taken.

But then, so was Emma. He frowned. "Emma," he said to no one in particular, just trying out the sound of her name on his ear. Alex looked around to see if anyone had caught him talking to himself. He laughed at caring about what someone else might think. He wasn't used to this. She did seem interested in him, although something wasn't right and he couldn't quite put his finger on it. Did she have some kind of hidden agenda? He had sensed something vague and disturbing but couldn't tell if it was vague and disturbing to him, or her, or both.

He'd met female dealers before, sharks, worse than men when it came to using artists. They made him nervous. Every artist he knew had a horror story about some dealer who'd taken the artist for time, money or work. He wasn't naïve about the art business, but Emma didn't appear to be motivated by such mundane matters. That was why he had to be careful. Her interest in art seemed a genuine interest, more so than many others he'd encountered. But he'd been fooled before. He just hated to think that he could be fooled again, especially in this particular case.

Not usually paranoid about reaction to his artwork, he found that he had a concern for her opinion that he could not have foreseen. He was unsure why this was so, given what little time they'd spent in each other's company, but there it was. Maybe she'd convinced him that she knew good work when she saw it. She'd had a strong and positive reaction to the murals. She talked a good game. More than likely, it was the image of her standing there—trying to hide her erect nipples. In either case, it was unusual for Alex.

It wasn't every day he met a dealer who was dressed in a see-through blue nightgown. He was, on most occasions, quite adept when it came to reading other people's motivations; with Emma, he had come up against something that was jamming his receptors. Maybe it was the coffee or the lack of food. There was an unusual electric quality in the air this morning; it had him almost unable to keep his seat while he drove. Traffic was bad in this town and that was contributing to this crackling, unsettled feeling. Alex turned into the bank's drive-through window three blocks from his studio and deposited his check without waiting—none too soon.

This would go a long way to keeping him in frijoles and rice for the next two months while he was working on his mural commission in Seattle. It would give him time to spend with Josh, in Texas, before he went. They had too little time together—traveling, as he did, from commission to commission and to his annual gallery show in Denver. He couldn't live on what they sold in Denver, but an occasional four or five thousand dollars a year made his life a little easier between commissions.

Fortunately, mural work had picked up over the past five years. He was making his travel and living expenses and child support payments. He was even putting a little bit aside. He had respectable earnings—not as much as he'd like, maybe, but then he had no solid complaints. His life was simple, his desires few. Someone hit the horn and flew past Alex in a black Camaro. Another horn went off, and Alex realized that he'd let up on the throttle—drifting, thinking about Josh and his work.

Back at the studio, downtown, he rushed around cleaning up the kitchen and putting his tools away. In the loft, he straightened out his meditation corner—he kept a small bronze Buddha to remind him that this too shall pass. But not only that, it was a beautiful little sculpture, and he could appreciate the work. Sitting in meditation made him feel balanced; he could've used a session right then.

Living in the same space with his work, he had to keep the place at least halfway organized. He'd been a bit lax lately, working every day out at the O'Briens'. Of course, his need for organization changed with the job demands of the moment. When at work in the studio, in the powerful clutches of his Muse, he was not responsible for the complete wreck that ensued—usually awaking from his reverie, four or five weeks later, with a dozen new paintings and nowhere to stand.

Nevertheless, he didn't want Emma to think him a complete slob. Well, slob or not, the place would have to do as it was, there was no sense giving Emma the wrong impression about who he was and how he lived his life. Besides, it wasn't really very bad to begin with. He would've painted the walls so they could view the paintings without distraction, but he didn't have time. Now, what work would he show Emma? The bell on the front door rang its tinny peal.

He went downstairs into the display area where he spotted Emma through the glass front of the building. She appeared nervous but was smiling, and he smiled back. "I'm glad you found me," he said, unlocking the front door. "1:00 on the dot."

"I am punctual," she said. Stepping in, she was confronted by a large horizontal painting on the central display wall. Similarly sized vertical paintings hung on both end-walls. Emma noticed they were all related in style. "These are not yours," she said.

"No, they belong to Randy Whetstone. Local painters can hang their work here. I like to show them. It's some exposure, for all the good it does in this town. And Randy's a friend who studio-sits when I'm doing a commission elsewhere. Come on, it's too hot out here."

The sun was burning through the glass in typical May fashion, and the swamp box was having a deplorable time moving the air around. Alex held back a curtain at the end of the display wall, and Emma passed through into the back where she noticed the temperature was quite a bit lower. "Do you like Randy's painting?" he asked. When she didn't answer his question at once, he prompted, "You can be honest."

"Well, it's not bad work."

"But would you hang it in your gallery?"

"No, but then we already have more accomplished painters doing this type of work, not to sound judgmental, sorry."

Emma found herself in a large open area. Both walls were paint-spattered in the shapes of the canvases that had been painted there. A broad staircase climbed the wall into the loft that spanned the width of the room. Above that, a skylight—large enough to park a truck in—flooded the area below in a natural, diffuse light. Beneath the loft was a small kitchen arrangement. Beyond that, paintings were stored in racks.

"Well, you're right. There are better painters doing that type of work. I just wondered what you would say."

"You told me to be honest."

"I did, indeed."

"Then, I don't make the final selection for the gallery. I do most of the screening, but we rarely take on new people. When we do, we don't do it lightly. We're very loyal to our stable of artists, and it takes lots of time, energy and resources to find them the right market."

"Can I get you anything?"

"Water, please."

While Alex was getting some ice, Emma investigated the space. Following a small group of abstract landscapes along the wall, she traveled up the steps into the loft where her attention was captured by the intriguing bronze Buddha. The redolent mix of incense and oil paint, burnt amber and burnt umber, permeated the room. Beneath the skylight's frosted glass, within it's shafted illumination, invisible motes of dust flared into life, flashing like novae for a brief, silent instance, before drifting extinguished into shadow.

She imagined what it would be like to spend some time here. "Very pleasant," she said as she descended to the foot of the steps where Alex was waiting for her. He handed her a glass of water. His gaze put Emma at ease, although his eyes, nearly the same color as his hair, had a compelling, almost unsettling, way of peering into her. He lingered a moment, looking at her lips. She wondered what he was thinking.

"I love this place," he said, changing gears and turning away. "It made a professional painter out of me. I was in the neighborhood before the city designated it 'the arts district,' and landlords began raising rents. While I was still married to Jennifer, we decided I needed professional workspace. We bought the place, thinking all the while that we'd probably never be able to hang on to it."

"It's a great space. Were you married long?"

"Ten years. When we divorced, I took over the debt in full and have been scrambling ever since. I worked as a scene painter for movies, opera, theater and ballet and became a muralist in the process. Before that, I was an easel painter and a house painter. Fortunately, my mural reputation took hold, and I gave up house painting. When I moved in here, my work grew not only in size, but also in breadth, depth and meaning. I learned the joys and sorrows of studio life. But I'm sure you don't want to know all about that."

She did want to know, but she only smiled, enigmatically. "May I see some more of your paintings?"

"Of course." He put his water on the table and headed for the storage rack.

For the next three hours, they studied his paintings. Alex removed them carefully from the racks. Emma helped to hang them. Then they looked. Each one took its own time. Her presence made them better, somehow, than he remembered them. He was unused to the sounds of laughter, surprise and delight in the studio. There was also quiet contemplation, sumptuousness of vision, perception and animation. They argued and conceded, thrust and parried, took a quick move up to see more thoroughly some intriguing detail, and a slow move back to get a better look at the overall picture. In the process, some lines were drawn, some lines were crossed and some lines were erased altogether. As the sun traversed the skylight overhead, promenading to the music of the spheres, they danced below, to the rhythms of color, line and form. Fading incandescence dimmed the corners of the room. Alex was the first to let go. Emma stepped back in the hush of the moment, unsure of what to do with her hands.

"Are there no more?"

"Oh yes, but I can't show them to you," he said, tapping the side of his skull with his forefinger and smiling. "How about something to eat instead?"

She looked down at the watch on her wrist. "Oh, look at the time," she said. "Well, why not? I owe you after all that."

Emma picked up her bag and stepped outside before Alex closed up. They walked down the street in rush-hour heat. At the Café Arles—over Greek salad, hummus, pita bread and a half-bottle of Merlot—they discussed the differences between easel and mural painting. Emma was drawn to Alex as he described the murals in the vicinity and insisted that he be allowed to show them to her. Under the influence of the wine, and in the afterglow of the studio visit, she agreed to go with him, even while sensing the possible danger of entanglement with someone who, she realized, she didn't really know all that well.

Together, they convinced Marti, one of the owners of the cafe, to fix them a picnic basket to pick up in the morning. As Marti waited their table, Emma had the insistent impression that she'd met her somewhere before, although she knew she hadn't. When they were leaving, she finally recognized that Marti was the woman in the mural who placed a bowl of fruit on the adobe wall. She had, of course, seen portraits before, but Emma assumed that Marti didn't know that she lived on in a second life, as a figure in a painting. Marti had been his inspiration, his Muse.

"A penny for your thoughts," Alex said.

"I haven't heard that phrase in a long time—just noticing Marti is the woman in the painting in my room."

"Oh, are you now? Very perceptive."

Emma insisted on paying the bill, although Alex made a good show of being offended that a woman should pay for him. She sensed that he enjoyed teasing her.

With rush hour over, Emma relished walking with Alex in the comparative silence.

"May I ask you a personal question? And please, tell me if it's none of my business. I'd like to know—" Emma stopped.

He stopped with her. "Yes, go on," he said.

She noticed Alex enjoying her embarrassment.

"Well . . . are you in love with her? I can't believe I said that. I didn't mean it the way it sounded . . . it just slipped out." She could feel her ears glowing red.

"It's okay, not a problem."

"What's the connection, for you, between the mural figure and Marti? According to the history books, artists often sleep with their models. Oh damn, I mean—I was just wondering what prompted your rendering of her? She's very beautiful. I could see how you might be in love with her. You seem very close. I've investigated some of these ideas before, but it always seems to come down to unanswerable questions about what's at the root of artistic creation. You know, all that stuff about the Muse. I guess you think me terribly naïve, or nosy."

"Not at all," he said.

They resumed their walk.

"Well, a little nosy maybe." He smiled. "But you see, it's like this. If I were to make a pass at Marti, her girlfriend Pris—who, by the way, made your meal tonight—would kick my ass from here to Timbuktu and back again. Pardon my language, but Marti and Pris are friends of mine who started out with the café about the same time I took over the building and . . . well, I've eaten one or two meals there—on the cuff—when I needed to. Marti has always served them. So it was natural, you see? My work comes direct from my life experience is all."

Emma felt her ears burning again and wondered what it meant, if anything, that Mary was also a figure in the mural. "I seem to have put my foot in my mouth all the way up to the knee," she said.

"Don't you believe it for a moment," he said.

They stopped at the side of her rented Crown Vic. Emma took out the keys, opened the door, tossed her bag into the car and turned back to Alex. His scent was alluring. Again, she felt something about him, something enigmatic . . . she wasn't sure what—danger maybe. She held out her hand, and they shook. He seemed reluctant to let go. She slid into the car and started the big motor.

"I'll see you in the morning, 7:00 sharp. We've got a big day tomorrow," he said. He closed the door and leaned down to her eye level.

She opened the window. "I'm really looking forward to it."

"Don't forget to wear some sturdy shoes and bring a hat."

She nodded, smiled, turned to check the traffic and, finding no excuse to stay longer, drove off. Alex stepped back and watched her all the way down the block where she stuck her arm out of the window and waved in one big sweep just before turning left out of sight.

He waved back, sucked his teeth and shook his head. He could see it was going to get messy. He'd just spent the entire day with another man's wife. "Not good," he said, heading back to his studio, "Not good at all." Here he was, speaking out loud to himself. And to make matters worse, he was going to see her again tomorrow.

Chapter Five

Across Eden View Street below, a 1998 F-250 Ford pickup truck, burnt-out primer gray, backs into the curb and parks. A heavily weathered metallic-blue and chrome camper large enough to sleep four, with its overhang bunk space above the cab, sits in the bed of the truck. Jack Lawrence notices the spot where the original factory decal, 'The Adventurer,' has now gone fugitive. He watches a man in a worn washed-denim shirt and a pair of gray industrial work pants descend from the cab and walk back to the end of the truck, to make sure he's close enough but doesn't extend into the red paint on the curb.

Jack notes the similarity in the man's appearance to his own—about six-two, shaggy steel-gray hair hanging over his collar, a taste for faded, cool-colored clothes and a slight paunch at the mid-section that reveals the full-blown onset of middle age. His lightly weathered complexion betrays a history of tobacco and alcohol. Sometimes, Jack misses his old vices. Satisfied that he has parked his vehicle to the rigorous standards of the San Diego police, the man disappears through the camper door in the back.

Jack gets his second cup of coffee from the kitchen, sits back down to his pad and charcoal and returns his gaze to the ocean. It's been a while since he's done any sketching. Unlike yesterday, the view from this apartment window is spectacularly overcast, although he can still make out Point Loma headland to the south.

Down the block, The Tradewinds, a gray, white, and blue high-rise concrete and glass juggernaut, is undergoing a new point and paint job. Dwarfing everything along this three-point-three-mile stretch of beach, the building leans stolidly into a light wind that's been steadily blowing shoreward from Tahiti since before Jack got up. In all their years of coming here, they've never experienced such inclement weather, certainly not this much rain, which Jack now remembers hearing above the sound of the ocean sometime before dawn. At another time, such weather would've been unwelcome.

Jack, ensconced in this new space, senses a coming change as he enjoys watching wind and rain whip the surface of the water into froth. He looks south towards the bay channel. The mist is so thick, the end of the pier dematerializes before his eyes. For several minutes, he just watches it fade in and out as the fog rolls into shore. Maggie's down there working. He hopes she's doing better than he is. Boy, is he rusty. He flips the page of his sketchbook. Sometimes it's just better to start over.

This trip, he reflects, has another first for them. This apartment building's been here a good many years. Though comfortable and well-maintained, it shows signs of better days, doorframes out of square, too many layers of paint on the railings. The mature palms, planted as saplings when the place was new, are lifting the corners of the concrete cool-decking of the pool in the courtyard below. The sign on the side, Rentals by the Week or Month, has prompted Maggie to point and say, "We need to check into that." And every year it's the same thing, the same inaction, indolence and rut.

But not this year. Their decision to take this apartment has already given him a new perspective. Jack is aware, though he doesn't like to think about it, that his life is going by at an accelerated pace. He's suffering some kind of personal dissatisfaction, tilted out of square with too many memories piling up, buckling his foundations. Something's missing. It might have to do with their inability to pursue meaningful change, even though he knows the importance that change already plays in his life. He senses the same in Maggie.

That's the best he can do with the fog. He shifts his attention inside, flips the page and begins a quick rendering. Jack surveys the interior of the room from his place at the table by the sliding glass door to the balcony, with the vertical blinds drawn all the way back. It's nothing special, innocuous in fact. The queen-sized bed he finds amazing—amazing that something so hard, and not even king-sized, can give him such a good night's sleep—especially with his back.

There is this eighties utilitarian functionalism about the pastel room, and in the ugly but solid oak furnishings, that he finds beautiful—the simplicity of it, he supposes. He captures it in clean, uncluttered lines. If he could afford it, he'd stay here with this ocean for months at a time. He'd watch it, listen to it, smell it, feel and taste it as if it were another missing piece of life that he and Maggie couldn't manage without, even though they live in the desert the rest of the year. He knows he couldn't be here forever; nothing is forever. Could he imagine not being here next to the ocean right now?

The word 'eternity' pops into Jack's mind along with the visage of David Rayburn whom he has not met, but the vision of whom is, at that moment, being sliced into narrow sections by the micro-mini blind as he shuffles by outside the kitchen window. He's heading toward the only other apartment on this end of the second-story verandah, an apartment that Jack thinks is unoccupied. He turns his sketchbook ninety degrees and begins a series of impressionistic thumbnails of David.

David, the second half of the Ruth and David Rayburn Seaview Apartments' management team, is wearing an expensive Islander shirt, printed in a bouquet of luscious, giant deep-red hibiscus. Although dry, protected by his burnt-bone, black umbrella, the shirt looks wet and gives Jack the startling impression that David is bleeding profusely. He's also wearing an oxygen ring around his head just below his nose, like a fallen halo. Disappearing behind his head, the plastic tube fits into a regulator on the canister hanging in the blue pouch at his side. With his slick tan crown and his monk's ring of cropped white hair, he could pass as Fred Mertz from I Love Lucy.

Just what could such an ill man do as manager, beyond listening to the tenants complain about weather and picking up the occasional piece of trash from the flowerbeds that surround the buildings? David is, he thinks, the interface for the services that come with the maintenance of such a facility, calling plumbers, electricians, air-conditioning and heating men with their tools and promises, excuses and fees, to come fix his decaying world. As if he, a mere mortal and a dying one at that, could, with vigilance, perseverance and a pure heart, albeit a sick one, call upon the gods to stave off the relentless entropy that's stalking him.

Jack puts his drawing tools down and sips his coffee. The first time Jack saw him, David was dozing in the orange and brown cloth sixties-style recliner. He faced out the floor length windows of the Rayburn's living-room office. Across the vast sea of brilliantly lit dust motes floating between them, Ruth Rayburn, his better half, checked the Lawrences into their rooms. David never acknowledged their presence in the overstuffed room. He slept the whole time, no doubt worn out by all that vigilant persevering with his bum ticker.

Ruth sat silhouetted by the sliding glass door that opened onto the sunset, holding an unlit cigarette while she worked at the desk under the staircase that, Jack presumed, led to sleeping quarters upstairs. A petite woman in her late sixties, she had a leathery, jaundiced complexion and thin, deeply wrinkled skin. Her arms were imprinted with small purple and yellow bruises at the inside crease of her elbows; someone had either recently taken blood or tried shaking some sense into her. She filled out the appropriate paperwork and cleared Jack's credit by sliding his plastic card through the electronic sentinel with a practiced flick of her wrist—a graceful gesture that reminded him of a character in Kundera's novel Immortality. With that, Jack understood that she, not David, was the true interface.

Having just arrived and expressing his envy at the Rayburns' luck to be living with the ocean just a step beyond the door, he asked Ruth, though a bit too loudly in the hush of the room, "How do I get your job?"

As if every guest before and every guest that followed continued to ask the same question, she replied in her small, uninflected voice, without missing a beat, "You'd have to wait until I die. I'd retire, but I have nothing else to do with my time."

In the cotton-like bubble of silence that followed, Jack noticed a fine crystal fish bowl the size of a large beach ball. Flattened on the bottom, it sat on a small table near the edge of the living-room area with its top correspondingly sliced off level to form a lip-less hole. It was filled to an invisible three-quarter mark with matchbooks—collected, as indicated by the sheer number in variation, description and kind, from every business in the greater San Diego metropolitan area. A single opened pack of Virginia Slims rested on top of the matches. The bowl reminded Jack of a crystal ball, and he wondered what kind of future it might tell for this couple if he could read it. And, he wanted to know, what was up with keeping such an inordinate collection of potential fire so close to a man who, though asleep, sat sucking his indispensable but highly volatile oxygen through a plastic tube?

The Slims didn't belong to David who no longer smoked. That wasn't to say that he didn't wish to; or even, as Jack imagines, that David wasn't right then dreaming of the days when he and Ruth, both heavy smokers, took the job as live-in managers. Had they entertained guests who, at a similar time in their lives, just wanted to have a little fun with some in-the-know people while on vacation in sunny San Diego? Were there discreet parties with too many Mai Tais, Martinis or Manhattans, the occasional exchanged room key never catching the attention of the other guests or the corporate owner—over the long run, demeaning and shameful behavior in a life that could've been lived to better purpose?

Was it, simply, over time, too many Harvey Wall-bangers, the compilation of minor indiscretions, the cheapening of relationships, the weakening of bonds, the loss of personal respect or, possibly, the slow accretion of guilt and ambivalence? Locked into destructive, mind-numbing habits, was it the loss of energy, drive, and desire for something better contributing to the slow strangulation of a marriage that finally collapses into silence, but for the daily exchange of their obligatory professional responsibilities? Were they yoked—ironically, even comically, in some deeply human way—to the consequences of just plain old wrong choices?

"My-oh-my, aren't I the moralist?" Jack says, casting his gaze out into the ocean. What of his and Maggie's choices? He's just fishing and knows it's entirely supposition on his part. This must be how writers create their novels. Dismissing this twaddle as the meandering of a lackadaisical mind brought on by such gray weather, he senses beneath it, somewhere, a loss that David and Ruth share, some sadness that dominates their life and relationship.

Jack picks up his materials, looks at his drawings and frowns. He tosses them back on the table. God, he's out of shape; his drawings look like beginner's work.

Jack assumed that although David had given up cigarettes for good, it was too late for it to be very beneficial to his health. How sad, Jack thought. With the oxygen-tube nozzles stuck in his nose, David couldn't even smell the ocean—something Jack had always loved.

He knew that Ruth would never give them up, no matter how dire the consequences. He supposed it must have been a source of perpetual, grating irritation between them; she could no longer smoke in the house, or in David's immediate vicinity. She probably had the feeling that the world had fallen off its axis and was wobbling its way through the universe, out of kilter. When she handed Jack his receipt and shook his hand, he glimpsed beneath the distracted gaze and glaze of her eye, a monumental insouciance so pervasive as to be almost malevolent. It was a feeling that he hoped never to experience.

As they were leaving the Rayburns' apartment, Maggie pointed out a small wooden box full of beach toys stuck in a corner of their back porch entryway.

"Wouldn't Mark just love to get those on the beach? We're going to have to bring him, sometime."

They often had this conversation when they experienced something fun. Maggie had the natural inclination to share it with those she loved. Somehow, they never seemed to translate that inclination into action, Jack thought, probably because at heart they were protective of their time together.

"You know," Maggie said, "I didn't see one photograph in that whole place, did you?"

"Now that you mention it, no."

"Why not? They're old enough to be grandparents. And, even if they don't like grandkids, they'd still have pictures, wouldn't they? A son or daughter, other family? But, nothing. Not one photograph."

"Well, they must have; the toys were there."

"Yeah, maybe. And maybe they're just there for the children of the guests."

Jack hears the sound of muffled voices and the closing of a door outside the kitchen, just before he sees David returning past the window. For a moment, the rain drips off the eaves onto the balcony in perfect cadence to David's footsteps descending the staircase. In the kitchen, Jack watches him cross the courtyard. He feels fragile, watching David move so slowly around the pool. He takes his coffee and returns to the table. The sketches of David could be worse; they're not as bad as they first appeared.

Yesterday, after Jack and Maggie unloaded the truck and brought their stuff into the apartment, he wandered through the sliding door to check out the view. Jack craned his neck around to see what was on the other side of the wall that separated the two balconies. There was a narrow balcony, the continuation of the one he stood on and another sliding glass door and windows. The blinds had been left open, but not pulled back, and the room was dim, even though at 4:00 P.M. the sun still rode high in the sky. There was no furniture in place, and all he could see in his quick reconnaissance, except for the beige carpet, were some rags in a pile and what appeared to be several metallic paint cans without labels. Maybe someone was working there, patching, painting and cleaning.

Somehow, it left him feeling empty—and old. And what of his painting? It's not the same thing. He likes to think his work is mature, intelligent and challenging, that his paintings are metaphors for life—edgy, full, intense— that they examine the beauty of being alive in a complicated world. Sometimes, he can't remember why he continues to do it. It gets harder to challenge himself, to discover something new as the years pass. He likes to think that these abstract excursions into the process of becoming, the dismantling of his ego, and the endless inquiry that it engenders, have taken on a complexity that could not have been imagined when he began. But in the end, he knows it's just painting—a way to get through his day—no more, no less important than anything else.

At the best of times, when consumed by the work, he's absent. There's no one in the studio. There's only this awesome and compelling flow of creativity. Without it, he's omnipresent, in the way of his own work and unable to stop dwelling on that discouraging fact. And even when the work is getting finished, so what? It would be going into storage with the rest of his paintings that no one is buying.

Jack's tired of thinking about it and misses those days when it was all for fun. It should be enough just to do it. It goes round and around in his head: the naiveté, the gallery scene, the dealers, the politics, the corruption, the hype, the submissions, the shows, the self-doubt. He has doubts about the quality of his painting and worries over the continual rejection, no matter how accomplished the work feels. It's taken him twenty-some years, but he thinks that he has finally gotten the picture. He puts his drawing materials away.

Across Eden View, the man emerges from the back of the camper dressed in his running shorts, shoes and a light-gray hooded windbreaker. Jack watches the man stretch. Incidentally, Jack notices that the rain has let up. He smiles as he goes into the kitchen to clean up. "Saucony Shadows," he says. "Ha! The same damn shoes I wear."

The underside of Crystal Pier always fascinates Maggie. She loves standing beneath the wet, dark timbers, among the forest of pylons wrapped in their canvas and concrete, with her camera in hand, the familiar strap around her neck. It never fails to sharpen her senses. The way the light surges through the space—filling it with reflections from the agitated surf, conforming to every nook and by-place within its domain—thrills her. The inevitable give and take of elemental forces, how the eye discovers the sensuality of it all, captivates her. Among these shadows, with the mist and spray wetting her face and clothes and filling her lungs, her years are washed away. She emerges transformed, desirable and passionate. Maggie feels a sense of release unfelt anywhere else. She slips her camera under her jacket to keep it dry.

She has hundreds of black-and-white photographs of Pacific Beach and the pier. Over the years, the pier increasingly figures in her work as a series of evermore sophisticated investigations of light and shadow. Maggie is a purist. She always shoots in available illumination. But today, the forces of darkness muddy the waters and douse the light. She doesn't care. Under normal circumstances, she wouldn't go out in this weather with her camera; but for some time now, she senses a certain restlessness in herself.

She sat this morning, drinking coffee, watching the ocean and listening to Jack snore in perfect time to the sound of the waves below; but now, she's drawn out to the pier and takes her camera along, in case she could capture something unique and unforeseen. The cloistered ambiance beneath the pier is always a good place for Maggie to sort things out.

Sitting on a dry spot in the sand, well back from the water, she peers into the gloom that shrouds her view of the ocean. Walking by her, along the path between the pylons where the city trucks haul out the seaweed, people cannot see her though they're close enough. Her dark gray sweats and light gray jersey obscure her form among the shadows that flicker against the mottled concrete wall of the pier. In perfect stillness, she's almost invisible. She sets the shutter speed of the old Pentax on open, focuses it up among the beams, holds it as still as she can and presses the button. She counts ten seconds and lets it close. Probably nothing.

Her first thoughts are always of Jack. They'll be together thirty years on their next anniversary. Is there something about their relationship that causes her unease? She loves him, and he loves her; but is it that simple?

As a child at home, she was a happy tow-headed, bashful blue-eyed girl. Her parents raised her to conform, attend church, follow the teachings of the Bible and get a good education. They wanted her to find a good husband, someone secure who would support and give her those things they found so hard to provide. Her parents were honest, hard-working, practical people who loved her. But now, she realized that parental love often demanded obligation and, on occasion, even the most loving, well-intentioned parents could turn a key and lock an obedient child into a life that was not in that child's best interest.

Throughout high school she dated neighborhood boys, and always her parents encouraged her to find a better sort. A sincere and honest girl who loved her parents and wanted to please them, she went out to appropriate places with proper young men in suits and ties from the offices where she worked. She was twenty-one, living at home with her widowed mother, and working as a bank clerk when Jack came along in his bell-bottom pants, shaggy hair and brazen self-confidence. She'd never met anyone like him. He thought he was an artist.

Maggie smiles at the memory. Getting up and moving out beyond the pier, she can see nothing but mist where the horizon should be—no line of demarcation between sky and sea. It's all one to her. She shoots a half-dozen frames in various directions, all ten seconds each, holding as still as she can. In this light, she'll probably be sorry she wasted all this film. She's trying to find the line that crosses her past, at which she can point and say, this is where I became who I am. If the gloom lifts, she thinks she could find answers to her questions, if not some interesting pictures.

Late one afternoon, on her way home from work in an almost empty cross-town bus, Jack got on, sat right next to her, leaned in close and promptly started talking to her as if he'd known her all his life. Unable to recall a word they spoke, she felt how flushed and disconcerted she was when, right before he got off, he asked if he could see her a second time. She marveled, thinking about it. She did something that she'd never do under any circumstances— she gave her phone number to a complete stranger.

Afterward, she was irritated that her mind, though it knew better, kept trying to remember when they'd seen each other before, since she didn't think that riding the same bus constituted seeing her for the first time. Such cheek, she thought. Later, when she discovered that he was three years her junior, it didn't bother her in the least—no matter what her mother had to say.

Maggie returns to her position under the pier and stretches her legs out in front of her on the sand. The weather appears to be clearing. Maybe she'll get some good pictures after all. Her relationship to Jack, she realizes, is not the source of her disquiet. He helps her change her life for the better, in many ways.

She knows that none of the occasional beachcombers drifting by can see her. Passing within feet, each one continues along as if they were alone. They talk to themselves, make strange faces and perform all manner of personal gesture that they would conceal from her otherwise. She thinks about taking their portraits, but doesn't feel like chasing them down for permission, hating to invade other people's privacy, almost as much as she hates them to invade hers.

One tall, angular young man, in a loose-fitting black cape with a large mop of long curly hair, is reminiscent of her son, Nick. Carrying his sandals in one hand and a fan-like palm frond in the other, he stops in front of her, raises his arms and dances an intricate jig to a tune that only he can hear. Now that Maggie looks closer, she doesn't see any resemblance to Nick.

She's startled that her impressions of the world keep shifting, always amazed at how different the world can look through a lens or from another point of view. It occurs to her that she's seen no joggers this morning or, for that matter, no couples. So far, all of those she has encountered are alone as they materialize and dematerialize, like ghosts in the fog. Nor does she see any of the gulls, sandpipers or pelicans that usually inhabit the beach. It's strangely silent but for the recurrent surf that, because of its interminable repetition, constitutes a kind of silence in and of itself, a white noise filtering through her like the fog. The weather is keeping them away. Ebbing and flowing, her thoughts and memories of their years, good and bad, come and go, tugging at her emotions, like the tide. No, Maggie's unrest comes from some other part of her life.

And what of Nick's coming home after those years on his own? What does she feel about his failed marriage and her grandson, Mark, who comes to stay with them? She loves them, but she knows she drives them to distraction, at times, always after them with her camera. Of course, there's less time for herself, less privacy. Is that a twinge of jealousy she harbors for his youth, his freedom, his potential, while he goes off to work or school or out to the coffeehouse with friends?

She worries about Nick as he struggles with problems that he cannot conceal in such close proximity, even though he keeps them as private as possible. His books, clothes and furniture are things foreign to her, belonging to another man; they make the house pinched, darker, claustrophobic. The dishes in the sink, the dirty ashtrays on the patio, his staying up all hours, the bad habits are back, pressing upon her in their triviality. She's learning to give up her need to mother him, to accept that it's no longer her place to worry about the hours he keeps or the bills he doesn't pay.

It's hard. Yet, since his return, she's getting to know him. If he'd not come home, she'd never have learned the depths of his personality and intellect. She'd have missed becoming his friend. Nick is no hardship on her. His coming home is giving her the rare second chance to witness his blossoming maturity. By letting go of him, she's liberating herself.

Maggie has forgotten her camera for the moment and finds that she's drawing pictures with her fingers, stirring the sand beside her. Soft, cool and damp, it's raked clean of the flotsam that dots the beach in both directions as far as she can see. Jack often puts sand in his paint for texture, a ground on which he builds his compositions. Jack, Nick and Mark are the sands and textures grounding her to life. Her pictures in the sand are not pictures at all. They're like the scribbles that Jack sometimes draws on his paintings— child-like scrawls, loose and expressive. The sand sticks to her skin like powdered cinnamon to buttered toast.

The gloom is lifting in the southwest. In the distance, she can see the flat shape of a great, gray battleship cutting its way out of the harbor from the naval base on Coronado Island.

During their last trip to San Diego, they went to the Coronado Hotel for her birthday luncheon: grilled halibut, julienne vegetables, buttered new potatoes and key lime pie. It was that year after Nick moved home, before they came to San Diego, when she noticed the first stirrings of menopause. She was fifty-two. Menopause, she thought. What about menopause? Sure, it was a good working hypothesis.

Why not? Jack bought a book for her before she even considered she was a candidate for it. Since then, they made a study of it together. Jack said he wanted to find out what kind of rollercoaster ride was coming. He was so serious in his need to understand what was going to happen to her. He didn't want to find himself at the mercy of her hormones; his own were hard enough to handle.

She had to laugh at his trepidation, but she suspected there was more to it than he'd say. Always the strategist, it was obvious, if war was going to break out, he wanted to be holding the high ground. He'd always shown a healthy respect for her character; he knew she'd take no prisoners. But now, she realized that his peculiar, precautionary behavior, albeit self-motivated, helped lead her into familiar territory. When the battle came, if it came, they could get to shelter together, out of the line of fire.

"Men-o-pause." The sound of her soft, rich alto is strange, melodious and comforting. "Just another glorious day in the life of we human females," she says, listening to the sound her voice makes reverberating among the timbers and rippling on the water. She brushes her hands together. With the tide coming in, the sun struggling to tear through the clouds, and this irritating sense of anxiety going nowhere at all, she realizes that she's glad to have had only one child. It's enough.

Maggie drifts back up the beach, stopping to shoot whatever catches her eye. Before crossing the sand to climb the cliff, she notices, standing at the crest of the shingle a few yards ahead, a young woman hugging a wrap tightly about her shoulders. Like a wraith with pale, translucent skin and dark curly hair whipping about in the breeze, the young woman is looking forlornly out to sea. Instinctively, Maggie raises her camera but then lets it fall back to her chest. There's more than a touch of melancholy in the way the girl hovers there, as if yearning for her lover who will never return. Maggie can't help herself; she lifts the camera, focuses and shoots. The image strikes her as one of the most poignant and touching things she's ever witnessed in her life.

Saturday

Chapter Six

Emma woke an hour before the alarm. She lay resting in the pale dawn, listening to the birds. Emma loved this time of morning. At home, it was the only time that was exclusively hers. There were fewer people out, and the world was a new place. She could read or sit with a cup of coffee on the patio and wake up slowly. Every other day, she walked three miles through her Palm Grove neighborhood—a beneficial time to think. This morning there was a lot to consider.

She'd returned to the Mountain Shadows after dark where she had found the O'Briens on the patio, eager to hear about her visit to Alex's studio. Now that she thought about it, it was embarrassing how she had carried on so about Alex and his work. Her behavior might've seemed strange, especially to Steve who'd been an acquaintance of her husband's for some years.

A tenured pharmacology professor at the University and a Teaching Fellow at University Hospital, Steve was also a consultant to the drug industry. The couples had met in Hawaii while attending a week-long conference on drug research sponsored by a number of major pharmaceutical firms. Emma and Mary liked each other immediately and afterwards maintained contact. Mary was planning to have a couple of small murals painted and hoped Emma could give her some advice about finding someone to do them. That was before Mary found Alex.

Six months later, when several of the big pharmaceutical companies sponsored a symposium on new drug therapies at the University in Tucson, it was unthinkable that the Brightons stay any place other than at the B & B. By then, Mary was excited to show the murals to Emma and wanted her professional reaction.

They knew nothing about her marital problems, and she didn't see any need to tell them. For the first time in many years, she experienced the relief and exhilaration of just being alive, although she suffered a returning, gnawing anxiety when she thought about Bob.

Emma's thoughts turned to Alex and their planned excursion. When the alarm finally sounded at 6:00 AM, Emma rose, showered, and blew her hair. She made coffee and bagged a couple of bagels to go for breakfast. Dressed in her jeans, Rockports, a pale yellow T-shirt and a straw cowgirl hat that Mary had loaned her for just this occasion, she grabbed her purse, coffee, bagels and was out the door. She caught the fleeting glimpse of a strange and different Emma looking back at her in the rearview mirror of the car when she stopped a moment to put on her lipstick. There was an improbable anticipation in her eye, but she would not venture to speculate on it for the time being. On the way, she caught herself speeding and slowed; she didn't want to arrive too early.

The offer of a full partnership in the gallery had come as a real surprise. In time, it would mean more money. However, it was still a sizable investment that would put a tangible dent in her finances. Then too, as an owner, she'd be bringing the job home with her every night. Maybe she didn't really love it enough to stay with it into the unforeseeable future. The gallery did satisfy a need in her, and she loved Gen, but she'd gotten a little weary of the commercial aspects of the business and sometimes found herself annoyed with the details of it all.

On the other hand, there was more money and control with greater decision-making power. She could bring in artists that she thought deserved better exposure. It wouldn't be fair to Gen, to take the offer, if she couldn't give one hundred percent to the business. At this point in her life, she wasn't sure just where her ultimate interests resided. So, she told Gen that she needed a couple of months to consider the offer, and that was where the matter rested.

She had discussed it with Bob, over their coffee one morning.

"I just don't see why you need to bog yourself and the family down with the responsibility—not to mention the investment required up front," he had said. "You know this venture of yours is diametrically opposed to what I want."

"What about what I want?"

"What about it? What about what Beth and Heather want? You know they like having you at home. They need you here. Are you just gonna drop them like a couple of hot potatoes and run off to do your own thing?"

"Bob, Heather's almost grown, and she's in Europe studying art—or have you forgotten?"

"I mean, when she gets back."

"When she gets back, she'll be leaving for college."

"She'll want you here when she comes home. And what about Beth?"

"Yes, Beth, well, Beth has got several more years at home, it's true, but she's just going through some teenage growing pains. She'll be fine. She's a good kid, and I won't neglect her. And you know that. Aren't you late for work?"

"Don't change the subject. Beth's growing up, getting surly and rebellious, and something needs to be done. If you don't do something, I will." Even though he knew better than this, he'd halfway decided to try and make it stick.

"I'm on it, Bob." The look she gave him withered any further chances he might have had along that line of attack.

"Well, anyway, we don't need the money is all I'm saying. My income is plenty. With my promotion, there's no need for you to work."

And that was right, she knew, as far as it went. She needed to work for other reasons, reasons that he conveniently chose not to understand.

This morning, however, driving through this sleepy desert town, on her way to meet a strange man and trek off into the hinterlands to God knows where, it dawned on her that anything was possible. The idea of doing something for herself—becoming an owner, being more independent, especially in light of Bob's veiled demands—was just too inviting, and she laughed out loud. It must be the sweet desert air that had her so intoxicated, she thought. The cool clear desert atmosphere seemed to crackle with an electric anticipation that came right up out of the ground, like a spring in an oasis. She was charged and refreshed by it as she traveled into the city.

Emma parked next to Alex's truck, in the lot across the street from his studio. She'd arrived ten minutes early, after all, and decided to sit for a moment to collect herself. Down the street, a couple of young people dressed in black waited outside the Café Arles where she and Alex had dinner the night before. The hair on the boy's head was spiked, like the ball of a medieval mace. The girl's head was shaved. Kids today, she thought, have a hard time discovering who they are, growing up in a world that demands they wear spiked hair and shaved heads. She thought of Beth and Heather and was grateful that she had two great kids. Well, anyway, last night had been an interesting evening to say the least.

The places that she usually frequented in L.A. were trendier. One could see just about every kind of person imaginable. The wild hairstyles and outrageous outfits didn't faze her. But to somehow fit into the scene here, and not feel out of place, was new for her. She rarely ventured into an area that appeared even a bit seedy, unless visiting

83

a studio with Gen. Traveling alone into unknown territory always made her nervous. And to think, here she drove right downtown in a strange city, all by herself, without a fear in the world.

The funky, artsy little restaurant had seemed so alive— the sound of glassware clinking together, the sound of silverware tossed with the dirty dishes into plastic trays being carried into the kitchen. The espresso machine made its own unique contribution to the hubbub, and Marti kept up a continual dialogue with her customers, the bus boy and Pris in the kitchen. Taped jazz played too loud for quiet conversation, so everyone expressed their opinions about music, literature and art above the voices of those around them. Over the evening, the din swelled and dropped as thoughts and ideas came and went. Of course, the arts were not the only subjects of conversation. During a lull, Emma and Alex overheard a girl at the table next to them explaining to another girl how she was going to rip the hair out of a third girl's head for messing with her man.

Marti's black and white photographs and a number of loosely executed oil paintings done by another local artist— portraits of the regular customers—were hung in every available space left uncovered by a 'special of the day' or a 'homemade chocolate chip cookie $1.00 each' sign. The paintings had attracted Emma's eye. Though hanging all over the walls in an unprofessional manner, they had a unique energy in the way they related to the place, something that she'd never identified before. Galleries in L.A. tended to be more sophisticated and serious, watching the bottom line.

But Café Arles wasn't a gallery. It was a gathering place where people shared ideas and artwork—the photos and paintings of their friends, good, bad or mediocre. These were the images the regulars wanted to see, images of the customers that belonged to the customers; in that sense, the images were the customers. It was curious that the Café Arles—and the paintings inside—had such a noticeable effect on her at this time in her life. It wasn't as though she'd never been in a café before. But being there last night gave her a new perspective and an unusual feeling about herself. Was it the people, the ambiance, or Alex that lent this renewed sense of possibility she had not felt for some years?

She had seen wannabes before. The art world was full of poseurs who sat around drinking coffee and smoking hand-rolled cigarettes, talking the talk, wearing crazy clothes and outlandish hairstyles, tattoos and piercings in every imaginable part of their bodies. Maybe some of them last night were artists in the making, and maybe not. Even in the best of circumstances and with all of the talent in the world, not many of them would be lucky enough to make a living at it. But it didn't matter.

For a true artist, it wasn't about the money or the fame. It was all about the courage to live a creative life, to keep your dream alive in the face of almost certain financial failure. She didn't know if she possessed such courage. Somehow, being there with Alex last night had given her a new respect for artists and a better under-standing from which to view her renewed commitment to the new Duncan-Brighton Gallery of Contemporary Art, Gen, and the gallery artists. She didn't know at what point in the past twenty-four hours she had made that commitment, but it felt right to her.

Just then, the tapping on her window nearly brought her out of her skin. Alex stood there with a broad grin across his face, holding a couple of knapsacks and a small cooler.

"I didn't see you go into the restaurant," she said, rolling down her window.

"That's because I went over early and had some coffee. We put lunch together, and I went back to the studio. Come on, let's go in mine," he said and walked around to the back of the truck.

"Don't you think the Crown Victoria would be more comfortable?"

"I don't think that vehicle would handle some of the roads we're going to travel today."

Emma locked the car while Alex stowed the gear in a clever box-like arrangement built in the bed of the truck, next to a strapped down five-gallon jug of distilled water.

"So, where are we going?" Emma asked.

"You'll see."

They drove through the heart of downtown, headed west on Speedway, and climbed into the bristling Tucson

Mountain foothills. The sun was up, the day was clear and the sky was miraculous. The desert was lush with expectation and promise. After reaching the outskirts of the city, Alex was the first to speak.

"Now, pay attention, Mrs. Brighton. If you don't pay attention out here, you could be stuck full of needles. And, I gotta tell you, they hurt bad. Believe me, some of these babies can put you in the hospital. I once knew a guy that fell off a horse and was dragged through a patch of that stuff and had to have over fifty thousand needles surgically removed from his body. He pulled thorns from his hide for over a year. He lost an eye, and the pain was unbearable."

"Some of them do look lethal, don't they? What's that one?" She pointed vaguely at the side of the highway.

"That is the ubiquitous prickly pear."

"No, not those. I mean these tall things with the white handkerchiefs waving from the tops, along the edge of the road."

"They're pretty, aren't they? Those are thistle-poppies. The ones with the purple blooms are Mexican thistles. You don't see as many of those. They're a bit shyer than their Russian cousins." Alex pointed out saltbush, yellow brittlebush, the red, white and pink fairy dusters and the different species of cholla—teddybear-long needles, buckthorn-short needles, tiny flowers, large flowers with various colors. "Don't get close to any of those," he said, "especially the jumping cholla. Vibrations from proximity can set them off. They pop right on you. Your first reaction is to pull them off, and before you know it, they're stuck all over, and you have no way to use your hands."

Emma already knew a few of these plants from visits to her brother's house in Scottsdale. Unwilling to spoil his fun, she didn't say anything. She liked watching and learning things from him. He'd make a good teacher, she thought.

"You do know that the tall ones with the brilliant white trumpet-like blooms are called saguaros, right?"

Emma just looked at him as if he had stuck his finger in his nose.

"Right, silly me. But I'll bet you didn't know that the Tohono O'odham people believe that each one of those saguaros used to be a real person? The saguaros are their reincarnated ancestors and deserve to be treated with the utmost respect, just like living people."

"Really? Why do you suppose that is?"

"Well, it might have something to do with the fact that saguaros are a source of several tasty foods; with their great water-storing capacity, they continue to blossom and fruit right through years of drought when many other plants succumb. So, if you think about it, their belief makes an excellent story for teaching their children to value a vital resource."

"Makes sense to me."

They stopped at Gate's Pass, left the truck and climbed up to the top of the ridge where they ate their bagels and drank their coffee with the other gawkers.

"That wide plain below us is Avra Valley," he said, pointing. "Those are the Coyote Mountains toward the southwest. Kitt Peak National Observatory maintains its facilities there. Those white things on top, glistening in the sun, are the telescopes. They're sixty miles away."

"You don't say. That's beautiful." She couldn't believe that she could see them so clearly from so far. Some days in L.A., she couldn't see her fist in front of her face for the smog. Well, that was an exaggeration, but not by much, she thought.

"And that's Baboquivari," he said as he moved close and put his arm around her shoulder. He pointed her view toward the sacred mountain at the heart of the Tohono O'odham Nation.

He was tall and smelled good. She raised her arm around his waist, and they stood looking at Baboquivari for several long moments. Then she turned to look at him.

He returned her gaze and smiled.

She looked down at her feet.

He abruptly turned her again, pointing her much closer to the valley below. "And that's Old Tucson movie studios where I used to work as an extra in the movies."

"Oh, yes? You were in the movies?" She lowered her arm and turned to look at him. Was there nothing he hasn't done?

"A couple of walk-on parts."

"Is that where we're going?"

"Oh no. Over there." He stood behind her and pointed over her shoulder as if aiming a rifle south-by-southwest, about thirty-five miles, to a low, wide range of mountains. "Those are the Sandarios. There's a long-abandoned settlement in those foothills. It's one of my favorite places. Some ancient people called the Hohokam lived in this area hundreds of years ago and left some very intriguing carvings in the rocks there."

As they returned to the truck, Emma noticed that Alex picked up some trash left there by others. He walked over and dropped it in a container without saying a word. This was an appealing quality. But more appealing was the way he fit his jeans. Oh God, she thought and tried not to linger on such distractions.

She liked to fancy that she hardly ever noticed men, sexually; but whatever she wished to think of herself, she was very attracted to them. She enjoyed feeling attractive, too; but then, who didn't? However, as a married woman with children, she never allowed herself to contemplate such possibilities. Acts of infidelity were, by definition, outside the realm of choice.

Bob was a decent man—though a dull one. He was generous with the girls, although he didn't spend much time with them. There was no doubt that he loved them, but in his distant, peripheral way. Emma was disheartened thinking about him. She wavered. She had loved Bob. He had loved her. Hadn't they been true to one another? Hadn't they cared for each other? She hated it. Bob thought it was enough to just make the money. Over time, he'd lost all enthusiasm for anything except work or a game of golf. At least he hadn't shown an interest in other women—as far as she knew. He traveled for weeks at a time. Even when he was home, he wouldn't go with her to the ballet or the opera or attend openings at the gallery. But then, she had no real interest in the things he liked, few as they were.

Emma occupied herself with these and other thoughts for the half-hour that it took them to cross the valley toward the Sandarios. Alex occasionally interrupted her reveries to point out a favored part of the landscape. She had decided to ask him to take her back, after they visited the petroglyph site, so she could arrange a flight back home by Monday. Bob wasn't due in Tucson until Thursday. If she left tonight or tomorrow morning, she'd have the time to sort things out before he left for the conference that she had decided to forego. Then she could get a fresh start in the gallery as the new partner. So, with all of this decided, why wasn't she happier?

Alex felt her consternation and remained silent, enjoying the ride and looking forward to the prospect of showing Emma the petroglyphs. He had no idea what she was thinking and wouldn't venture to guess. Whatever battle she was fighting, it was probably best for him to keep his silence. This was something he enjoyed doing, anyway, especially since he was out in the desert on a warm spring morning with a beautiful and captivating woman at his side. He couldn't think of anything that he would rather be doing.

Then again, there was his forthcoming trip to visit Josh. He missed that little boy. It had been too long. When Friday rolled around, he'd be cruising along I-10 to be with his son for at least two weeks. For that matter, why not move there when he was finished in Seattle and be with Josh on a more permanent basis? There would be someone to lease his studio; good space was always at a premium in Tucson. Perhaps it was time for a little change in his life. He made a mental note to do some research into the kinds of work and real estate he might find there. The only thing preventing him from moving any time soon was his commission in Seattle. And the only thing better than his visit with Josh would be that Josh could live with him on a permanent basis. Some day, maybe.

He chanced the occasional glance at Emma. He realized that she'd never been far from his thoughts since meeting her. It occurred to him that he'd better try to keep a handle on those thoughts. The day was going to get hotter before it was over, and he needed to keep a cool head. Nevertheless, he had definite qualms about this situation; there was something about her way that he couldn't fathom and that was so intriguing, it made him wary of doing the wrong thing. He was drawn to her. As they neared the end of the washboard hardscrabble road that wound its way up into the foothills, he knew he had to find out what this feeling meant because whatever happened with Emma was going to have to happen by Friday. On that day, he was leaving to see Josh. There wouldn't be another chance.

Alex brought the truck to a stop after miles of sandy arroyos, rocky ridges and groves of buckthorn cholla. He stepped down from the cab and brushed off the backside of his jeans. Feeling a bit ruffled from the jolting of the ride, Emma climbed out of the truck. She stood and looked back across the rising plain of Spanish dagger and scrub to the great sandy expanse of the valley they'd just crossed below.

It was incredible to experience such deep, open space like this, without a cloud in the sky. Unfortunately, she thought, this was the kind of space no longer found depicted in serious abstract painting. Alex's work was an exception. Emma recognized that this landscape was another source of his inspiration—another muse—the same kind of space she'd seen captured in some of his paintings.

A pair of red-tail hawks climbed the thermal updrafts into the cerulean sky, above the face of the mountains. In the flat distance of the central part of the valley, a couple of large dust devils twirled and danced like dervishes in the dusty-gold midday heat. Back along the Tucson Mountains, carpets of desert chicory and primrose were scattered across the land, like throw rugs. The great forest of saguaros, with their crowns of waxy white flowers flashing in the sun, had made this part of the country famous. This little patch of ground in Sonora was the only place on Earth that they existed. Alex felt kinship with this giant cactus because he, too, had made this desert his home.

As if they'd been doing this together all their lives, they moved around to the back of the truck to assemble their gear. Emma watched, open-mouthed, as Alex removed a shotgun from its case in the back and slung it across his shoulder.

"I'd hate to meet a big cat up here in the rocks without a decent noisemaker," he said. "Don't worry. It wouldn't hurt the cat, just sprinkle a little salt in its rump—only if it decided to try and eat us."

Emma still didn't know quite what to make of this.

"There's been lots of rain this season, and there's plenty of game; we're not likely to even see a mountain lion, much less be threatened by one."

Emma relaxed. In for a dime, in for a doughnut, she thought.

"Besides, they're all sleeping in some cool shade way up among the rocks by now—I hope. By the way, be sure to make some noise as you walk and watch where you put your feet." He spoke in his most authentic western drawl: "Rattlers are territorial and don't take kindly to trespassers, ma'am. And, since this is matin' season, they'll be out in force, so keep your eyes peeled."

After her initial shock, Emma, the city girl, noticed there was also a snake bite kit in a well-stocked first aid case in the back of the truck. Alex was prepared for emergencies, and it was reassuring for her to discover this about him. She'd wondered earlier why he was wearing a large sheathed knife strapped to his waist, and now she got an inkling of insight as she imagined herself, bitten on the calf, lying on the ground with Alex stooped over her, slicing the wound open and sucking the poison out. Obviously, it wasn't a fashion statement. It was not there to make an interesting match to his worn Stetson with the wide brim that, in this sudden, burgeoning heat, made more sense to her than it did before.

"Here, take this," he said. He handed her a canteen, one of two he took from a custom-built white box cooler in the back of the truck.

She unscrewed the top and took a demure sip.

"It's more than we need, but better safe than sorry. You don't ever want to underestimate the heat in this desert, even on such a great day as today. You dehydrate in no time, and then you're gone. It's a miserable way to die."

"Say, what's in that box over there, if you don't mind my being too nosy?" she asked as she capped her canteen and pointed out another custom-built wooden container.

"Nothing. It's where I keep my paints and gear."

"You paint in the field?"

"Small works. Sometimes, that's the only kind of painting I can do. There's nothing like sitting out in a quiet spot, getting it down on canvas. When I get tired of the studio, it's rewarding to go sit under a tree, slather around some pigment, and capture the landscape."

"I didn't see them at the studio."

"I never show them to anyone—those I keep."

"Why?"

"They're personal—not very good, mostly—just what I do for fun."

"I'd love to see them."

They stood for a moment, eye to eye, feeling the current passing between them.

"Do you ever paint with watercolor?" she asked.

"Sure, for quick notes and small pieces that I like to turn into studio paintings or murals. But I prefer oils or acrylics for large work." He handed her the knapsack with their lunch. "Did you bring another shirt, something with long sleeves?"

"No, this is it."

"Then here, put this on." He tossed her a bottle of number thirty sun block. She dutifully obeyed, then slung the knapsack onto her back, strapped her canteen over one shoulder and her purse over the other, like a pair of cartridge belts, and replaced Mary's straw hat on her head. "How do I look?"

"Absolutely stunning."

Her eyes sparkled. Her cheeks glowed. Emma was beaming. Alex couldn't take his eyes off her. In that instant, they heard no sound. Everything was perfectly still. There was no telling how long they might have stood looking into each other's eyes that way.

The thunder of two Davis-Monthan fighter-jets passing overhead abruptly broke the silence and shattered the spell. Alex put the snake bite kit into the knapsack with their lunch and locked up the truck. With a final check of their gear, they set off with Alex in the lead. As they walked, he occasionally stooped and picked up a handful of stones that he tossed out in front of him as he walked.

"It lets them know we're coming and gives them a chance to clear out before we get there," he said over his shoulder.

"Good idea," she said.

Watching Alex from behind, she couldn't help but be aware of his lithe, animal-like grace as he stepped around the rock and rubble in the nearly non-existent path. Having sexual thoughts about him embarrassed her—not because of the sexuality, but because she was unable to stop. She'd had these thoughts since she first saw him. That irritated her. This was not her normal behavior, and it wasn't flattering to acknowledge that she was a sexually frustrated woman. She became suddenly angry with Bob and, true or not, to her mind, it was his fault. She hadn't felt a sexual craving for Bob, like the one she was presently feeling for Alex, in many years; it disturbed her. The idea that her self-control seemed non-existent, in this instance, made her throat and ears turn red.

Maybe it was just the heat getting to her. It was going into the high nineties, possibly over a hundred today. Who wouldn't feel this heat? Just then, with her head down, watching her feet, she ran right into Alex, too engrossed in her thoughts to notice that he'd suddenly stopped in front of her.

She brought her hand up to her mouth and stepped back.

Alex turned to her as he cleared his throat. "I was just going to point out that over beyond that large outcropping of rock up ahead is where we're going."

Emma dropped her hand to her side. The motion caught his attention. His eyes fell to her lips. Unable to resist them, Alex leaned forward and kissed her. Quickly, they came together along the length of their bodies. Emma reached up around his neck. His lips moved over her face and mouth, and he pulled her to him. The heat of his body passed through her clothes into her. Emma kissed him again, crushing her lips on his. She felt the tension falling from her body.

Moments later when they parted, she leaned back into his arms and laid her head upon his chest. They stood, lightly swaying on the long, dusty slope. For the first time in days, Emma wasn't thinking about anything. Her mind was as clear as the sky. She held on to the moment, to this timeless clarity, captured by the smell of his body as it mingled with the lingering amber residue rising from his shirt. Some nameless ambivalence in her had withered under the sharp sun and blown away on the breeze, only now revealed in its glaring absence.

Alex wondered if he should regret his impetuousness. He'd been wanting to kiss her since she stood blinking her eyes in surprise at him that morning he first saw her in the Mountain Shadows. This would probably alienate her for good, although he was encouraged by the fact that she was still holding him like he was the only thing that mattered in the whole universe. He'd wait until she made a move before he decided what to do next.

But he envisioned them packing it in for the day, heading for home—a silent ride, each nurturing their own thoughts and regrets—with Emma just wishing to be away from him. The light scent of her perfume and her sweet animal odors rose with the heat of her body. He couldn't remember when he'd smelled anything so enticing. He kissed her again, this time softly on the top of her head.

Emma pulled back from his embrace and held him by the elbows. "Don't you have something you want to show me?"

He looked at her, wide-eyed. "Up there," he said and pointed. "There's still a little way to go."

"Well, shouldn't we get a move on before this heat gives us both a stroke? It's already made us a little crazy, don't you think?" She smiled broadly up at him.

Smiling back at her, he turned and started for the tall escarpment above them. It occurred to him that even though he was the one walking in front, she was in the lead. Alex was comfortable with this surrender. He didn't know another woman with whom he'd consider sharing the lead. He'd always been an independent man. That might just possibly be one of the big reasons why his marriage had failed. Maybe he was unable to trust completely, to let go of total control. He couldn't stop thinking about her kiss; her lips were so full. He kept reliving it in his mind and almost stepped on a rattler. Alex didn't hear it rattle, but then, maybe it didn't. They didn't always warn you when they were about to strike.

Several steps behind, Emma dreamily watched him climb around boulders blocking the path. Taking time to negotiate the trail in her own way, she saw him walking peaceably along when he suddenly jumped into the air, back to the left of her. Too late to be of much help, she tried to catch him as he fell among the rocks.

"What's wrong? Are you hurt? What is it?"

"Nothing. No. Just a rattler. I thought he had me. I almost stepped on him. He didn't strike; at least, I don't think he did." Alex stood and re-slung the gun. He straightened his shirt and slapped the dust from his clothes.

"Where is it?"

"Just behind that rock." He pointed. "Keep your eyes open. Where there's one snake, there's likely a mate close by."

They moved up to the rock and found that the snake had moved off ahead of them. They followed and watched it move away from their path.

"A nice one, huh?" he said. "Must be four feet long. Diamondback. A beauty. I wonder if there's another around." They made a short but thorough search of the immediate vicinity; finding nothing, they sat down for a moment, to let their hearts resume a normal rhythm. Alex removed the shotgun from his shoulder, along with his knapsack, and draped his arms across his knees.

Emma took off her knapsack and opened the flap to see what Alex had brought for lunch. She tossed him an apple and retied the flap.

"Did you see the size of that beauty?" he said.

"Was it a large one for its species?"

"Big enough to ruin my life for at least a month, if it didn't kill me first." After he thought more about it, he said, "Well I doubt it would've killed me, although it might have made me wish that it had."

"You should be more careful," she said. "One never knows what evil lies in wait." She smiled.

They ate their apples, drank some water, re-slung their gear and moved up the slope.

Emma looked around the open space but couldn't see a petroglyph anywhere. The ground had leveled off and become a broad shelf at the base of the escarpment that they saw from below. It looked completely untouched, without the slightest hint that it was a special site. Could there ever have been a settlement here? The area was pristine; it seemed this was the first time any humans had ever set foot on the place.

"Where are they?" she asked.

"Over there," he said, pointing to a fissure concealed at the base of an escarpment, forty to fifty feet high. "But don't go over there just yet.' He removed his knapsack and pulled out a flashlight.

"I don't see anything."

"You will." He handed her his knapsack. "Stand back, I want to check it out before we go in." He moved over to the opening; it was small, nearly undetectable from all but this one angle of approach. He gathered up several hefty rocks and tossed them inside, one at a time. When nothing happened, he went in behind them. From her angle, it appeared as though he bent slightly and disappeared into the rock itself.

A moment later, he reappeared as if by magic. "It's okay."

"I still don't see anything," she said as she joined him. But suddenly, there it was. She grinned at him, and he grinned back.

He loved the expression she got on her face when she discovered something new.

She quickly returned his knapsack and removed hers. She took out the flashlight. "So, this is why you brought these and the candles, too. How did you find this place?"

"Joachim, an old friend of mine, brought me out here. He's a member of the Yaqui tribe, out at Pascua Village. This site is sacred to his people, and he wanted to share it with me. He knew that I'd show it the proper reverence. He told me I should bring no one out here, unless I could trust them to respect it and keep it secret. So, will you swear to keep it secret forever, or will I have to kill you?"

"Ha, ha . . . I cross my heart and hope to die," she said. "Can we go in now?"

Turning on their flashlights, they entered the cave single-file with Alex in front. They stooped sideways to pass through the narrow opening. Once inside, the space opened into a large cavern. It was cool, longer than wide, and went back twenty or thirty yards. Off the main area, smaller fissures—all of them large enough to pass through comfortably—led out in several directions. Alex looked for evidence of habitation and relaxed when he found nothing but a few scattered remains of critters—a jack hare, a pack rat, and a couple of chuckwallas—that must have crawled into the cool shade to die.

"Whenever I come here," he said, "I'm always amazed that no big cat has taken up residence and even more amazed that there's never any evidence of bats."

"Why is that?"

"I'm not sure, but Joachim claims that the spirits of his ancestors live here, and no living creature would dare to violate the sanctity of their home. That's as good a reason to explain things as any I can imagine."

"Well, what about our being here?"

"We're guests."

After her eyes adjusted to the comparative dimness of the flashlights, Emma noticed the sparkle in the surface of the rock. Even more impressive were the paintings and carvings she saw there. As they sloped gently upward over their heads into the shadows, a whole world of painted, stylized images came to life before them—a chronological pictorial history of this region, all mixed together. In beautiful, warm earth tones—red and ocher, sienna, browns and blacks—there were conquistadors on horseback and Jesuit padres with their crosses, as well as birds, small herds of cattle, lizards, antelope, trees and cactus. People were depicted giving birth, harvesting crops of squash and maise, and fighting to defend their villages. Geometric grids and spirals of different sizes in profusion, obviously made by different hands, surrounded them. Direct and shadowed handprints of all sizes made incredibly complex patterns. Emma instinctively felt that the enigmatic patterns represented familial relationship.

"Groupings of families together . . . why not?" she said. "It would make sense."

"Who can tell? Although some of those images are self-explanatory, the experts have no proven idea what prehistoric paintings and carvings actually mean."

An hour later, they took a break to eat their lunch and drink a split of May wine from plastic cups. Then, for the next two hours, Alex led Emma throughout the different chambers. Aside from all the artwork, the cave, itself, was a marvel to explore. She was completely absorbed by the stories and the possibilities that suggested themselves to her, trying to unravel the various pictographs, petroglyphs and paintings.

"Do you know if there is any meaning to the fact that all three different kinds of rock art are mingled together here?" she asked.

"Here, look in this book," he said, handing her the field guide to cave art that he had brought along. "Not that it will say anything about this particular site."

She tried to compare what she and Alex interpreted from the individual images on the walls against what the book described about cave imagery, in general. Of course, she couldn't know for sure what was in the minds of the artists, but she thought that she and Alex had begun to understand a little something about these ancient people. "They were a lot like us, weren't they?" she asked.

"They seemed to be—just trying to survive and raise some kids in a tough old world." In the back of the book, she discovered a list of the known petroglyph sites in the United States. Even though Alex had mentioned something about it, she was surprised when she realized that this site was not listed.

"Now you know why I had to swear you to complete secrecy on pain of death," he said. Warriors with shield and lance chronicled the Pima rebellions against the Spanish above them. Apaches raided peaceful settlements in this area upwards of two hundred years after the Spanish arrived. Scenes of violence commingled with poignant scenes of pregnant women, and women and children with baskets of food. The pictographs and paintings were not all made at the same time or by the same hand. But all of them reminded Emma of the great cave paintings of Lascaux, though these were not anywhere near as old—one kind of an historical record of human residence and activity. In the smallest chamber, farthest from the entrance, there were several indecipherable works—which Alex believed, though couldn't prove, were representations of the woolly mammoth and the giant ground sloth—contemporary to the images in other parts of a much older European Neanderthal world.

Emma felt connected to these ancient artists and yet distanced from them in ways that were imminently painful to consider. She felt joined to but rejected—denied in some basic, primal way—from the personal reality experienced by all people regardless of the times and places in which they lived. These artists were, somehow, more in touch with themselves and better able to express their reality than she was able to express hers, or so it seemed. She was bereft by the poignancy of it. It engendered a tremendous longing in her, an anguish that she hadn't felt since giving up her art. She had not truly realized, until that moment, the emptiness that resided in parts of her life. Emma would never have guessed that she'd have to leave home and travel to another state, and visit a cave, to find herself so far from the reality of her own being.

I can do this, she thought. Yes, she could do this and, just maybe, come to know who she really was. She could reconnect to life in the world in a more meaningful way, as she had when she gave birth to the girls. Painting, she understood—as she gazed up at those specters from the past so elegantly displayed above her—was what she was born to do. This was how she was meant to tell her story. Among the shadows, she'd come face to face with the fact that she had willingly given essential parts of herself away. Could she get them back after all those years? Was it too late? She choked on the irony she felt for the wasted time—for those things that she'd once loved and that were now missing from her life.

Alex moved closer to her.

Turning to look him square in the face, with tears welling up in her eyes, she snapped, "Why did you bring me here?" Before he could answer, she turned and strode from the chamber.

Gathering his gear quickly, he followed her from the dark. He had looked upon and tasted that which was forbidden. Sweet though it had been, it now felt like he had swallowed a mouthful of sand. Maybe the ancient spirit who dwelled in the cave was punishing him for his presumption. Maybe he shouldn't have kissed her. "I don't want you to do anything on my behalf," he said, then stowed his gear in the back of the pickup. He was surprised at the exasperation he heard in his own voice. "Well, damn it all to hell anyway. Just when things were going so well between us."

"I'm sorry," she said. "It's my fault. I'm married, and I love my husband. I shouldn't have done this. I'm very embarrassed. It was wrong of me."

"This means I'm not going to see you again?"

It was unlike Alex to give into emotions, and whenever he did, it made him stupid. Wiping the sweat from his face, he realized that this was not the time for either anger or stupidity.

Emma, too, was sweating profusely from the hike. She removed her hat and wiped her brow with the shoulder of her T-shirt—already wet in places that accentuated her breasts. "I was going to invite you to show your work with us," she said, "but under the circumstances, I don't think it would be a very good idea. So, I'd be more than happy to write recommendations or even call a few people I know who would treat you very well. I owe you that much."

"You don't owe me anything." He tossed her a roll of paper towel from the back of the pickup then drank from his canteen in large swallows. "Did I ask you to show my work?"

"Well, no, but it's very good work. You should let me help you find a spot in L.A."

"Do you always tell people what they should do with their lives?"

Emma didn't respond.

Alex didn't know why he was being so rude, so pigheaded; she was married for Pete's sake. There was never any real chance that she might fall in love with him. How had he allowed himself to indulge in thoughts of love, of living happily ever after with her and Josh? It was ludicrous from the start. He locked his shotgun away.

Get what you can get out of it, cut your losses and count yourself lucky, he told himself. Let her call some galleries. Why not? Having a few extra bucks in your pocket could only make it that much easier to spend time with Josh. Right now, that's really what you need to be doing. You don't need to be running a tour bus for a sun-crazed tourist who doesn't even know her own mind. There's no reason to hang around here until Friday. Do your laundry tomorrow and leave the next day. Get as far away from this woman as you can, as soon as possible, and good riddance to it all.

He was being uncharitable, but he didn't care. Alex couldn't remember the last time he was this pissed over anything. He wasn't entirely sure what had made him so mad. The fact that he was this upset made him even angrier. So much for his Zen peace and serenity. It was just that as they descended from the cave, he had gotten more infuriated with each step so that by the time they'd arrived at the truck, he felt like exploding. It was all he could do to contain himself.

Alex's earlier prediction about their ride back to her car proved to be correct. They were quietly immersed in their own thoughts. When he tried to discuss what had happened in the cave, Emma politely told him that she didn't want to talk about it. She thanked him for the studio visit and for showing her this wonderful site, wished him well in his career, and reiterated her desire to be of help on his behalf. Beyond that, they maintained a peaceful silence.

Back at her car, Alex tried one last time. "Look, I'm sorry about what I said earlier. You're right—I should look for a new gallery in L.A. The extra money will not be unwelcome, and I'd appreciate whatever you might do for me. Come on, let's have a beer and talk about it. We could go have some Mexican food at a little place I know, just two blocks from here."

"No thank you. It wouldn't do us any good, and I have to get back to the Mountain Shadows and try to reserve a seat on a plane home tomorrow."

"You have to eat," he said. "Besides, I hate to part company this way. Couldn't we just have a cup of coffee somewhere?"

"It's better if I go now. It'll be easier for me. We have nothing to gain and more turmoil if we drag it out."

"That's not true, but okay. If that's the way it has to be, that's the way it has to be, though I'd like it to be otherwise. You can't solve your problems by running away from them, you know, and that's what you're doing."

"You're wrong, I'm going home to solve my problems and I don't want to discuss it any more. I'll send you copies of anything I do with the other galleries in your regard." With that, she stuck out her hand. But as he reluctantly took it, she had second thoughts and reached up and kissed him lightly on his cheek. Then she got in the car and left him standing in the lot.

Even with her good intentions to get a plane ticket back home, Emma found that she couldn't bring herself to go directly to the B & B. She was in need of a shower, but didn't want to face Mary and Steve and have to explain things to them. Whatever they knew or suspected about her, they'd offered nothing but support and encouragement. Mary was sympathetic and seemed to understand something of what Emma was feeling, although Emma was more than a little mixed up about it, herself.

It was still mid-afternoon, and having found that she made a wrong turn when she left Alex's studio, she wasn't exactly sure where she was at the moment and drove around downtown, trying to get her bearings. The big plush Ford's air conditioner brought the temperature down so low, her damp clothes became uncomfortable. She changed the settings and began to look at things more calmly.

She was right, of course, to leave it alone. She had no business, whatever her desire, destroying her family in the process. Imagine, kissing a man—a younger man—out on the side of a mountain. For that moment, she was bold. She'd never been that bold before, not that she could remember.

The thrill of his kiss came back to her, with a longing. She could still feel his big hands pulling her close into him. She remembered the hardness of the muscles on his back and his shoulders and the heat she'd felt through his damp shirt as she kissed his mouth. Emma recognized her street, made a swift turn and headed for home. She wanted to get out of her damp clothes and into a long, cool shower. "Get a grip, Emma," she said. "Get a grip."

Alex was bereft. There was nothing he could do. All of a sudden, he really missed Josh. He went home, took a long, tepid shower and made plans to get out of Tucson as soon as he could.

Chapter Seven

So, how far did we go?" Maggie asks.

"All the way, except for Pacific Beach north of the pier," Jack says.

"I know that, silly."

How many times have we done this? Well? And you never remember how far it is. Six miles. Six point six miles to be exact, if we do the whole north end above the pier, which is point zero three miles all by itself. I'm not counting the distance we travel from the apartment to the pier, that's approximately point one five miles."

"Oh," she says, slapping him on the arm. "I remember."

"Then what did you ask me for?"

"I just wanted you to tell me, like you always do."

"Well I was just getting ready to, but you asked me first," Jack says, looking disappointed.

Maggie's always asking him questions. He likes to impress her by telling her things she doesn't know, and she doesn't mind. She's learned some interesting things from him—like the fact that the small depression beneath her nose, above her upper lip, is called a philtrum, and that the small lump of flesh at the front of her ear, which in part shields the opening, is called the tragus. She's often amazed at what Jack seems to know. Sometimes, however, he's lying to her and just acts as if he knows. Then she enjoys getting him by the short hairs and exposing his ignorance. Sometimes, he's just pulling her leg because he knows that she's gullible. So, she has to be on the lookout for his phony explanations. She hates it when he gets one by her. He always makes such a big deal of rubbing it in, trying to embarrass her.

"What do you say we stop at Ralph's and get something to take to the beach for a picnic this afternoon?" he asks.

"I want to stop at the shell shop first and see what kind of shark this tooth came from." She takes it from her pocket as they cross the sand. They're heading toward Gene's Shell Shop—across from Crystal Pier. They didn't walk so much the last time they were here; they didn't have the energy. This trip is different. Having more energy, they try to go to the beach every morning by 9:00 A.M.

At the top of the concrete steps just south of the pier, they stop to look at the ocean. Overhead, a small flock of brown pelicans glides by in a staggered V formation. Maggie hands the shark's tooth back to Jack, and he puts it in his pocket. The beach is getting crowded. Tide's out, but the waves are cresting between two and three feet. Surfers are already out in force. And though it's not officially the season, he can tell that their favorite spot will, no doubt, be taken when they get back. Lifeguards have sectioned off the areas where swimming is allowed and, as a convenience to the swimmers, they've been allotted the beach closest to the bathrooms. With weather too perfect to remain at home, even the dullards, who are generally more inclined to stay in and watch the tube, are going to show up today.

"You know we ought to get us one of those umbrellas," he says and points to an older couple looking for a spot on the beach. The man is stumbling through the sand, loaded down with beach chairs, bags, a cooler, straw hats, towels and an umbrella that's flipping up and down, balanced as it is between his elbow and ribcage, trying to make his way between the people on towels and blankets who are stretched out in every direction at his feet. The couple looks around uncertain which spot they should take; apparently, a couple of feckless morons have taken their favorite place. They shuffle around the beach a few more times, this way and that, but end up right where they started.

"That's going to be us some day," he says, "staggering around with our meager possessions hung around our necks, like a couple of mucklucks, completely baffled and without a clue. We already look like them, George and Betty Smith, with our straw hats, our cooler and our little chairs just like theirs. Another ten years, you think? Think they're older than that? Was it written in the Big Book of Life someplace that humans have to act the same way, dress the same way, go through all the same things at the same time of their lives, in the same way? God, it's depressing."

"Oh, stop it. What? Do you think you're so special?"

"Well, no. I . . . "

"Do you think just because you're a painter, and you're staying at the beach for a whole week, and you have a black shark's tooth in your pocket that makes you something special?"

"No, but it's a nice one, you have to admit," he says in his own defense. He grabs her in a big bear hug. "You don't have one," he teases, nuzzling her ear and turning her around and around. "And I have another nice one, too," he whispers, not referring to the shark's tooth.

He lets her go, and they head toward the shell shop, crossing the little plaza of tall palms, benches and showers by the steps—where people rinse away the sand before leaving the beach.

Maggie always feels a little guilty going into Gene's shop because she knows that she and Jack don't intend to buy anything, and Gene always looks so disappointed when they leave empty-handed. Jack, on the other hand, enjoys disappointing Gene because he entertains the conviction that people should not remove natural elements from their native environments, especially for commercial reasons. They should be allowed to return to the natural order by decaying right where they drop. Jack, himself, however, can't resist and brings back pockets full of shells every time they go out. By some convoluted reasoning that only Jack could come up with, he believes Gene to be a pirate, a thief and a scoundrel for looting and pillaging Mother Nature's treasure trove and selling it in his shop. Maggie's never comfortable asking Gene for information about the shells, even though she'd love to know more about where they come from and why they have such beautiful designs in them. She doesn't want to take his time or give him the impression that she might buy something.

Outside on the deck, a half-dozen display racks made from driftwood—with fishing net stretched about them like spider webs—entice prospective buyers into Gene's lair. Wind chimes and clackers made of shells and drift-wood are strung around on cord, like circus flags and plastic pennants. Small lamps, cobbled together from windowpane oyster shells, sit next to the larger ones that were fashioned from various types of shells, decorously arranged and hot-glued on bases made from bigger shells. Painted rocks, fossils and minerals from oceans around the world are sitting artfully arranged on the floor.

Wicker baskets full of the commoner shells, like those found in just about any shop anywhere, are everywhere. Bags of mixed shells, shrink-wrapped wicker platters full of shells, some species of which were found right there on Mission Beach—though many more were imported from other marine provinces around the world—were designed as gifts. She knows a lot more about them than she did years ago when they first started coming to the beach.

Strangely enough, most of them show no signs of ever being in the ocean at all; she assumes some of them were raised for the market on farms. With all of their spines intact, no chipped edges, no faded colors, no signs of the wear and tear of living in the harsh ocean environment, there's no trace of the animal that once lived in them. A small bushel-basket sits off to the side, full of reduced items that were broken—either in shipment or by some careless lookers who managed to break them and sneak out before getting caught.

Gene believes in educating his patrons. A typed sheet with Xerox pictures hangs by the door; the text reads:

The Shell Oil Company makes The Great Scallop, the most familiar and best to eat, into its logo. The Variegated and Mantle scallops shame the Great Scallop in their rich colors. Of the surf clam species, there's the great Tivela— pieces of which Maggie remembers picking up on her first trip to the beach and thought were shards of broken crockery, until she found the animal still alive in one with its cream-colored shell rayed with soft purple. Maggie just loves the names of these animals: Venus, Nut, Bittersweet, Volutes and Cones, Harps, Ceriths and Augers, Periwinkles and Nerites. The more common Limpets, Sand Dollars
and the highly polished Mussels, Asses Ear Abalone's mother-of-
pearl.

She can't get enough. And, wow! Would you look at that? Sitting beneath the typed sheet right by the door is a sign with an arrow pointing down, identifying it in bold as well as italic print—the largest clam shell in the world, The Tridacna Gigas—the giant clam, with razor sharp edges, living in the warmest waters of the Pacific—the largest clam on record weighed over five hundred and fifty pounds. It produced a worthless pearl weighing more than thirteen pounds.

The sign also gives a lurid account, in small red print, about the diver who, unfortunately, discovered this particular clam when it clamped down on his leg, cutting the artery. Alas, he forgets to tie a tourniquet at his thigh. Although struggling heroically to saw off his own leg at the knee with a fish knife, in his mighty effort to escape the vice-like grip of the giant clam, he's devoured alive on the sea floor by the savage, man-eating, ravenous sharks drawn there from miles around by the blood in the water.

That Gene will tell you anything to make a sale. Or, Maggie wonders, could that really be true? It's even better on the inside; there are cases and cases of shells: Abalone to Zebra Shell—Tritons, Whelks, whorled Recluz's Bullseyes. Trumpets, Turbins and Helmuts, Queen Conch reigns over the Caribbean and the Scorpion Conch rules the Pacific. Cowries, with porcelain-like   finishes and striking colors, rest next to the Eyed, and the East African stolid Cowries, the Dawn and the Money Cowries, used as a means of currency. Little Egg and Egg Cowry. Though not truly rare, there's the Golden or Orange Cowry, one of the most gorgeous of its genus.

The Cowries are Maggie's favorite. On the wall above the case, she reads about others that Gene does not keep in the shop: the rare Brown-Toothed Cowry, the Fulton's

Cowry. Of the White-Toothed Cowry, there are only five known specimens as of the date of printing on the poster that now, as she looks at it closer, reads 1973. Keepsakes, she thinks, things to keep for the sake of memory of time spent at the seashore. Touching them, she feels her connection to a source infinitely older than herself, though the feel of one in her hand is comforting in a way that she could never describe in terms other than the physical. She could spend hours looking—unreasonably, they give her such a feeling of optimism—but she notices that Gene is watching them, hoping to spot the moment when to come over and help them make the right selection.

On the back wall, near one corner, Maggie discovers a freestanding bookcase that is new to the shop. She can only assume, after several minutes browsing, that Gene is eyeballing her with that disapproving scowl because of the way she's opening the bindings of his books. Well, tough, she thinks and picks up A Field Guide to the Shells of the Western Coast of the Americas that she decides to purchase—although he doesn't know that—and flips it all the way open, pressing back on the pages to get a real thorough look inside. She flips cavalierly through the book.

Gene grits his teeth, forces a grin into service, and is almost beyond restraint to come over and put a stop to what she's doing. Serves him right, she thinks. But then, somehow, he manages to take hold of himself and look busy, rearranging the inexpensive earrings and necklaces made of shell that hang on the pegboard behind his counter. The customer is always right; Gene likes living by the seaside.

Beside the bookshelves, Jack is looking into a glass display case that's lit on the inside by a small lamp. Maggie takes her book and joins him in his appraisal of the locked case. A half-dozen black sharks' teeth, just like the tooth Jack found, litter the white velour cloth inside. At the back of the case, some tags identify the specimens before her; she can't believe what she's reading. If true, Jack's find is, in fact, an inky-black thirty-million year-old extinct Megalodon shark's tooth that could be worth as much as three hundred dollars. They turn and stare at each other with their mouths open.

"I feel like a rich man," he says. "Come on, I'll buy you some lunch."

"You can buy this book, too," she says. "I didn't bring my purse with me."

"I walked into that one, didn't I?" They move over to the register where Gene is picking nits and shuffling papers. He's almost beside himself when he notices that Maggie has a book tucked under her arm.

"Can I get you anything else? No? I've seen you folks in here before, haven't I? You were here last year, right? I knew it. Never forget a face. That's a good choice to identify the shells out there. Have you found any interesting ones?"

Jack couldn't resist pulling the shark's tooth out of his pocket, along with a twenty-dollar bill. Maggie watches

Gene's irises click open, quaver, narrow and then glaze over as he looks at the tooth and makes change for the book.

"Nice," is all he says.

Outside on the walk, Jack looks at his watch. He enjoys looking at the shells, however, unlike Maggie's optimism, he gets a strange commingled sense of nostalgia and foreboding that makes him uncomfortable. There's something disconcerting about being there. Time slips by so quickly that he feels himself thrown forward into some distant future, and that he's been there before. Or time drifts so slowly that he feels he's waiting for something, though he doesn't know what it is—and wouldn't want it even if he did know. So many questions. He looks at his watch, again. Thirty-five minutes. Imagine, gone just like that. Is that what getting old comes down to? Jack wonders.

There's something about sameness that they find comforting—the same motel time after time, the same beach at the same time every day, the same route on their walk visiting the shell shop, Ralph's Market, north end of the beach, then south. Revisiting the same restaurants, eating the same food, accompanied by more subtle and insidious routines that they no longer notice or think about, all contribute to their malaise. Could it be that they desire only to spend their lives killing time?—languishing in those agreeable habits that make it possible to escape the rigors of thought and the perturbation of doubt, but which leaves them devoid of passion, living life in the comfort of the familiar. Thank Zeus that every time they come here, there's always something different about the place.

One year, their favorite fish market and oyster bar, Ahab's Seafood, went under. Jack loved the irony of eating lobster and New England-style chowder on the Pacific. Next year, the replacement went under. Well, it wasn't that good anyway—too trendy for Maggie's taste, with the college girl waitresses in their wonder bras, clingy tops and short-shorts.

Last year they discovered a little Japanese fast-food place—a tiny, wrinkled old woman did all the cooking in the back. She made great bowls of Udon soup full of roast pork, veggies and noodles. This year, it had a 'for rent' sign in the window. Did she pass on to a better place, or did she give away too much for too little and just went bust?

The Shell station, at the corner of Grand and Mission Blvd., so convenient for gassing up, gone, along with The Spice Rack next door where they liked to eat their last meal on every trip. Tacky, old-fashioned red-checkered tablecloths had covered the well-used wooden tables that sat on a creaky plank floor. Cheap plastic flower garlands draped around the ceiling made the place resemble a gazebo. They loved it anyway. And the food—they would never forget the food: Sinful muffins with poppy seeds, blueberries or zucchini; all kinds of napoleons, biscotti, eclairs, doughnuts; a dozen different kinds of cookies, tarts, cakes, crêpes and waffles with fresh berries or syrup of all flavors and bacon or sausages. And the Eggs Benedict with ham and hollandaise, or Eggs in a Nest of corned beef hash, washed down with the delicious but naughty champagne mimosas that got their day off to a rosy start. Not to

124

mention the desserts, the homemade ice creams, pies and chocolates that were all indescribable. He could still taste them; they made his mouth water.

Six or eight years ago they tore down the whole end of that block; it had stood empty until last year. Now, there's a Starbucks, a print shop, a juice bar, a game room and several other small, hip new-age beach-gear shops clustered around Ralph's grocery—barnacles on the back of a giant crab—and these are beginning to age. The old always makes way for the new. People eat healthier today. There's no doubt that the good old Rack had to go. And there's no getting around it; change is inevitable. The real question: What's coming next and what can we do about it?

"Hey Maggie, look who's up ahead. Remember that Ford truck parked beneath the window that I pointed out to you yesterday? Well, see this guy coming with the bags? That's the fellow that's been living in the camper."

"Really?"

"I saw him park right next to the 'No Overnight Parking' sign. He's been parked there since yesterday. That must be nice—   drive right up to the ocean and stay a week without paying rent. If   I tried that, they'd haul me off to jail and throw away the key."

"Say, he looks a bit like you, don't you think?"

"Not really. I'm better looking than he is."

"I wonder what he does all day?" Maggie returns the man's smile as they pass. "Did you see that? He smiled right at me."

"Yeah, I saw it. And I saw you smile right back, you hussy."

"You know, I think I've seen him before; I was under the pier. It was raining. He ran by wearing a light gray jersey. He didn't see me."

"Oh? Well, I saw him this morning while you were in the bathroom. I forgot to tell you. He came out of the truck with a backpack, one of those collapsible aluminum lawn chairs, and a small folding table. He went down to the end of the walk where he stood for a few minutes, until he turned north and left."

"Well, what would he be doing with all that?"

"Looks like he was headed over to the north end to paint. That's where I'd go."

"Not very imaginative, are we?"

Maggie takes his arm, and they cross Mission Street, heading for the beachfront walk where there's less noise and hassle. Here the traffic is a cacophony, a hip-hop holiday hustle. Car horns are blaring. Bumper to bumper, buses and trucks halt with their hydraulics hissing and screeching like a flock of squabbling gulls. Their smelly rubber tires "thrub" the asphalt tarmac in a circular cadence, raising volumes of dust, smog and debris. People are yelling, jostling, bumping, pushing, tripping over each other's heels along the street. Skateboarders weave confusion into the mix, in and out of the throng. The wheels of their boards click and clack in counterpoint over the uneven concrete sidewalks. An occasional temper flares in all the commotion.

Under the spell of sunlight—bouncing whitely through the sharp sea air, tinged though it is with exhaust—Jack and Maggie play one of their little games while they walk. They make up stories about people they see. Based on the clothes, the expressions, the general vibes that the people emanate, the Lawrences try to guess who they are, what they do for a living, the most important thing in their lives. Maggie recognizes that Jack's hooter radar is online, but she ignores it, or tries to. Jack thinks he's being discreet, but he rarely fools Maggie.

In Ralph's, these intrepid hunter-gatherers go about the business of securing their afternoon vittles. They decide on that distinctly American cornucopia known as the salad bar, a luxury that always makes Jack grateful that he was born in the good old U S of A.

"Americans," he declares—and he doesn't care who overhears him—"can walk into a store on just about every corner, of every street, in every city in the whole damn country and buy food from all corners of the globe. There are kiwis from Australia, snails from France, sardines from Norway, rum from Jamaica, watermelons and tomatoes from Mexico, not to mention all the exotic spices and condiments in the world to flavor them up.

"Two thirds of the world's population are struggling to eat, but Americans have at their fingertip, for minimal expense, more than they can possibly consume—so much is just thrown away. Americans waste more food, material and power than any people on the planet. Does it make a man proud? It never ceases to amaze me just how spoiled Americans are. They take it all for granted so easily. No wonder the rest of the world hates us. It makes me want to puke."

Maggie doesn't like hearing it, but she never complains. She gets the things she needs and ignores the tirade.

At the checkout, Jack watches in disappointment as an older man takes the last umbrella from a large box on the aisle. With the groceries evenly divided, and double bagged into extra reusable bags for easier carrying, he pays the cashier, and they head back to the apartment, re-crossing Mission to walk along the ocean walk. There they can escape the traffic noise and fumes and enjoy the view. Crossing Eden View, they see that the pickup is parked in the same place.

"We're going to have to keep our eyes on this guy," Jack says. "Maybe he's not a painter at all. He could be a cat burglar, robbing all these apartments while their innocent, unsuspecting holiday visitors are at the beach. He's shifty looking, don't you think?"

Just as Jack finishes saying this, the man descends from the back of the camper dressed in a pair of highly polished black loafers, crisp dark slacks and a cool, colorful short-sleeved shirt that enhances the silver of his hair. The man smiles again in Maggie's direction and nods to Jack as they pass each other, heading south in the direction of the pier from which they'd just come.

"Aha! What did I tell you? See those clothes? Pretty spiffy for a painter. I didn't see a splatter of paint anywhere."

"I think he looked rather handsome in those clothes," she says.

"You think he's handsome?"

"He's got a great smile."

"Yeah, I noticed."

"He's probably meeting a woman for lunch."

Jack wonders how this guy could have gotten so dapper, so fast, in that cramped little camper shell. Does he have some kind of mini-shower in there or what? But he says nothing. In fact, they both remain silent until they get back and put the groceries away. Jack pours water from the pitcher in the fridge while Maggie sets out small plates of food—hummus, bread, onion, olives and tomatoes. They eat on the balcony and watch the sea, trying to absorb the full immensity of what they're experiencing.

"Do you want to go up to La Jolla and see that Joan Mitchell show sometime this week?" Jack asks.

"Why not? We could stop off and get a look at the beach there, maybe even take a swim in the cove."

Maggie recalled the first beach they visited together before they were even married. It was a short time after Maggie's father had died. North Carolina Beach was just an hour's drive from where her Dad had grown up on a farm. Every summer her family had driven from Detroit to visit her father's family. Jack and Maggie spent two whole weeks of sheer bliss in a big old rambling beach cottage on stilts in the sand. They went off in the early evening light, down to the boardwalk where they bought fresh doughnuts and stood watching—rapt in fascination, in each other's arms—as the machine spit the circular rounds of batter into the bubbling fat below; only letting go of each other to eat the sweet glazed confections, almost too hot to touch. Hotdogs, cotton candy and sno-cones, too, they munched the burgers and drank the beer, almost getting sick on the Ferris wheel and the Tilt-a-Whirl—holding on to each other for dear life.

After dark, strolling back along the beach with the sounds of the amusement park dying away behind them, stunned into silence by the stars, they stopped to listen to the ocean and make out in the sand. Who would not love the heavy petting, investigating the intimacy of such personal discovery?—learning the depths of each other with tongues and fingers and all the surfaces of their skin as only the young learn the first time, gasping for breath, hearts pounding.

At stolen moments during the day, Maggie felt constantly interrupted by the prying eyes and minds of others when someone was always looking for them and might've caught them, alone at the cottage, off down the beach or out of sight behind the dunes. Even without the consummation of intercourse, there was something extremely pleasurable for these initiates, even deep and thrilling, in the risk of exposure when sneaking around for the kind of ecstasy they found only at the brink of ripping off their clothes.

Maggie thought it was on the beach in North Carolina that she first knew that she loved Jack. They'd only been dating for a few months when she invited him to go. Her Uncle Perry convinced Maggie's mother that it was a good idea for Jack to come, knowing that Maggie liked him more than she had anyone for some time. Otherwise, she would be the only one with no one of her own age along for company. Then, too, Uncle Perry could always use help with the sixteen-hour drive. He was on the trip with a wife, a sister and a niece, and he needed, as he put it, "to have another male around, just on general principle." Besides, it was a four-bedroom cottage.

But now that she remembered it, she realized that Uncle Perry must have known how depressed she was, indeed, how down they all were over the loss of her father at such a young age. This trip, coming when it did, was the perfect medicine for what ailed them. It gave them time to reflect, to be distracted from the pain and sorrow. And Jack must have looked like the best distraction imaginable for Maggie. Uncle Perry had been right.

Maggie knew it was the first time Jack had ever seen the real ocean. Ever since, he has been unable to dissociate sex from the sea, not that he's found any need to try. Everything about it—the moisture-laden light breaking into prisms of color as the water broke over the wave, the scents of salt and seaweed baking in the sun, the crying of the gulls, the black starry sky over black open water—made him horny. She had to laugh at him.

The second time, they traveled to the ocean on the coast of Maine several years after they were married. Horny as lobsters in mating season, they made love on every beach they could find, clear down to Boston. Likewise, Maggie credits their honeymoon journey to Niagara as the initial cause of her compelling desire to have sex in the open air under a waterfall.

Now, after thirty years of marriage, their lovemaking begins with the first slipping of his hand between her legs at the kitchen sink before breakfast every day, continuing all day when they're together. And when apart, they keep the constant touch alive in their minds, in their thoughts, until the final lovemaking begins under the covers, or in the early morning hours when an errant, hot-rodding teenager on the prowl through the neighborhood awakens them. It's an irrational, undeniable need that strikes in the odd hour and that only the other can satisfy.

After lunch, they shower together and make love for the second time that day, an unusual occurrence that Maggie attributes to the regenerative powers of the salt sea air and plenty of sleep. They nap, and she's the first to rise. After washing her face with Noxema, she holds a cool damp cloth against her swollen labia before dressing in her suit for the beach. Maggie is not unused to such ardor from Jack, but their sex life is changing. Now, they're lucky to make love four times a month and even then, Jack is sometimes incapable of orgasm. Of course, Maggie's pleased that he can perform for an extended time, but then that's never been one of their problems. He's always been able to satisfy her sexually.

Maggie knows that when aroused, she's what Jack considers a hot number, though she's not what he'd call a voracious sexual athlete. She's enthusiastic and energetic and, as the years go by, seems more inclined to have sex, even though her interest in sex is changing with the dropping of her hormone levels. It takes them both longer to be aroused. At home, the daily grind takes its toll on their love life as it does on every aspect of living.

Later, in the kitchen, Maggie gathers their picnic stuff together. She sits on the end of the bed and wakes Jack by massaging his feet.

"Do you ever miss falling in love?" she asks.

"Mmm," he moans.

"Remember that feeling?"

She's not going to let him off that easy, he realizes.

"You know, the first time you see someone and spend time with them? Then all of a sudden, you can't get enough; you just have to be there with that person. You can't wait. You just want to be with them all the time."

"But we are in love."

"I know that! No, I mean falling in love, not being in love. You know how it happens."

"I know that, over the years, you and I keep falling in and out of love," he tells her, opening his eyes. Her massaging the same spot is starting to irritate him. He gently pulls his foot back and lays the other one across her lap.

She hardly notices. "It's not the same. There's nothing like the first time. Do you ever miss it? Do you ever think about falling in love with someone else?"

"What's the point? I couldn't tell you even if I did."

She slaps his foot a quick, stinging blow to his instep. Then suddenly pushing it away, she jumps up and heads into the kitchen. "Come on, let's go, it's getting late."

Downstairs, getting their beach chairs from the back of the truck, they run into David Rayburn in the parking lot. He tells them that Ruth had a sudden medical problem in the night and had to go to the hospital where they admitted her for tests and observation.

"It's cancer, of course, but at this point they don't really know what stage or what's happening to her except that she's in a lot of abdominal pain," he says. He looks distracted as if he doesn't quite know what has happened to him, or he doesn't recognize his surroundings and is trying to get his bearings. He's breathing harder than usual, puffing for air.

"I'm so sorry to hear that," Maggie says. "Is there anything we can do?"

"Oh no, no, nothing," David murmurs. "But thank you. I just thought I should let you know." He looks from one face to the other and back again and turns and heads toward his apartment. He stops at the edge of the grass to pick up a piece of trash then disappears through his office door.

The sand on the beach is too hot to cross in bare feet. Unlike the human inhabitants, the gulls stand one-legged out on the wet sand, keeping their temperature down. They only venture back into the hot dry dunes of the beach at the prospect that some careless human has left a tasty delectable of some sort in an unguarded tote bag. Jack and Maggie stand and look out upon the expanse of the ocean.

It's as if the beach were inhabited by a colony of walruses. And, as for sheer numbers, if this were a typical Saturday in the off-season, Jack would hate to see a Saturday in the on-season. All of the big males are plopped out on their territories, scratching and sunning themselves while the young bachelors hang out in gangs, displaying for the seasonal young females who are dressed in even skimpier beachwear than the boys. The youngsters are into everything. Adolescents, with sleek perfect bodies, chase each other and play paddleball at the water's edge. The mature females lounge sedately with their books, sitting in their nylon and aluminum chairs; or they lay propped up, relaxed under their sunbonnets and umbrellas while watching a child or two who needs attention. Even so, they're not too busy to keep their suspicious eyes on their mates, the big males, whose darting eyes are popping out all over the beach.

Jack and Maggie find a pleasant spot just north of the service ramp, not far from the bathroom that sits on the cliff above. Laying out their towels and setting up their chairs, they settle into an afternoon of relaxation and pleasure—rubbing on the sunblock, reading, napping, and watching the people who Jack always claims to despise. In fact, if the truth were told, he actually loves them, though he finds them so disappointing. It's just that he can't stand to be in their company for any length of time except at the beach. Around five, they break out the picnic—cool green salads, sardines in soy oil with jalapeño peppers, juice, cheese, apples and Fig Newtons.

"Well, do you ever miss falling in love?" she asks, resuming her interrogation, now that their picnic is over.

"Back to this, are we?" He pulls Kundera's Immortality of the beach bag. "Sure I miss it, but what can we do about it? Are you going to fall in love with someone else any time soon? You'll let me know, won't you? Maybe you would like to fall in love with Pablo."

"Who?" Maggie grabs the Fifty Shades of Gray paperback from the beach bag.

"The guy in the camper who keeps smiling every time he sees you."

"Oh, him." She lipfarts. "He's too old. But if I find someone, I'll let you know," she says and grins at him.

Some moments go by while they read.

"God! This is one of the worst books I've ever read," she says.

"Well, that's too bad; this is Kundera's best."

Out beyond the surf, the water's beginning to take on the silver glint of the late afternoon sun as it broaches the horizon. Maggie puts her book away, removes herself from the chair, shakes off the stiffness from sitting too long in the same position and stretches out face down on her towel.

Jack continues to sit and watch the girls around him, wishing he could shake his Kundera at them. Maggie might think he's just ogling the girls, but Jack derives a great deal of pleasure from watching all sorts of people. They're endlessly fascinating to him when he stops long enough to consider what it is they're actually doing in front of him—

time spent that he usually doesn't think he can afford except when he comes to the beach.

"Maybe you really are burnt out on your job," he says.

"You've been there a long time. You always say how much you still like the people."

"I do, but it's over twenty years now and it's the same every day. I know I'm lucky. It's a great place to work. It's just that I need more time. If I could have another day off, if I could afford to take a pay cut or get more time instead of a raise, I'd do more with my photographs. I never have the time to just think about what I'm doing with them. You're lucky that you have every day in the studio all by yourself with no interruption. You know, better than anyone, how much concentration creative work demands."

"This is true. But it's not all fun and games out there, you know?—especially when I'm not making any money. I feel like I'm not contributing in any real way. All the time in the world doesn't make it happen. In fact, sometimes, it's just the opposite. But I know what you mean."

Jack stands up to stretch and watch a group of boats passing south toward the entrance to the bay. He's never able to figure out if this particular class of boats is pleasure craft, fishing vessels or charter boats. Certain Navy ships he knows on sight from war movies, and he can usually identify the commercial tankers from shows he's seen on TV, but he can't tell at these distances when they're the

Navy's tankers. Just like some of his and Maggie's problems, they're too indistinct, too out of focus to tell anything specific about them except for their general shape. There's a lot of traffic out there and, damn—he slaps his forehead—he forgot his binoculars again.

Overhead, a local television station's news chopper is flying south, trying to meet a deadline of some sort, he imagines. But he and Maggie have no deadlines now—just being here. Jack notices that the crowd is thinning out as people begin leaving for the day. He sits back in his chair, massages his calves.

"You know, we're better off than a lot of people," he says.

"I know," she says. "Nick and Mark are both healthy. We're not in bad shape either. We've nothing to complain about, really."

"Well, we're not making enough money."

"How much is enough? All our basic needs are met."

"Sure, but we haven't saved much for the future."

"No, but then we're not destitute either. Like you said, we have more than a lot of people."

"Yes, but somehow we're still not quite satisfied, are we?—not completely happy."

"Is anybody? What is being completely happy anyway, and how long does it last?"

"Who the hell knows? I'm tired of thinking about money. Listen here, young lady, it looks like you got some sun today." He's pointing out her pink arms. "It's been over an hour. You want to go for a swim?"

"That doesn't matter. I wasn't waiting to go in."

"I know." He jumps out of his chair.

"Watch what you're doing, you're getting sand in my suit!" Maggie turns, props herself on an elbow and brushes sand off her cleavage.

"Yeah, sorry! Hey, great suit. Can I feel it?" he asks as he bends down and begins to run his hand over her mons Veneris.

Twisting around, she gets up quickly.

"I think it looks warm enough to go in," she says, although   she hugs herself in a shiver. The sun is descending rapidly toward the open sea. They move down the shingle to the surf where it's lathering the beach, kicking across the hot sand and herding gulls as they go. After a day like this, as the last golden rays of sunlight strike long, almost horizontally across the sky, nothing in the world makes them as truly conscious of the moment as that shiver they get when they first put their big toes right smack into the chilly water.

Sunday

Chapter Eight

For whatever reason, not one she could remember, Emma put off trying to get a ticket back to L.A. the night before, telling herself that she had plenty of time to do it today. But by the clock on the table, it was already ten, and she hadn't even gotten up to use the bathroom. She knew from booking her previous flight that she'd already missed the first plane back this morning, and there were only three in the day. However, this was Sunday, and she wasn't sure how many flights there were or what times they were flying. Still, it didn't matter. There was always tomorrow.

Emma hadn't slept this late in years. It felt good to just lie in bed. It must be this climate, she thought, because this was her second late morning since she arrived. Would she ever get used to this? She doubted it, but she was probably wrong about that. She'd been wrong about other things in her life over the years. Life was illusory, and Emma was no exception when it came to being fooled by appearances.

The hike must've really worn her out. She stayed in bed, rummaging through memories of yesterday's fiasco and staring up at the stars on the ceiling. They were painted illusions as were the rest of the images floating on the walls around her. The ceiling beneath the paint was textured in a standard wall pattern that belied the illusion painted there. Why hadn't she noticed the textures? It amazed her that she failed to look beneath the surface of things. It occurred to her that that was probably true in other areas of her life as well. What else had she missed?

When it came to walls, she'd seen the texture before. She even knew how the plasterers created it—quickly slathering plaster compound onto the ceiling and walls with their trowels, much like oil paint on a canvas, leaving the ridges, welts, pocks and dimples in big swathes on the dull-gray sheet rock. So, she knew all about wall texture and thought she knew about illusion.

But today, illusions of all sorts, like the murals, aggravated her. The colors were too intense. The overall scene was too vexingly male-view dominant. She found them meager, lacking substance, too syrupy and unsophisticated for her palate—another banal vision of southwestern Arcadia. Was there not enough banality in the world already without adding to it with murals like this? The women were too perfect, the men too manly. Where was the gritty reality, the irony? Where were the telltale signs of chaos and decay? Where were the seeds of evil? There was no snake in this Eden. All the fruit—mangos, grapes, bananas and papayas— was perfectly ripe; no corrupting apples here; no Caravaggio painted these murals. The men and women on these walls would never age. Everything was static, unchanging, dead—preserved just as she saw it for all time, or until someone painted it out.

"Oh, Alex, it's just not possible," she said and got out of bed. "Perfection doesn't exist, and you can't make it seem like it does—no matter how expertly you create the illusion." In the perfect world, no doubt, she'd be a great painter, and they'd fall into mad, passionate love and be with each other for the rest of their lives.

"Fat chance, Emma," she said, then put on her robe and headed for the bathroom. "Now I'm talking to myself. Great."

In the dining room, ten minutes later, she found a note from Mary, telling her to help herself to anything she could find in the kitchen. She wouldn't be back until late afternoon. Emma had a leisurely breakfast of cereal and fruit at the dining room table. As she ate, the relentless beauty of the Catalina Mountains reminded her of the Sandarios and the caves where she and Alex had had such a marvelous day, until she had started feeling sorry for herself. Maybe eating a small wedge of raspberry-cheese Danish with her coffee while she browsed through the Sunday paper would make her forget all about that embarrassment. She didn't want to think about yesterday or Alex; but lately, there was no controlling her mind.

She took the paper, Danish and coffee and went out to the patio. The air was sweet, but the day was heating up fast, and she wouldn't be out there long. It didn't matter. She was just too antsy to stay inside for the time being. When she had told Alex that she was embarrassed about her actions, Emma was being truthful. But she'd lied to him about loving Bob, although, at the time, it was true in her mind. Her image of her adult self was changed irrevocably and, for the present, there was nothing on the horizon to replace it. She was Bob's wife in name only.

How she came to this discomfiting state of affairs was mystifying. How does one get oneself into this kind of quandary? There was no one thing she could point to and say definitely that this was the cause—this was the point where she became the woman she was today. At least the Danish didn't disappoint. Maybe a little gallery hopping wouldn't disappoint, either.

Alex woke early in an uncharacteristically bad mood. He didn't bother to shave, shower, or comb his hair. He'd had a bad night, and his eyes reflected his lack of sleep. Splashing water in his face to wake up didn't help much. He dressed in yesterday's clothes and walked down to the Broadway Hotel coffee shop for his coffee—plus three eggs over easy, four strips of bacon, hashed-browned potatoes, two slices of heavily buttered toast and strawberry jam. He didn't go to the Café Arles for his breakfast; they didn't serve such fare. A meal of that nature was unusual for him, since he had given up meat and fried foods years before. He knew better, but he did it anyway. Sometimes, a man just had to do something that he knew was going to hurt.

He drank his coffee and watched the faces of the people sitting in the booths and along the counter—familiar faces, most of them—people he'd seen in the neighborhood for years now, although he really didn't know any of them. They nodded in recognition, sometimes, in passing on the street or in the restaurants. They were the people who made up his community. Some of them looked hopeless, without funds or the possibility of acquiring any. He never talked to most of them. They didn't have any more answers to the big questions than anyone else. He lived with them in a broad sense and wondered what it would be like to leave them here and move to Texas. Not much different, he supposed.

People like these, like him, lived in every city in the country. He always felt pretty much at home anywhere he went. He'd miss most of the gang at the Café Arles, no doubt. But it would be a little while before it was necessary to think about moving on a more permanent basis. There was Seattle to contend with, and that prospect was exciting to him. Now that he considered it, it was probably what was needed to get this woman out of his mind. Nothing like a colossal public art project, with the risk of total humiliation, to clear his head and get his priorities in line.

The waiter refilled his cup without being asked and dropped the Daily Star on the table in front of him. "Thought you might like to look at this while you finish your coffee," he said.

"Thanks," Alex said.

"Are you done with those?" the waiter asked, pointing to Alex's dishes.

Alex nodded.

"Is there anything else I can get you?"

"Nope, that'll do it, I believe." When he reached over to pull out a section of the paper, he smelled the day-old perspiration in his shirt and thought he could smell Emma there as well. It reminded him of standing out on the

Sandarios and holding her close to him. She seemed always there, just below his consciousness, popping up unexpectedly when he let his guard down. It had been like that all night.

He blew over his cup and sucked air to cool his coffee as he drank. He lowered the paper and looked out at the empty streets. Downtown early Sunday morning was his favorite day for that reason. Damn it all, he thought. Was there anything he could've done differently? He was following her lead. Whatever her situation, she was in control and knew what she wanted, or did she? Emma was refined and intelligent, knowledgeable about art. She was conversant, curious and fully engaged—thrilled in the cave with the petroglyphs. Perhaps it was an illusion. What if she was a total psychological and emotional wreck? Stranger things had happened in his life. Was he just being paranoid?

If he was, it was no wonder. Just look at those headlines, he thought and lifted the paper—same old crap on the front page, never any good news. The murders, the pedophile priests, that moron Trump, he was sick of it all. His stomach rumbled. He took a napkin from the table and wiped perspiration from his face. Burping helped settle him. He put his cup in the saucer and pushed them away.

So what was this all about, really? She had seemed comfortable with their intimacy and yet, it was only a short time later that she had that strange reaction in the cave. He noticed it slowly growing as they walked from chamber to chamber. Her eyes lit up at his suggestion that the faint and indistinct images in the rear cave dated much earlier than the others. Humans living in that area so long ago had left images that she could see, and it had positively enthralled her. She had seemed truly happy in his company.

There was nothing left to do, but stop thinking about it and get back to making his travel plans. He folded the paper, paid his bill, bought a pack of Tums and stepped out onto the sidewalk. Suddenly, it seemed a prudent course of action to not waste any time and hurry back to the studio. It looked like he was going to start paying for his transgressions sooner than he thought.

Well, so much for the avant-garde, Emma thought, as she walked around the members' group show at the Kitchen Sink Gallery—one of several small co-op art galleries in Tucson. In comparison to artists in L.A., or even to someone like Alex, their show was mediocre with only a couple of moderately interesting pieces. Ego-driven and dripping with irony, most of the work exemplified the worst of what was being shown in the major art centers in the U.S. Emma wasn't stuck in the past. She was as interested in new work as anyone in her field, but sometimes she deplored where the art market was headed. As a dealer, determined to uphold certain standards, she knew she didn't have to give up 'quality' for 'new' when she began work in the new Duncan-Brighton. She and Gen had talked about such things before, and it was one of the reasons that Emma had decided to take her offer.

Outside on Congress Street, she looked around to get her bearings, then headed for the Museum. On the way, she walked by a tiny, brightly-decorated Mexican restaurant. Unable to resist the smells emanating from the doorway, she stopped to peer inside through an old screen door. The place was full, although an older couple was vacating their table. Suspecting that the younger couple coming along the walk behind her was also headed for the restaurant, she slipped in quickly, sat at the empty table and smiled at herself. Something good might remove the bad aftertaste from that mediocre Kitchen Sink show.

The chalkboard menu on the wall over the counter in front listed only five items, all in Spanish. From years of living around Hispanic culture in L.A., she could make out chili rellenos, pollo asado, carne seca, arros y frijoles and menudo. When the tiny, bright-eyed Hispanic waitress popped over, rattled off the daily specials listed on the menu and requested her order, Emma couldn't decide and asked for a combination plate with a sample of each.

The girl wore a colorful skirt and blouse, reminding Emma of the women in the murals at the Mountain Shadows.

"That's a pretty outfit you're wearing," she said, as the happy young woman began clearing away the dirty dishes.

"Gracias, my Nana made it for me," she said and headed to the rear.

Emma's eyes followed her all the way back through the doorway into the tiny galley kitchen where a thin, stooped, white-haired Hispanic man in a long white apron and chef's hat cocked to one side was singing and dancing little steps. As he stirred the pots, Mariachi music blared with static from a radio on the shelf above his stove. Another young woman in a white apron was also laughing and singing with the music. The girls might have been twins; they looked that much alike.

The chef danced Emma's young waitress around the small space as she gave him the order. Stopping to ladle out the food, he turned to see who had ordered everything on the menu. When he saw Emma watching him, he nodded and smiled, then turned back to his stove, resuming his chicken-scratch two-step. The girl sat the plate in front of her and told Emma to save room for the flan.

Thirty minutes later, stuffed like a turkey and paying her bill, Emma noticed the words 'El Cocinero' at the top of the menu board and smiled. She had no idea what it meant, but thought it was a fitting name for this cozy little place. The lunch had lifted her spirits, and Emma couldn't remember the last time she'd eaten such good Mexican vittles.

Outside, in the glare of the afternoon sun, Emma realized that she had to hurry if she was going to see the Museum show before it closed. But she couldn't move any faster and felt like a duck waddling along the sidewalk. She thought about her impromptu lunch at the little restaurant. It was so spontaneous, not like her at all, not to mention that she had just eaten an hour or so before.

Besides the food, Emma had loved the little murals in bold primary colors all along the walls. They were painted with love and a sense of joy, and their earthy quality reminded her of the murals at the Mountain Shadows, in feel and motif. Lush plant forms, ivy and wisteria vines trailing around the doors, an occasional design reminiscent of the hand-painted tiles, idyllic scenes of Mexican village life—simple depictions that meant something real to the artist who had created them. Like the food, they represented a desire to make her visit to the restaurant a tasteful experience, a true sensual and visual delight. Primitive and unarguably romantic, if not downright corny, the paintings were clichés, but they communicated a message from the painter directly to the viewer.

And she had felt it. She felt as good viewing the art as she did eating the hot, spicy food. After years of working with artists, and taking classes at the university, she understood painting from an academic and esoteric point of view, but here in Tucson, she'd seen painting in a new way. From the ancient rock art of the caves, to Alex's informed and elegant abstractions, to these small but enchanting enamel wall decorations, she experienced an insight into the rationale for paint—a new notion of what painting might really be all about. Another aspect of the impulse to make art, to create, was becoming clearer in her mind. So caught up in the nuance and intricacy of the commercial world of art, she'd somehow misplaced her own intuitive grasp of what art, in general, and painting, in particular, could mean, at their core. She'd lost something long ago that, oddly enough, she was now beginning to need.

Ten minutes later, she was inside the monolithic concrete cave of the Tucson Museum of Art. Emma paused to allow her eyes to adjust to the dim light and slightly chilly ambiance of the space. For a moment, she fancied that she could feel and hear the subliminal throbbing of infernal machines laboring far beneath her. She paid for her ticket and crossed the lobby to the freestanding Plexiglas box full of dollar bills that prompted her to be at least as generous as previous patrons. She dropped in five more bucks, resisting the impulse to crack it open, take the money, and run.

Just beyond the donation box, she saw the first of a series of paintings—hung in a row, along the first leg of several ramps sloping at right angles that descended into the nether regions below. Standing at the top of the ramp as if on the promontory of some vast underground cavern, she could see the rest of the show lined out along the walls, at different levels beneath her. For a moment, just before looking over the edge, Emma thought she might see a lake of bubbling brimstone at the bottom. How strange was that? Was she hallucinating? For some strange reason, the place made her uneasy. Maybe it was the artwork.

On the wall to her right, the first painting was by a painter she didn't know—a big dreamy abstraction of floral patterns reminiscent, in size only, of the large flower paintings of Georgia O'Keefe. It lacked the substance of Georgia's hard-edged no-nonsense realism and sharp eye. This kind of slick, sweet sentimentality should be punished, Emma thought.

As she moved down the row, the next piece, though technically proficient, was an equally uninspired rendering of a young cowgirl, herding a small group of cows and their young calves through a torturous ravine, with the monsoon breaking over the mountains behind them, threatening to trap them before they could escape the coming deluge. The card said that the daughter of a nationally recognized cowboy artist had painted it, but Emma didn't recognize the name. She was aware that not all work hanging in museums was there because it merited being there. Sometimes, for other reasons that had to do with commercialism, favoritism and nepotism, merit was, occasionally, the last consideration for inclusion into the hallowed halls of Art.

Moments later, at the first landing, Emma paused to say hello to the security guard whose nametag read Dante. She decided it was fortunate that they were closing at four; it would be a very long afternoon otherwise. In fact, it turned out to be a significantly shorter afternoon than she'd predicted. Dispensing with her usual modus operandi, Emma breezed by each painting looking for one thing only—a sense of truthfulness, a sense of complete and utter inevitability. She was looking for that one element of authenticity that she found present in the rock paintings that was also present, in another way, in the restaurant decorations. She found it hung towards the back end of the show. It was a small self-portrait, in oil, by a painter named Bea Tyler. She stood in front of it, caught up in the intensity and truthfulness of its vision.

Every painting in her own small collection possessed this same quality, as did the paintings she'd seen at Alex's studio. Each one was inspirational and revelatory. The style of the work was of no consequence; it didn't matter what it was about. That one irreplaceable element was present, or the painting was a failure. She had to have been aware of it, of course, but she couldn't have put it into words before today. They were spiritual.

How she hated that word when applied to art; it conjured all the wrong associated images. What great paintings had in common, and what made them exceptional, was that they all expressed the spirit of the artist without adornment. Lacking that, a painting was simply an exercise in paint—dead. This should not have been such a revelation to an art dealer. Obviously, out in the greater world, in this postmodern golden age, any talk of a painting being spiritual was undoubted blasphemy, and, in fact, Emma knew that painting had reached its zenith. But although there was nothing new to be added to the discipline, there was still much to be learned from it. How long had she been studying art history and never before understood this one fundamental insight? Everything depended on one's point of view. Perhaps she'd found her own special way of seeing. Everyone had one, or should. Now that she thought about it, her world was changing, becoming new, strange and mysterious right before her eyes.

The Museum, this palace of the Muses, was full of ghosts; they were hung on the walls like so many painted sheets. This edifice had become a mausoleum. "Don't take it too seriously," she remembered her mother saying, "It's just an interesting diversion to practice until you can find your real work in life." Well, her mother had it half-right. You can't take it too seriously. "You can't take anything too seriously," Emma said aloud. Stepping away from the shades of the museum into the full golden glow of the late-afternoon sunlight, she felt just like Persephone on her long-dreamed-of maiden return from the underworld.

"So, it sounds like you had a busy day," Mary told her as they took their tea out on the patio. Cool night air flowed down from the canyons of the Catalinas.

"Yes, and I still haven't called the airline to get my ticket changed, so it looks like I'll be here another day—if that's okay with you."

"Stay as long as you like. You're scheduled until Thursday anyway. I'm going to miss having you around the place. Oh, by the way, Alex called earlier. He asked how you were. He's leaving sometime tomorrow to go see his boy. I think he wants to see you before he goes."

They pulled their chairs together and sat facing the mountains that were fading into the darkness.

"No, I don't think I can see him again."

There was a lull in their conversation until Mary spoke. "I know it's none of my business. If I'm prying just tell me. Has something happened between you two?"

"No . . . well, yes. I think I'm falling in love with him, and I can't do that now. It's so confusing." Emma couldn't believe that the words had just slipped out of her mouth as if she fell in love with someone every day of the week. And to be so open with Mary, she didn't know what to think. The thought that she might be falling in love with Alex had never taken such an explicit shape in her mind before this moment. It was a palpable and surprising truth.

"So, that's it. You have seemed a bit high-strung the last day or so," Mary said.

"Oh, have I been unbearable? I'm sorry."

"No, no, nothing like that. No, just that you seem a bit distracted. I would never have guessed what you just told me. Although, now that it's out in the open, I'm not entirely surprised. The two of you have such a lot in common."

"Yes, well, that may be true, but it's complicated right at the moment."

"I can see that. What are you going to do about it? That's the big question."

"Well, fortunately, things haven't gone too far between us, and I do have issues to get straight with Bob. There's the gallery, of course. Gen offered me a full partnership, and I've decided to take it. Bob's not going to like it, but that's just too damned bad. With Heather in Europe, and the problems I've been having with Beth, I can't get involved with this man, not now. It's impossible. People don't just fall in love like this."

"That's life, Emma. Remember what John Lennon said: 'Life's what happens to you, while you're busy making other plans.'"

"I know, but it's not fair—all these years with Bob. I mean—I don't know what I mean."

"Life isn't fair."

"You're right. That's not fair to Bob or to the girls. It's just that—how can it happen to me now? Why can't my life just be simple? Never mind. It's ridiculous, I know. But that's not all. Today, when I was looking at the only good painting in the women's show at the museum, I realized that I've missed something that was very important to me when I was a kid. Now, it's too late."

"What do you mean?"

"Sometimes your dreams don't come true, that's all. I wanted to be a painter. Today, I realized for the first time in my life that I could've been a good painter. Most of those women in that show were my age. My mother exposed us to art, took us to the museums. How could I have missed the signposts? How could I have given up my dream that easily? Well, that's past, I guess. It would take too long to catch up. And I'm too old to go back to school at this point in my life."

"Why not go back to school, if that's what it takes?"

"It's too late. Heather might feel that I'm intruding into some private aspect of her life. Besides, I have Beth and the gallery."

"Listen, our dreams are all we have to tell us who we can be. If we don't pursue them, then we're usually pursuing someone else's, and that always leads to disaster. Just what do you think I'm doing here?"

"Here? You mean the B & B?"

"Yes! This is my dream. I'm going to retire here, on my little ranch, with friends like you coming to visit. When I was little, I dreamed of being a cowgirl. And now, here I am—not really a full-fledged wrangler yet, but I do have four good horses. I've learned to saddle and ride and muck out stables, just like a real hand. I'm a lot different than when I first came out here. True, I still work as a nurse, part-time, but that won't be forever. This would never have happened, if I did what you're thinking about doing. I'd be growing old and bitter and getting as sick as my patients because that's what happens to us when we deny our dreams. Don't get me started." She laughed, took a sip of her lukewarm tea, then frowned. "Change often creeps up on us unnoticed."

Emma looked up at the Catalinas as they metamorphosed into silhouette against the night. They were changing slowly with the rising of the moon. She sensed their immense presence. Above her, the sky was full of stars, flickering through the prism of darkness; the atmosphere was shifting the light, incrementally, photon by photon, between the myriad colors of the spectrum. What message were they sending? Suddenly, somewhere close, a pack of coyotes began to howl. Emma was startled by their eerie calls.

After a time, Mary asked, "What do you think they're singing about?"

"Mmm, beats me," Emma said.

"Well, I'm not sure, but if I had to guess, I'd say they're singing about their dreams—about what the night brings them scented on the air—prey or love. I'd say they're singing about desire."

They listened to the coyotes' song without further comment until it stopped.

"Not to be too blunt, Emma," Mary said, "but I have the sad suspicion that one of your dreams is about to slip through your fingers . . . forever. He's leaving for Texas first thing in the morning."

Chapter Nine

I don't believe in love," Jack tells her unexpectedly. The beach seems deserted for a Sunday morning, Maggie thinks, as they pound the sand, walking where the surf recedes. His statement has a false ring to it—one that she's come to associate with his way of talking when he's about to trick her with some kind of phony-baloney.

"How can you say that? What about us? Don't you love me?"

"Of course I do; but that doesn't mean I believe in it."

"What are you talking about? How can you love me, if you don't believe in it?" She walks beyond Jack who's examining a half-eaten gull carcass that has washed up in a large tangle of seaweed on the previous tide.

"How can I not love you?" he says, catching up to her. "You're so lovable."

"Yeah, right! So, what are you trying to say? If you don't believe in love, what do you believe in?"

"Pussy," he says, then laughs out loud.

Maggie can't believe she lets him drag her into such inane conversations, especially when she can see it coming; but then, he's been doing that to her ever since they first started dating. It's just one of their little bonding rituals, a bit of glue that keeps them together. Truth to tell, though she doesn't let him know it, Maggie enjoys the camaraderie. She follows him as he veers off their path along the water's edge toward their favorite restaurant on the boardwalk, The Sundowner.

The hostess seats them by one of the ocean windows, in full view of the promenade of scantily-clad figures—a plethora of muscles, boobs, bulges and butts—skating, biking and parading along the boardwalk in front of the grand oceanic panorama beyond. An early thirty-something couple is making out in the booth in the corner. To Maggie's amazement, no one seems to notice. The couple's antics wouldn't have made any real impression on her, if their kisses hadn't started to anoint areas better left to other venues. If things went any further, clothes were going to be removed.

Jack leans over to Maggie. "Can you believe that?"

"They can't be married," she says.

Jack just looks at her—until she continues.

"I wonder how long they've been together."

"Not long by the looks of it. They seem in a hurry to get to know each other." Jack chuckles, looking at the couple. "How can they be so oblivious?"

"I don't know, but I sometimes wish I could be that free about things."

"I wish you could too," he says, chuckling again. "See the lip-lock she's got on him? Have they no shame? My God, he has a handful there." He looks at Maggie, his eyebrows arched.

The waiter arrives with lemon water and menus, recites the specials for the day, then disappears into the kitchen as quickly as he arrived.

"It looks like the party's being moved to another location," Maggie says, referring to the two lovers who've grabbed their check and headed for the register at the door. "You think they're in love?"

"It looks like lust to me."

"I'll bet they're falling in love for the first time."

"Oh boy, here we go again."

"Seriously, tell me. Why won't you discuss it?"

"You sure are persistent, just like a snapping turtle. You'd rather have your head chopped off than let go. What is it with you lately? Feeling a tad insecure? We've had more sex this week than we had all last month," he whispers. "I'd think you'd be feeling pretty darn good about yourself."

"I do, I do, I feel great. But it's not about sex."

The waiter returns to take their order.

"I'd like to order whatever that couple had for lunch," Jack tells the waiter, who grimaces in pain because he has only heard that one about six zillion times.

They order a dozen oysters and chowder and sink back into the booth to watch the waves and the birds and the people going by.

"Will there be anything else?" the waiter asks.

"Just time enough to eat and a check when I'm done," Jack says. "Oh, and Tabasco for the oysters." Turning back to Maggie, he continues. "Look, I fall in love every day. Every woman that catches my eye, I fall in love with. I find them beautiful. It means nothing. I find something attractive in almost every woman I see. It's the way nature made me. I'm supposed to look and be attracted. But I also find flowers beautiful and killer whales. So what?" he says, then blows and slurps on a spoonful of chowder.

"Yes. But you can't sleep with a killer whale."

"I can't sleep with every woman I see either."

"No, but you'd like to."

"So what? Don't you ever see guys you'd like to sleep with?"

"No, actually I don't. Does that surprise you?"

"Oh, you see them all right. You just won't think about it, that's all. If you did, then maybe you wouldn't be in such a sweat. What about that UPS guy that comes into your office? You're always talking about him."

"He's a nice guy. He's good-looking with a very pleasant personality and always has something cheerful to say. All the girls like him." Maggie blows at her chowder.

"Yeah, I'll bet they do. And, what's with this girl business?"

"If you'd pay attention, you'd realize I'm talking about the feelings we get when we're attractive to other people. The fact that we're getting older doesn't mean that we no longer have a need to be desired or appreciated."

"Oh, for Pete's sake, is that what the hell you're going on about—feeling old—nostalgia for the wolf whistle? Oh, hi."

The waiter who had sidled up to Jack, unnoticed, delivers the oysters with a flourish of his towel and, as an afterthought, plops down four small bags of oyster crackers that he forgot to leave with the chowder. Jack opens a bag of crackers for them to share with their chowder, which is finally cool enough to be eaten.

Maggie puts the unopened bags into her purse to feed the gulls later. "Don't these look good," she says and squeezes a lemon wedge over everything—oysters, lettuce, ice, the cup of cocktail sauce in the center of the metal platter. They dig in, swirling those slimy crustaceans around in cocktail sauce with their little three-pronged forks before slurping them down; the brine runs over their lips. They go fast.

"That sure was tasty. I could eat six more of those, easy. Feel like dessert?"

"I'd rather wait until we get to La Jolla and have a piece of that mud pie at the Hard Rock Café, but I could use a cup of decaf."

"Good idea. Hey, it just occurred to me that that waiter never brought the Tabasco. Never mind; what say we skip the decaf here and have it with the mudpie? I guess the waiter will show with the check, up there, at the register." Jack grins at her.

She grins back.

"He didn't really earn it, was all I meant," Jack says, after they pay their bill and step out on the stoop. "It just irks me to tip someone for sloppy service."

"Well, why did you then?" Maggie asks.

"I don't know. Maybe I hate to look like a cheapskate."

"I guess you'd rather look like a grump, instead, griping over leaving a tip, and a skimpy one at that. You should have told him, not me—and spoil my mood."

"Okay, okay, I give up; you're right," he says. "Next time I won't tip at all."

They strike out for the boardwalk.

"Stupid jerk! Watch where the fuck you're going!" Jack hits the brakes and then the horn when another truck lurches onto La Jolla Boulevard right in front of them.

"That's great—just what I love to hear," Maggie says, "you, blasting the horn and screaming at the top of your lungs. "He can't hear you!"

"Did you see that asshole? Damn near creamed us." He checks his rear view mirror and shifts back into second. "Lucky we weren't smacked from behind. We could've been killed!"

"But we weren't, so calm down. You know, you get angry over any little thing lately."

Jack takes a couple of deep breaths and puts it in third. "I don't know, things just set me off. I get so pissed, especially when these stupid assholes are driving like maniacs."

"Well, you're acting just like them. We can't go anywhere without you becoming enraged and calling somebody an asshole. I'm getting really tired of hearing you go on like that. I can't take it. Just look how my hands are shaking."

"I know, I'm sorry. You don't have to tell me. I don't feel right for the next two hours. Some jerk runs a red light in front of me, and I just go livid. I wanna kill him." Jack turns right on Pearl Street and climbs the hill. "You know, I always thought that as I got older I'd become more tolerant, but it seems like I keep getting angrier. I feel tired a lot, too. Must be the big mid-life crisis! Maybe it's time for a twenty-year-old mistress and a Harley. What do you think?"

"I don't know, but you'd better do something because this is getting to be a nasty habit, and I, for one, don't like it very much."

"Well I don't like it either. It takes a lot out of me."

"Then do something about it." Maggie purses her lips and vigorously smooths out the wrinkles across one thigh of her khaki shorts.

Turning right around the corner on Girard Avenue, Jack stops abruptly and waits to pull into the parking space being vacated by a huge black Mercedes. A little white-haired old woman who can barely see over the steering wheel is backing out slow and straight, holding up traffic in both directions.

"Don't say it," Maggie says as he turns to her. She knows how Jack feels about incompetent older drivers, and in this case, she'd have to agree. This woman does not belong behind the wheel of a car.

Flustered by the blaring horns and sitting diagonally in the middle of the street, the woman pulls back into the same space.

"Oh, for Pete's sake," Jack lets slip, unable to contain himself. Driving by the Mercedes, he wheels the truck into the open slot two cars beyond. "Now, let's go look for that Buddha you promised me."

"I thought we were going over to the Baker Gallery." She nods at the place across the street.

"They don't appear to be open—it's Sunday, remember? Let's walk down to Kiln Street and see if that incense shop is still there. They might have a Buddha we could get cheap."

"Have you forgotten where you are? There's nothing cheap in La Jolla, least of all Buddha."

Walking past the Mercedes, Jack notices the old woman looking around with an expression of sheer terror on her face. Although the traffic has cleared, it seems she cannot decide to pull back out and drive away.

"Maybe I should help her get out into the street," Jack says.

"Forget it. Remember, 'no good deed goes unpunished.'"

"My, my, aren't you the heartless one today?"

"Not really. It's just that you can't help someone who doesn't have the good sense to not be in that situation in the first place. She knows she shouldn't be driving, but here she is. Some people have to learn things the hard way. You're better off to leave her to her problems. You've got enough of your own."

"That's rather cold, isn't it?"

"I don't think so. She's being totally irresponsible and endangering others. She deserves what she gets."

"But she's so old. She needs the help."

"My point, exactly."

"Don't you ever make mistakes?"

"All the time."

"Well?"

"Well, what? Not only is she endangering others, she's relying on other people to get her out of her mess—a mess she wouldn't be in, I might add, if she had acted responsibly and stayed off the road."

Jack pauses. "Well, you do have a point there, I guess." Jack and Maggie look at the woman and then at each other and shake their heads.

"Come on, we gotta find Buddha," she says. "He'd know what to do."

They turn and walk down the street, stopping occasionally to look at window displays. Maggie walks at a slower pace. He's always in a hurry to get where they're going. Maggie's interested in seeing things along the way, and wonders if it's her habit of searching things out as a photographer that informs her manner of locomotion. She likes to wander aimlessly; Jack is always headed straight to the point of interest.

When they were first married, Maggie told Jack how impressed she'd been by the speed and sense of purpose with which he moved. On a date one snowy night, she was especially taken with his jumping out of the car and clearing the windshield, in the space of a red light change.

"Why don't you slow down so I can see what's in these windows?" she says. "Are you in a hurry?"

"Well, no, I was just going to the incense shop, and I'm not sure exactly where it's located."

"If you're in no rush then, maybe I could get a look at these clothes." She points into the window of a women's apparel salon. Maggie glimpses, almost unnoticeable in the shadows behind the display, a very elegant, polished, coifed woman who, at first, appears to be one of the mannequins. On closer inspection, however, Maggie realizes that the woman is appraising her and Jack in a haughty manner. When the woman realizes that Maggie can see her smirking at them, she twists her sneer into a condescending smile and disappears into the darkened recesses of the store.

Maggie looks down at her own clothes. She remembers how she used to love to shop, always buying the best she could afford. She liked expensive, well-made garments with shoes and bags to match. But looking up at her reflection in the glass, with Jack fidgeting around on the sidewalk behind her, she's reminded that there are people who never outgrow their need to feel superior to others. Maggie feels sorry for the woman in the shop. She turns, walks to the curb where Jack's looking across the street, and takes his arm. "Come on, let's go."

"Hey, wait a moment. See that garage door? You should've seen the car I saw go in there. Let's go look."

"I thought we were going to search for Buddha."

171

"What? Now, you're in a hurry? It'll only take a couple of minutes. See anything you like in that store window?"

"Not really."

"Oh?"

"The atmosphere's too rarefied for me."

"Yeah, I know what you mean. Have you seen how many Jaguars there are in this town? I've already counted four, just since we got out of the truck. There are probably more Jaguars in this town, per capita, than any other town in this country. And Rolls. You remember the Rolls dealership over on Prospect, or was it on Pearl?"

Having crossed the street against the light, they stop to peer into the darkened garage. They enter beneath the elegantly lettered sign, 'Ken's Klassic Kars.'

"Mind if we look around?" Jack asks a couple of men in overalls, standing next to the cherry-red Stingray convertible, just inside the door.

"Help yourself, but please don't touch," says one of the men who Jack assumes to be Ken.

"Sure, no problem, thanks."

Jack immediately recognizes two of the six cars in the room—the Corvette and a forty-nine Ford coupe. The Ford he knows well from a model he once put together as a kid. Eventually, he also recognizes a Jaguar XKE, a Dusenberg, a Maserati and a Mercedes Gull-wing. They all gleam like jewels; you could eat off the motors.

"Boy, these are some really old cars," Maggie whispers to Jack.

"Can you imagine what one of these costs?" Jack whispers back.

"I've no idea. Why are we whispering?" she says.

"No reason. That Maserati alone has to cost you $250,000if it costs a dime." Jack doesn't really know that for sure. He's read somewhere that cars like it, and certain models of Ferraris, are extremely high-ticket items and he makes a guess at what they might cost. Maggie, he notices, looks a bit incredulous—like she does when she's unsure whether he's trying to pull a fast one or not. She doesn't question his authority. He has a hard time imagining someone would pay this kind of money for a car—one that only seats two people—when he could just barely get his mind around paying $48,000 for his house back in the seventies. He's scandalized to discover that this particular Dusenberg, having once been owned by the King of Sweden, would sell for over a half a million dollars, and maybe more, to the right collector.

"Thanks," Jack says and waves to the two guys who are still engrossed in their conversation, next to the Jag.

"Find one you like?" Ken calls back.

"All of them," Jack says. Outside, they pause to let their eyes adjust to the light. "I just got a big whiff of the ocean; how about you?"

"Yes, the breeze must be just right," Maggie says.

"Maybe it's because of the smell of the oil and exhaust in the garage. It was so close in there. But, hey, if you could have any one of those cars, which one would you want?"

"The Jaguar, I guess. It's my color—blue, like my eyes."

"I liked the Ford. We couldn't even manage the upkeep on the others, much less the money to buy one in the first place. Probably couldn't even keep up the Ford, definitely not the Jag. But I really have no desire to own one. If I did, it'd just be something else to worry about. Somebody's going to steal it. Somebody's going to key the paint out of sheer maliciousness. Couldn't drive it anywhere without worrying if I'd get it back home in one piece. Give me my old truck any day. But they sure are beautiful. Do you ever wish we had their money?" Jack waves his arm around to include the whole community of La Jolla. They cross Girard with the light this time.

"Nah," Maggie says. "Money's not going to make you happy, if you can't be happy without it."

"You know, life's really unfair. I work my ass off, year in and year out, just to make unique paintings that nobody buys. Then somebody like Mendoza comes along, makes up these little moony-faced Indian children and gets stinking rich—so rich he has to burn all his paintings because he doesn't want to pay the inventory tax on them."

"Stop your whining," she says, stopping on the curb. "Whoever said life was fair?"

Looking up the hill, they turn and start south along the sidewalk.

"Well, why should these people have more than me?" he whines, once again waving his arms. "I'll bet that little old woman with the big car has more money than God. Why should the rich have more than anyone else? You can't tell me they deserve it more. You know, I always thought that if I worked hard, I would have all I needed. But here I am, headed for my sixties, no closer to financial security than the day I was born."

"Well, you sure sound bitter about it. You choose the path you follow, you know. No one forces you to paint."

"That's true. But that's what I do. That's who I am. I was born to paint. I wish I was made to do something else, but it's in my DNA. Besides, art is important work—certainly better than making money in some dead-end job, simply so you can kick back and put your feet up until they cart you away. I want to create something to last beyond me, to touch someone. Doesn't following my dream to be a painter help elevate the human race?"

"I've never understood your desire for immortality." Maggie stops to admire some Persian rugs in a store window.

"What do you mean?" he says, joining her. "Boy, those sure are some good-looking rugs. Just look at all those rich colors. I'll bet some poor, starving, overworked, underpaid little children made those in some godforsaken Third World sweatshop."

"Are we going to discuss that now?"

"I guess not. What were we talking about?"

"You have this part of you that wants people, complete strangers even, to admire you, to remember you after you're dead. What're you trying to prove?"

"What makes you think I'm trying to prove anything?"

"Well, let's see now. What about 'deserving as much as everybody else' and 'elevating humankind'? Sounds like ego to me. You do it for yourself and leave the rest alone. It's not for you to say what's important for posterity."

"Listen to you!" Jack stops dead in his tracks. "You sure have my number today. What makes you think you know so much about it?"

"I don't," she says and turns to face him. "But you only get like this when we come to some place like La Jolla. Can't you be happy with what you have?"

"Maybe—no, not really." He continues down Girard toward Kline. "I'd like to have more, so I could stop worrying about not having enough."

"Just how much is that?" She catches up.

"I don't know. When I stop and think about it, I remember all those hours I might have spent doing something I hated, just for the money. I think about how good my life is and how much I have to be thankful for, but I get nervous that I'll lose it all somehow. You know I work hard. I feel like I deserve to have what they have, and I'm angry that I don't."

"I guess that's how it is as we get older," she says. "We have to remember that we've got a good life, better than many if not most. I make photographs, as good or as bad as they are. You make beautiful and meaningful art, and it just gets better with age. You're a master painter, even if I'm the only one who tells you so. We've made choices and this is our life; we can't let fear stop us now, or turn around mid-stream and head in the opposite direction." She halts abruptly to emphasize her point.

"I know, I shouldn't whine like this, but I focus on all the money that I don't have, and it makes me crazy," he says, stopping with her. "I don't even want to think about it."

"You have to remember to keep your eyes on those things you have that are important, and stop thinking about those things you don't have."

"How can you see this so clearly? And why do I get so confused?" he asks. They resume their walk, left at the corner, going west on Kline Street.

"That's just today. Tomorrow, you'll be the one telling me to keep my eyes where they belong because I will have forgotten."

They come to a stop at the corner of Fay Avenue and Kline Street.

"Damn," Jack says. "I thought we would've hit that incense store in the last block, so I guess I'm lost. Maybe it's up that way." He points south along Fay Avenue, grabs her by the hand and starts to drag her across the street with him as the light changes green.

"Hey, slow down. Just use your phone and Google it." She pulls free. "Let's be really bad and go over to the Hard Rock Café and eat a cheeseburger."

"Okay, but let's get the truck and drive down there. Maybe we can find that shop on the way."

Two doors past the corner on Fay Avenue, they stop right in front of the shop they're looking for. In the window, capturing Jack's attention is a large dark-bronze Shiva, dancing within a circle of flames—the incarnation of space and time in evolution. A singular small fire sprouts like an artichoke from the palm of his hand. He plays finger cymbals with his other and dances with perfect, yet fearsome, equanimity sculpted into his face—his leg raised with ankle bent in the pantomime of creation. As a painter, Jack feels a certain affinity for the figure.

Books on meditation, mysticism and the religions of the East are arrayed in small stacks, levels and columns around Shiva. Many other small bronze figures, from the pantheon of Hindu deities, and a number of strangely crass, highly polished but poorly made diminutive brass Buddhas strike Jack as very incongruous in this setting.

Inside, a cheerful, horse-faced middle-aged woman offers to be of help. She reminds Jack of his seventh grade art teacher, Miss Roberts, who once told him if he would leave the girls alone, he could some day be a great artist. Maggie asks her for directions to the restroom and makes her way to the back while Jack wanders around.

Prayer wheels, beads, small handbells, finger cymbals and candles of assorted colors and sizes are on display. If one was looking for a book on mysticism and meditation, as well as herbal medicine, psychology, philosophy, self-help and spiritual growth, there's an extensive library running along the wall. Books on Buddhism, Islam, Christianity and other religions of the world stand binding-to-binding along the shelves. On the opposite wall, behind a counter containing the larger and more expensive gemstone clusters, are the less expensive channeling crystals, hung from chains and leather necklaces, along with a section of CDs and tapes for New-Age stress reduction. The soothing music of whale song is playing over the shop sound system.

Nag Champa from India is wafting in the air—fullbodied but not too sweet, one of his favorites. In fact, one reason he feels so comfortable in the store is that he's already familiar with its smell. Jack likes the variety of incense he finds—patchouli, aura cleanse, apricot snow, pine-glade, sacred sandalwoods and ambers, sweet and golden frankincense and myrrh. For room cleansing or specific ceremonial use, there are sticks, powders and pellets. He likes the variety of censers—small soapstone temples and boats carved by machine, probably on an assembly line somewhere in India—as well as the wooden sleds and the bronze and brass incense burners, also crudely fashioned in some foundry in the Near East. Farther down, a section is devoted to oils and emollients for massage and aromatherapy. When Maggie rejoins him, he's rearranging the items on the shelves to suit his own taste, just for the hell of it

The shop is lit by small, expensive display halogens clipped to artfully arranged, exposed steel-wire conduits snaking through the open ceiling. Various counter and glass display cases—with silver and gold broaches and other jeweled pins fashioned in the shapes of crabs, horses and bulls—call out to be noticed. All the houses in the astrological heavens are represented. Jack slides up close to Maggie and catches her drooling over an expensive gold-mounted topaz scorpion.

"You do know that we're living beyond our means and really can't afford this. If we don't come up with some way to increase our income, we're going to be in trouble when you leave your job. It's not going to last forever."

"No? Hey, don't you think this scorpion is just about the most beautiful thing that you've ever seen in your life?—except me, of course."

"Oh, look over there," Jack says, escaping across the room to a table display of small bronze figures. Catching his eye is one bronze unlike any other in the shop—six inches tall, the big brother to the crass miniatures in the window. Sculpted in clean, simple but elegant detail, it's compact, solid and finely wrought. Jack cannot remember seeing one this beautifully made before. A light, buttery gold bronze, obviously Indian, this Buddha of moderation—neither too starved nor too indulgent—is the perfect, serene enlightened one.

"Well, I found it," he tells Maggie as he picks it up. "Look, it's beautiful, but it's sixty bucks—a little more than I want to pay. Although I haven't seen one better sculpted anywhere, have you? I love it."

181

"When has a lack of money ever stopped us from spending it on something we loved?"

"I know just where he wants to be," Jack says, inspecting it from every angle.

"It's settled then. Happy Birthday! Let's buy that Buddha and some incense and get out of here."

Outside, Jack tells Maggie to wait for him while he goes back to use the restroom, but he doesn't really need to use it. He wants to purchase the topaz scorpion that Maggie pointed out earlier. Unaware of his presence, the saleswoman is bent down at the display table where Jack discovered his Buddha. The cabinet doors are open below, and she's holding one of the dozen or so remaining replicas that she's about to place in the exact spot where the other one sat so serenely.

By the time they pick up the truck, eat and pay their $4.00 entry fee, it's almost 3:00 P.M. They have little more than an hour to view the Joan Mitchell retrospective at the La Jolla Museum of Contemporary Art. Jack's miffed at himself for not getting there sooner. He has a fondness for the painters of Mitchell's generation—strong abstractionists, though not as ego-driven as many of their predecessors.

Inside the newly-remodeled gallery, the open marble space is inviting in its hush. Except for the occasional security guard, stationed at the door between galleries,

Jack and Maggie are alone with the paintings. Moving from one piece to another, trying to get an overview of the show before settling down to look closer, they split up to follow their own inclinations toward individual works.

The simpler, almost monochromatic pieces are most often based on Mitchell's feelings and remembrances of certain places or things. Jack is drawn to the dark, lush, moody blues and greens from a series of paintings called Canada—a place Mitchell often visited as a child with her family, a place that meant much to her child's eye. A pristine garden of delight, it called her back over the years, compelling her to make these haunting objects; although, she never traveled there as an adult. 'River,' 'Tree,' 'La Grande Vallée,' 'Field for Two' and 'Bluet' are all paintings evocative of this paradise on earth. He's drawn to all of them.

At quarter to four, he's in the back gallery where two large halls converge in the corner of the building, and the entire west wall is made of glass. It overlooks the sculpture garden below and the ocean beyond. The architect who contrived this encounter with nature had no idea that Mitchell's paintings could make such a strong impression. How could he have known that Jack would be so emotionally charged by Mitchell's work?—or that, combined with the sheer force of such a magnificent view, it would cause tears to come? Jack sits on the bench in the center of the room, stunned into silence. Caught up in this emotional maelstrom, he doesn't sense Maggie approaching from behind.

"You, too?" she says quietly as she sits by his side.

"I don't know if it's the paintings or the view, but it almost knocked me down when I walked in here."

Maggie hands him a tissue from her purse and takes another for herself. "It's the paintings," she says. "I've never felt such strong emotions from looking at paintings."

"They remind me of the first time I saw a Van Gogh. It was in the Detroit Institute of Art, my first visit to a museum. I was just a kid, walking through the galleries, awed by the hushed atmosphere, room after room, and then there was this . . . jewel. It was the most incredible thing I had ever seen—a self-portrait of Vincent. I loved it immediately. I knew right then that I wanted to be a painter. You can tell by looking that she felt exactly the same way about his work. These paintings show her debt to him—our debt. It's almost like their spirits are walking around in here, together. It's amazing. Can you feel it?"

"Did you see the blue painting called 'Edrita Fried?' That was the one that finally got to me."

"Oh yes. It just boggles the mind. The intensity of the color—she was in despair over the loss of her longtime friend. You can feel the power. That's what I want from my paintings—to touch people, engage them, make them feel that moment of recognition. It's not even that. It's more. It takes you out of your self-consciousness. It sounds so stupid when I try to talk about it."

"I feel the same thing. When you're working, you simply forget yourself, but you're right, there's no talking about it."

He leans over and whispers to her, though there's no one else in the room. "You know this is second-generation abstract expressionism—a term Mitchell hated, by the way. We can't paint like this anymore. Make no mistake; she knew how unfashionable Ab-Ex became over the last years of her life."

Maggie leans in and whispers back, sharing a secret of her own. "It didn't stop her though, did it?"

"Oh no, in fact, regardless of the way her style changed, she held true to herself." Sitting up, Jack continues in his normal voice. "She didn't do badly by it either. But by all of the accounts that I've read, she'd have been lost to despair without painting. She painted to survive. And now, I can see that I'm just so much like her. I have no choice—a painter is what I am."

They sit watching as the sun goes down and the mist rolls in.

A security guard—a young, blonde woman with a big warm smile, whose nametag identifies her as Angel—has come up behind them unnoticed. "Sorry, folks, we're closing now," she says. "Some view, huh? With these paintings and that view, I never get tired of sitting here,

185

looking out of these windows." Abruptly, she turns to lead the way back to the front.

"It's Eden, all right," Jack says.

"You should see it when it's storming," she says, without looking back over her shoulder at them. "It's like being right in the middle of creation, standing there, looking out those windows."

Later, at the entrance, she seems rather distant, somewhat cold as she shows them out, pulls the doors shut, weaves a steel chain through the handles, and secures them with a lock. They stand outside, stunned and perplexed, as she turns out the lights and disappears into the darkness. They are trying to decide what to do next. They suffer the stink and noise of the late-afternoon traffic, and a surprising, unimaginable ache—the ache of having been expelled from paradise for no apparent reason other than divine caprice. Or was it, rather, just the unfortunate concursion of time and space?

Monday

Chapter Ten

Though it felt like it and had all the appearances of one, it was not a dream. Never mind that Emma was in bed or that it was still dark outside. Had she slept? Could she be dreaming and still be awake? She wasn't sure. The night passed slowly, in any case. She couldn't sleep; she was too energized—her synapses sparkled, bubbled and popped like champagne. She felt intoxicated.

But if Emma was intoxicated, it was not from champagne. She had not been drinking, of course. Although for a time during the night—how long a time? she wondered, looking at the digital clock by the bed—champagne seemed to have bubbled and flowed all around her. She'd been waiting for the clock's alarm—living these alternative realities as if she were a character in a novel, projecting herself into the future—contemplating the gallery, Alex and the chance that he would be gone before she could see him again. These scenes played themselves out in the dark in front of her, over the course of the evening, like a Fred-and-Ginger movie—each, just one of many possible futures that could come to pass given the best that chance, coincidence and her own honest efforts could offer. Over the night, these visions had swept her up and away as time dragged by.

At the moment, the most recent scenario she experienced was the gallery scene with all the excitement of the crowd that she imagined had turned out for the evening. The black strapless gown she wore possessed her figure, tenaciously, flaring generously down into flamenco ruffles trailing along the floor. Her hair rose magically to the crown of her head in a loose frothy aggregation of wispy curls. Divers errant strands played about her face and neck, accentuating the flawlessness of her cheeks and throat that were flushed with the thrill of such gala festivities.

Art critics from the major publications were out in force. Art Forum, Art News, and Art in America all loved the show. The Mayor of Los Angeles was in attendance. The Duncan-Brighton Gallery—cool white walls and Carrera marble floors—had, it seemed, achieved stellar recognition literally overnight. There were wall-to-wall people. Best of all, Alex's paintings fit into the gallery more divinely than she could've dreamed possible. She needed to see him and tell him of her decision.

"Emma!"

Emma turned around and was surprised to find Mary and Steve O'Brien, from the Mountain Shadows in Tucson, making their way to her through the crowd.

"It's so good to see you; you look great," Emma said. They spoke louder to be heard over the sound of the harpist who was playing Debussy's Claire de Lune.

"You look fantastic," Mary said.

"Stunning," Steve said.

"I can't believe you came all this way." Emma air-kissed them about their cheeks.

"Well, Alex is our favorite artist and besides, I had to come to L.A. You'll never guess why in a million years," Mary said.

"Well . . . " Emma said, her brows arching.

"I'm riding in the Bronc Busting Competition in the Los Angeles County Rodeo at the fairgrounds tomorrow. Isn't that great?"

"I really love to watch her compete," Steve said. He gave Emma a huge grin and a nudge of his elbow.

"Really? You're not kidding me?"

"Really, it's true—tomorrow, cross my heart and hope to die," Mary said.

"I can't believe it. Aren't you a little too old? I mean, aren't you afraid of getting hurt?" Emma grabbed Mary by the elbows and held her at arm's length, fixing her with a mixed look of amazement and concern. "You really are following your dream, aren't you? Wait until Alex hears about this." Emma hugged her. "You were so right. I decided to follow your advice. I'm going back to painting. I can't wait to tell Alex."

"I saw him over by the food, earlier, enmeshed in a circle of beautiful women," Steve said.

"Will you excuse me? I just have to find him," Emma said.

"Well, the show's wonderful. The paintings are great. I noticed he's already sold most of them. We're leaving soon, so say hello to him for us, in case we don't catch up with him before we go," Mary said.

"I'll tell him you were here. Good luck on your horse."

"I'll need it. You come back to Tucson when you want to get out of all this big city madness. Bring Alex with you."

"I will."

Cameras were taking unauthorized pictures everywhere. On her way across the room to find Alex, she heard her name being called again. Her brother, Eric, and his wife, Colleen, were standing in the middle of the gallery. To come all the way from Scottsdale, when they didn't even know Alex, Emma thought remarkable. She heard her name again.

"Emma!" Gen smiled and waved to her from across the gallery.

She returned the wave then searched the crowd for Alex; she caught a glimpse of Marti. What a beautiful woman. That green dress was an absolute stunner. The gorgeous willowy blonde in the short, slinky gold lamé standing next to Marti was undoubtedly Pris. She was staring daggers into the squat, bald man next to them. Marti's décolletage floated voluptuously just below his nose, enchanting him to distraction.

Alex was gone. Emma hurried across the room. The crowd pressed in on her and, again, she couldn't escape an encounter with a patron who wouldn't shut up. Finally, when Emma turned away, she was face to face with Beth.

"Oh my God!" She couldn't believe the apparition before her. Beth was dressed exactly like Emma except Beth's jet-black lipstick matched her nails. Her hair, though pulled up, had been shaved on one side to reveal a small, ugly black rendering of an animal, indelibly inked into her scalp. A dozen stainless-steel rings hung from one ear and a single ring pierced her opposite eyebrow. The oversized, elbow-length gloves and high-heeled shoes completed her ensemble. Beth's appearance reminded Emma of when she and Heather were little girls playing dress up in Emma's old clothes. Memory tugged at her heart.

"What is that above your ear, Beth Anne Brighton?"

"It's a cow, Mother, so don't have one! Okay?"

"Is that a tattoo? And what in the world do you think you are doing here in that costume?"

"Lighten up, Motherrrr. Daddy brought me over to see the bad man's art show."

"Bad man? What are you talking about?"

"The bad man who destroyed our happy home. Daddy is very upset."

"So, here you are, finally," Bob said as he grabbed her elbow and turned her around to face him, none too gently. "I've been looking all over creation for you. Why didn't you stay here? I thought I made myself clear about leaving L.A. without me."

Emma couldn't endure the closeness of the room or the phalanx of partygoers pressing in, gawking at her in this dilemma. She was going to faint. Bob grabbed her lower jaw and held her face toward him. He glared at her. Was he going to slap her?

Beyond his shoulder, Emma spied Heather wearing a black beret and painter's smock.

"No, no, no," Heather mouthed. She was wagging her finger and shaking her head. All the people looking at them were shaking their heads and fingers, like Heather. How embarrassing! Heather looked ridiculous in that outfit. What was she doing home from Italy? Emma tried to speak to her, but nothing came out of her mouth.

"How could you, Mother? How could you?"

The clock finally went off. Though she was looking directly at it when it happened, she didn't see the numbers as they changed. It shone: 4:30. Emma was back to reality.

She became aware of the pale early light sifting through the sheers at the window. "Oh Alex, don't go to Texas yet," she whispered. If she hurried, she could shower, pick up a peace offering somewhere and get down to his studio before he left. She didn't know when he planned to leave town today, but what she did know about him was that once he made up his mind to do something, he didn't tarry. He was probably already up, getting things together. She hurried.

Speeding along in the big mauve Ford, Emma noticed an all-night grocery at the corner of Oracle and Orange Grove and turned sharply into the parking lot. She wanted to get something, anything, a gift to offer her apologies for the way she'd been behaving. A fruit basket would do the trick, if she could find one. It would give them something to share for breakfast. She walked past a pay phone and considered calling Alex to make sure that he'd be there, but remembered seeing the paper with his number on the night stand next to her bed.

She knew that she really didn't have to apologize, but it would make her feel better if she and Alex could part company as friends. She zipped from counter to counter palpating plums, bananas, kiwis and mangos, until there it was, just what she needed, a small ready-made basket of fruit, wrapped in cellophane and tied with a small bow of red ribbon.

Outside, pearlescent clouds shredded themselves over the mountains in the early light of sunrise. God, it's too beautiful for words, she thought. But then, things always looked better in the morning. Emma remembered talking with Mary about following her dream. Later, when she was lying there trying to go to sleep, it all fell into place. It wasn't too late. Her life with Bob was finished. She'd start over. Emma understood what it meant that Heather had grown up and was leaving home for good. For the first time, Emma knew that she was strong enough to accept it and was happy that Heather had found her love of painting so young.

In the meantime, Beth needed her. Well, that was not a lasting problem. Beth was a good child and Emma intended to help her find her way, whatever it took. With a little care, understanding and intelligence, all of these issues would be straightened out. It had been a long time since Emma had felt this confident. She knew such profound change would disturb Bob. However, if he were as smart as she thought he was, he'd see that this was best for all of them.

But it didn't matter. She couldn't remember being this happy in recent months. And to think that this joy she felt stemmed from her decision to become a painter. In fact, she realized now that she'd been suffering a low-grade depression for the past couple of years. It was a cliché, she knew, but there was no time to lose; life was too short. She also knew that somewhere there was a clear path ahead, and she would find it. That thought gave her a tremendous boost of courage.

Stopped at the light at River and Oracle, Emma couldn't help noticing the young man sitting in a pickup truck in the next lane, bouncing around and singing to the radio. It was so loud she closed her windows, which only muffled the beat to a thumping that vaguely matched the rhythm of her own heart. She recognized 'Stairway to Heaven.'

Just as the light changed, the man, who was grinning like the Cheshire Cat, gripped the steering wheel with his white-knuckled hands, looked directly at her, nodded to the beat of the music and took off. From the way he looked, he could've been piloting a rocketship to Mars. His head snapped back against the whiplash cushion above the seat. Emma, too, put the pedal to the metal and sped down Oracle, twenty miles over the limit, only to be frustrated when caught by the next light. The man in the pickup, however, ran it red, evidently approaching the speed of light, moving too fast, too far beyond the decisive point to decelerate his craft at the cautionary yellow.

Emma sensed it was true for her as well. There was no slowing, no turning back. Her need for speed might've had something to do with Einstein's formula describing energy, inertia, mass and velocity, something she began to understand in view of recent developments in her life. She sensed this undeniable urgency and gauged relative distances to time lost, delineated new worlds of exploration and crossed circumscribed barriers of light and space.

Her newfound relevancy and wonder at this Unexpected thought and feeling pushed her onward. New notions of viability, love, and relationship propelled her into the future where she—an unlikely but worldly time-traveler seeking to change a previous timeline—was captured in the karmic maelstrom of cause and effect. No matter how she cut it, she'd been irrevocably altered. Time itself had been altered because the speed of thought at which she lived her life, and the distances of emotion she'd traversed in the past four days, had been altered. She felt the world change. She'd arrived, however circuitously, at a new starting point in her life. Better late than never.

She knew that she must get to Alex. There were things she wanted to tell him about her, and things she wanted to know about him. She was bursting with a need to relate to him these astounding experiences that she had. The sight of his old truck sitting in the lot, glowing in the after-dawn light, for instance, she thought was one of the most encouraging sights that she'd ever seen. She wanted to tell him about it, about everything, although she was giddy with the lack of sleep. It occurred to her that Alex might've decided to fly to Texas and asked one of his friends to drive him to the airport.

Emma twisted the rear-view mirror toward her and gazed into the two sharp, pale blue points of inquiry that were her eyes. She didn't know what she hoped to find there. They told her nothing, but she deduced that there were unanswered questions beyond those windows. Although she hadn't stopped to put on her make-up, she had more color in her face than usual. Pinching her cheeks, she fluffed her hair, took her basket and left the car. What would he think about her showing up, unheralded and bearing gifts?

Emma drifted and darted across the panes of glass of his storefront studio windows. At first, she was just a dancing point of energy, a small electric figure with purse and basket, approaching rapidly in reflection. She watched herself growing larger, further defined, clearer, coming more sharply into focus—a diaphanous, blue-violet vision, glistening brightly in the sun, crossing the street. She didn't stop to think about what she was doing, fearing that she might lose her nerve. When she reached the curb, Emma continued right up across the walk, until her finger was pressing with all necessary force and the loose bell plate was sounding its annoying, sporadic tinny-buzz—a tremendously hopeful announcement of her presence.

Inside, Alex was still deep in a dreamless sleep. The sound of the bell was clattering around in his subconscious. He dismissed the noisy intrusion as just another in an intermittent but unending stream of transient bell-pushers who were unable to pass by temptation. He refused to wake immediately. He'd not had much sleep, spending most of the night in fractious debate with himself over when to leave and what to take with him to Texas. Usually, Alex had no trouble prioritizing the events of his life. Things generally set themselves in order, and there was little he needed to consider before he acted. Usually, it was all very simple.

Today, however, his indecisive mind couldn't get past the fuzzy thoughts that kept intruding. Should he stay another day, or should he go? Should he call that blasted woman who'd burrowed into his consciousness and wouldn't allow him any peace, or should he wipe his mind clear and just forget it. This wasn't like him. He did make one decision, however, and that was to call his son to let him know that he wouldn't be there as planned.

She had been definite about her intentions the last time he saw her. There was no reason for him to be hanging on like this—not to mention that he'd already made up his mind once and decided to leave as soon as he could get things in order. So why couldn't he do it? What kept nagging at him so persistently? These and other demons had been at Alex most of the night. It was only now, when they'd grown tired of torturing him and left him in peace, that he'd finally fallen into a pure deep sleep. If only that infernal bell going off somewhere would stop ringing, he could drift away. It was extremely insistent. There it was again. A small tendril of alarm wormed its way into his conscious world, and he followed helplessly along until . . .

"All right, all right, I'm coming!" His voice cracked into silence. He dragged his body off the futon and felt his way over to the chair where he picked up his jeans and slipped them on over his usual morning woody. Have to be careful there, he thought and opened his eyes, to make sure he didn't do some irreparable damage with the zipper. The bell rang again.

"This had better be good!" He hobbled barefoot down the steps of the loft. Rubbing the crust of sleep from his eyes, he peered through a small opening between the curtain and the door where he couldn't be seen. He rubbed his eyes one more time to make sure of what he was seeing.

Emma! He turned away and started to walk back to the stairs of the loft, and just as abruptly, he turned back and looked again through the gap.

She rang the bell one more time. A scene in black-and-white—ripped right from the pages of some tawdry Harlequin romance—flashed across his sleepy brain, like an old Tracy and Hepburn movie:

—They threw themselves into each other's arms in a delirious frenzy of kissing and grappling. His bare chest rippled and crushed against her. Restrained by the fabric of her blouse, her luxurious bosom heaved against him, and all the while their lips and tongues searched eagerly for ears, faces and necks. He lifted her into his sinewy arms, thrust his way through the curtains and took her, willy-nilly, up into the loft. He laid her roughly on the mattress, ripped the clothes from her writhing body and made wild, fervent love to her. Finally spent in the heat of unrestrained passion, they fell to sleep entwined in each other's arms— faces aglow, drifting and sleeping and drifting deeply, deeply into love ever after—

Alex shook the ridiculous scene from his head, vowing never again to read the stuff that he found at the laundromat while he waited on his clothes to dry. He pulled back the deep-purple curtain, went through the opening of the wall, took the keys from his pocket and unlocked the front door. Bare-chested, bare-footed and—thankfully— flaccid, he stood there with a crown of hair spiked out in all directions, the deposed king from the land of Nod.

Emma stood outside, shifting from one foot to the other and back again, unsure what to say or do next.

Alex was speechless, but felt relief at the sight of her. "Come in."

She pushed the basket of fruit into his hands. "I wanted to see you before you left and apologize for my behavior on Saturday."

"Not necessary."

"I know, but . . ."

"Would you like some coffee? I can make some in back. Let's get out of the public eye here," he said referring to the glass windows in which they were standing on display, like a couple of department store mannequins. Back in the studio, Alex put the fruit basket on a small table in the kitchen. "Would you care for something now?"

"Coffee would be nice. I don't want to hold you up. I know you're going to visit Josh today." She stood there, uncertain what she should do, feeling a little uncomfortable in the same space she'd felt so at ease in before.

"Well, I'm not ready yet, so I'm not leaving today."

Emma couldn't hold her sigh of relief.

"I decided to call Josh and tell him that I need a couple of days to get things squared off around here. He'll be a little disappointed, but I think he'll forgive me. It seems like I'm always disappointing him." He poured water for coffee. "Sit down, sit down. Make yourself at home."

"Thank you. It's been a rather hectic morning already. I didn't want you to leave with the way things were."

He excused himself and popped up the steps, two at a time, for his T-shirt and Birkenstocks. "It's okay, don't worry about it," he yelled down to her. "You know, I was disappointed with how things went. I didn't know exactly what I had done to anger you."

"It wasn't you. That's why I'm here. It's this, this wonderful, crazy, fearful change in my life."

"I must admit I'm puzzled, especially seeing you at the door with a fruit basket." He came back down and resumed scooping coffee into the filter.

"I know it's early. I thought you'd probably be up, getting ready to go. But I had the most remarkable dream last night—well, it wasn't really a dream. Whatever it was, for some crazy reason, I just felt that I needed to tell you about it. Mary told me you'd called the night before, and I wanted . . . it was late. I was in a muddle; it was everything, all swirling around in my head."

"Really, it's okay. I wanted to see you too."

201

For several moments, they sat and listened as the coffee steeped through its filter and dripped into the pot. The aroma was almost as intoxicating as the silence. Alex got up and washed a couple of cups, set out cream and poured.

"This isn't easy," Emma said. "I had all these things on my mind, and now, I don't know what to say. There are so many new experiences and feelings. How can I begin to tell you how the last few days have changed my life?—when I'm not even sure how it happened. Two things I know for sure, but neither one has anything to do with the other. I've decided to paint again. It's been a long time, maybe too long, but I have to see if I can."

"Do you mean you want to paint professionally?"

"I want to spend my life making paintings."

"I've gotta tell you, it won't be easy."

"I know. Believe me, as a dealer, I've seen enough painters to know the score. Maybe I won't be good enough. But at least I'll try." She straightened her back and shoulders, sitting higher in the chair with her hands around her cup on the table in front of her. "I used to draw and paint as a child and kept at it when most kids had lost interest. I loved it. I'd forgotten how much, until this weekend. My mother used to paint in watercolor. She was quite accomplished. Did I tell you that?" She sipped her coffee.

"No, you didn't mention it."

"She had real talent, but she never believed in herself enough to pursue it full time, even though she loved it. I think she was most happy when she painted alone. I watched her through the window. She loved her paints, easel and brushes—would sit for hours in the garden, with an indescribable expression playing across her face. But she gave it up for my father because it took so much time away from him. Those were different times."

"Hopefully. But becoming a painter's not just a matter of doing what you want." Alex said this rather more firmly than he intended.

"I suppose. But all my life, I've had this dream. When I was in college, my family told me how inappropriate it was for me, as a woman, to become an artist. But I was determined. I told no one of my decision. I couldn't."

"Did you feel isolated?" He sipped his coffee.

"Oh yes. I was studying art history—courses I would've taken anyway. But as it happened, I got pregnant with Heather and decided to marry Bob. I was so young. I didn't think I could do both—be a mother and a painter too. My own mother discouraged me. She said there wasn't room in my life for Bob, Heather and painting as well. My determination evaporated. I can't believe I was so spineless. That was it . . . until this weekend when I saw those wonderful murals of yours."

"You're not trying to tell me that it's my fault," he said with a big smile across his face.

"Oh, nothing like that." She smiled back. "But I felt those murals—just like I felt those cave paintings—and knew that I've been missing a big part of who I am by denying it as I have. I don't know why it took me so long, but here I am, realizing for maybe the first time in my life what it means to be me." Emma leaned back and sipped her coffee.

"Well, you have to be who you are, that's for sure." Alex leaned forward on his elbows, sliding his cup out of the way. "Many people never find that out. Sometimes, even when they do, they don't do anything about it. Change is too difficult for some people—they're afraid. It means upheaval and chaos, taking control of your life, crawling out on a limb."

"I'm terrified and thrilled, all at the same time."

"Painting can break your heart, let me tell you. Can you take the rejection and failure coming your way? And it is, believe me. There are no guarantees."

"I know. I mean, I think I do. When did you know you were a painter?"

"Oh, that's a long story. You want some more coffee? How about some of that fruit you brought along? I'll tell you about a dream that I had when I first thought I wanted to paint seriously." Alex found a large knife while Emma washed her hands at the sink. He set out a plastic trash bag for the peelings before pouring more coffee. Emma sliced the fruit.

"Like you, I loved making art long after my classmates and friends had given up interest. I never stopped, though I went long periods between projects. When it got hard, I didn't do it, until driven to do something, good or bad. It was mostly bad. I was a dilettante. At one point, some years ago, I dreamed about it." Alex peeled a banana and began to eat it.

"Me too, last night. It was about you, among other things—not a dream as such, or maybe it was. I don't know any more. But go on, I'll tell you about it later."

"At the time, I was doing a lot of theater work; I dreamed I was in an empty theater. It was late. I was alone, looking for a place to show my new paintings. I'd been climbing and looking all over that theater for what seemed like hours."

"Did you work in theater for a long time?" She quartered an orange and pushed two pieces across the table to Alex.

"Long enough. I climbed the stairwell in front of me. A landing turned a ninety-degree angle and ascended into a glorious white room. A spider web spanned the entrance to the top floor; a huge black widow sat right in the center. What do you suppose that was about?"

"I'm not sure, but I don't like spiders." Emma ate the flesh of the orange, licked the sticky juice off of her fingers and tossed the peels into the bag.

"I could see no walls, just this incredible light and space that seemed to go on as far as my eye could see. Out in the midst of all that space, about ten feet tall and standing on its hind legs, stood the biggest bear I had ever seen. It offered to embrace me, stared into my eyes and knew what I wanted." Alex paused to sip at his coffee and look at Emma.

"Well, what happened? Don't leave me hanging."

"It was clear. I could brush aside the fear and dance with the bear, or I could turn and descend into darkness without claiming the light for my own. That's when the dream ended."

"Amazing."

"The dream's as clear right now as when I had it."

"It's very vivid."

"And, it was as clear as the nose on my face that there was no turning back. I was a painter. And here I am, still a painter, boring you silly." Alex finished his banana and started the orange.

"Not in the least. Do you always dream so profoundly? It hasn't been that clear for me."

"Well, I don't know. It seems all those experiences of yours have been working on you in a very synchronous way. You're certainly making some hefty life-changing decisions. What more can you ask for?"

"Since you put it like that, I can see things coming into focus."

"It's not every day we discover our passions. Just remember, life can be a lot of fun if looked at from the right perspective. I can't encourage you to become a painter, but then I can't discourage you either. Everyone has to make choices for themselves. That's what living is—that and cleaning up these dishes," he said, finishing his orange.

Alex got up to wash his hands and clear the table. Emma helped him. They finished putting things away and stood by the sink, next to each other.

"Is there anything else I can help you with?" Emma asked.

"Not that I can think of, but no doubt something will come up if I give it a little thought. Is there anything I can help you with while I'm thinking?"

"Well, now that you mention it, would you take me up to your loft and show me your Buddha?"

"My what?"

"Your Buddha."

"That's what I thought you said. But don't you want to tell me the second thing you decided last night?"

Smiling at him, Emma walked around the table, took his hand and led him to the stairs of the loft. The morning sun filled the studio with a glorious warm light. Though it didn't take much, she coaxed him up the stairs. His mouth hung open. He looked as if he had something important to say but couldn't find the appropriate words.

"All right," she said, "if you insist, but I'd rather see your Buddha first. Are you sure you're not going to Texas today?"

"Oh yes, positive."

"Good. That gives us the whole day. And I think we're going to need it.

Chapter Eleven

It's Monday. We have to leave the day after tomorrow, so come on, get up," Maggie yells from the bathroom.

"It's not even seven o'clock. I haven't had my coffee yet."

"I know, but you have to see this, Jack."

"I thought you were going for a walk."

"I did and saw something I think you'll find very interesting."

"I have something I think you'll find interesting," he says, propping himself up on his elbow.

She comes out dressed in her bathing suit.

"You're not going swimming this early?"

"Come on, get up. I want to show you something on the beach." She puts shorts and a top over her suit.

"I am up." He flips back the covers and waves it at her. When he realizes that she's less than overwhelmed at the grandeur of his member, he gives up, covers himself and says, "But I haven't eaten anything."

"We'll take some fruit and coffee with us. Hurry. We have to get our stuff out of the truck, and I don't want you to miss this."

"It's too early." He moans and crawls reluctantly from under the covers. "I wish I understood the physics involved in the creation of this bed. How can something be this hard and feel so good? If I knew that, I'd be a rich man."

"You are a rich man. Quit groaning and get moving. The sun's climbing, and I want to be down there while the beach is still in shadow."

"God, it's cold," he whines.

Put on your sweats and quit clomping around like that. You want to wake the whole building?"

"Oh, don't get your fuzzy in a fluff. I can only move so fast—and I'm not clomping around."

Ten minutes later, they're quietly pulling their door closed and tiptoeing down the steps with their beach bag. They cross the courtyard beyond the pool to get the rest of their gear from the truck.

"Awfully early for David to be gone, isn't it?" Jack says. He notices David's car missing from its slot as he disentangles the beach chairs from a plastic milk crate in the truck bed.

"Maybe he's still at the hospital. I wonder how Ruth is doing. I don't think she's been here all week."

"And I don't remember seeing David's car when we got back from La Jolla."

"You think he spent the night there?"

"I guess. She must be in a real bad way."

"Well, I don't know, but I hope she gets better."

"You don't even know her."

"So what? I feel for what he must be going through."

"You don't know him any better than you know her."

"Have you never heard of compassion? Can you imagine me in the hospital? How would you feel about that?"

"Don't even start this," Jack says, locking the tailgate. He picks up his gear and heads for the beach with Maggie in tow. "I hope she gets better, too, for both their sakes. I hate to see anybody suffering or alone. But that's the way life is. If you're not suffering with some God-awful disease, stress has you by the balls, and people are going nuts all around you. Then, even if you manage to escape that, old age and sickness arrive to kick your ass all over the place.

Your parents die, and all of your friends end up either in a hospital or dead. Your teeth and hair fall out, your spine curls up and you get hemorrhoids. Life's bloody marvelous." Jack affects a half-assed English accent on this last thought.

"Boy, aren't we cheerful today," Maggie says and stops.

"You did drag me out of bed with no cuddling, and no coffee, you know."

Maggie hefts her gear up to her chest and just looks at Jack who also stops and turns back to her when he realizes that she's no longer accompanying him. "And what's with that bloody English accent?" she says.

"Just trying to make my point. Anyway, you started it."

They complete the short walk from the parking lot past the north end of the apartments in silence.

Overlooking the beach, they watch a few couples, loners, solitary joggers and the people exercising their dogs. It's cool in the shade and Jack shudders with the chill.

"Okay, what was so urgent that you had to get me out of my nice warm bed this early?" he asks. He notices the single figure sitting in a lawn chair at a small folding table—

looking out at the ocean. "Is that Pablo—the guy from the truck? What's he's doing down there?"

"Guess."

He turns, gives her a puzzled look, then focuses back on the scene below them. "Looks like he's holding the table down with his elbows, the way he has it rocked back like that. I can't tell from here, with his back to me. Is he painting? Doesn't look like it."

"No, he's writing, silly."

"He's writing? But I thought he was a painter."

"He's a writer, like Nick. I went down there to see what he was doing. I walked by, and he smiled at me. Then I doubled back up here to get you. Let's go down."

"Go farther, we don't want to crowd him," Jack says when she begins putting her chair on the sand. They move until Jack feels comfortable with the distance between them. "I guess we're going to have to give him a new name," he says. "How about Shakespeare?"

"Can't do it; there was only one Shakespeare."

"Okay, how about Hemingway then?"

"We could still call him Pablo—for the poet."

"No, he has to be a novelist."

"Hmmm, so let's make it Fyodor."

They settle back into their chairs to enjoy the breeze and watch Fyodor scribbling in his notebook, looking out across the ocean for long moments, then scribbling again.

In the shadow of the cliff behind them, Jack feels apart from civilization—sitting on a shelf between worlds, below the very edge of the continent. He knows they come to the ocean, whenever they can, to escape the inexorable passing of time and experience the sense of it expanding. Suspended above the fray, twist and neediness of being, they savor this transitional space that pulses with life and infuses them with an energy they can find nowhere else. The energy of the natural world in its austere and implacable indifference expects nothing of them. They are just who they are. There are no rules, no proctors—only the ocean, the sun, the sand and, of course, Fyodor. They share a cup of coffee and sit mindful of the world's fragility and impermanence.

"You know Nick's leaving again soon, probably the end of summer," Jack says.

"Why did you bring that up now? I was having such a lovely time sitting here, wriggling my toes in the sand."

"Sorry, no reason. It's just that I was thinking about time and eternity and Fyodor; it made me think about Nick because they're both writers. I'm going to miss him."

"Me too, but I wish you hadn't brought it up. You remember when he first left home?"

"How could I forget? Like shot from a cannon—like shit from a goose—like . . ."

"Okay, okay . . . I never thought I'd get used to it. My one and only, gone. Then, when he came home—after how many years?—I thought I'd never get used to having him in the house again."

"We sure are stuck in our habits, aren't we? Can't change anything without a lot of gut-wrenching emotional hoop-la. We're turning into a couple of old farts! I hate it, just something else to deal with."

"Like my job," she reminds him. "That's going to change sometime, and I don't think we're ready for it."

"I know. You keep bringing that up. But that's what life is, isn't it—constant flux, like that water out there— perpetual agitation, coming and going on the tide."

"Yes, well, it's going to be just as hard to see him go this time as it was the first time, if not harder," she says.

"I'll miss seeing him on the patio, drinking coffee, smoking those foul-smelling hand-rolled cigarettes and writing in his notebook every morning. I don't like to think about it, but I'll manage, I guess. I'll have to."

Maggie pulls the thermos from the beach bag and pours them a half-cup.

"You know what I'm going to miss?" she says, taking the first sip of the hot brew before giving it to Jack. "Our little talks on Saturdays. I love to sit and discuss his latest exploits or the subjects he's studying. He explains things so well. But other times, you'd swear he didn't have a brain in his head."

"It's like he hasn't got a lick of commonsense when it comes to some things. He's so smart with his books, but so naïve about the world—like that time with the dentist . . . "

"Don't even get me started. He can be so senseless and stubborn sometimes, you just wonder who he gets it from."

"But I'm going to miss him anyway," he says and hands the empty cup to Maggie.

She pours them a second half-cup, sips it and hands it to Jack.

"We were just as brainless as he is when we were his age," he says, removing their books from the beach bag.

"Speak for yourself."

"And without half the education." He hands her book to her. "You know, it was a real eye opener to discover ourselves there, turning into a couple of mummies in our cozy middle-aged domesticity, glued to the tube—a couple of eggplants, really. I realized that I hadn't been reading very much. He reads all the time. Just trying to keep up with what he's talking about is almost impossible." He sips his coffee. "All of a sudden there was this breath of fresh air blowing the cobwebs off my brain. I was intellectually engaged again. We were dying by degree. I think he may have saved our lives when he moved back home."

Several birds, slicing through the air overhead, draw his attention south along the beach. A couple of people are throwing something up into a cloud of fluttering gulls hovering and swooping above them. Giving the cup back to Maggie, Jack puts his book back in the bag, stands, moves over slowly—trying not to kick sand in Maggie's direction—and begins to do stretching exercises.

"At any rate, Nick certainly changed things," she says. "It was very exasperating at first."

"I know, but the hard part was learning that I needed to keep my concern for Nick to myself and butt out of his business." Jack grunts with the exertion of over-extension. He relaxes a moment, realizing that he had better go easy before he pulls a muscle. "I have to accept Nick as a grown man and stop trying to father him. Those parental habits are hard to break." Jack pauses to catch his breath. "You guide and protect your child his entire life, and then, all of a sudden he's grown up. If you're smart, you realize that horse won't ride any more. You just have to let go and stop doing it."

Maggie pours out the coffee dregs and screws the cup back on the thermos without comment.

"It's not easy," Jack continues. "It makes life so much easier if we just treat Nick as our friend. Has he mentioned where he wants to go to school?"

"He said something about doing his graduate work in Oregon or Washington. Said he grew up in the desert and thought it would be fun to find out what living in a rain forest is all about.

"As a writer, Nick can live and work anywhere in the world. Sounds pretty good to me." Jack flops down in his chair, a little winded from his jumping jacks.

"I can tell you what sounds good to me," Maggie says as she puts her book away and stands. "I have to use the bathroom. Can I get you anything while I'm up there?"

"You brought water didn't you?"

"It's in the bag."

Picking up her sandals, Maggie crosses the sand and ambles up the concrete ramp where city garbage trucks enter the beach. Jack watches her stop at the top and put on her sandals. After, she recedes from view along the sidewalk behind the cliff. She's still beautiful, he thinks and takes the water from the bag to drink. After putting the water away, he retrieves an orange, peels it and looks at the ocean while he eats.

Jack never tires of looking at the ocean. The vastness of the world's waters is something he likes to think about. Somehow all that water gives him a feeling of hope, surrounding and connecting everything on the planet, filling every accessible niche. When he's at the ocean, things seem brighter. Maybe it's some magical quality of the light, but maybe it's something else too—the mother of us all, the cradle of life. What he doesn't like to think about is the trash and garbage that he and Maggie find washed up on the beach when they walk in the mornings. But the day's too beautiful to dwell on such stupidity. Jack lets his mind wander back to Maggie and the other oceans they've visited over their years together.

The first great-water they saw as newlyweds was the Atlantic, off the coast of Maine. It was entirely different from North Carolina Beach. Rocky and rugged, Arcadia National Park is an island, the easternmost point in the United States. It was cold, even during summer. They went for tea one rainy afternoon and watched the ping pong matches at the Jordan Pond House. Later they drank White Russians in the piano bar and listened to a comedian who did a remarkable impression of Jerry Lewis—his one claim to fame.

He couldn't say there was much of a beach anywhere around the island. However, Jack couldn't trust his memory about that; it was so long ago and, at that time, he was unaware, as most young people generally are, of the world around him. Then too, they were only there for a day before moving on down the coast. But the rocks, the crystalline blue water and the sharp cutting wind he did remember. It was most bracing, the ocean constantly crashing into foam on the rocks. Thunderhole was where he crawled down the sheer face of the cliff, hanging on where Maggie couldn't follow—heights bothered her—just to get a peek into the cave below. It was full of boulders—spheres the size of beach balls—being violently polished into tiny sparkling beads of sand by the relentless Atlantic, repeatedly pouring itself into that awesome pocket of rock. The sound alone was worth the climb.

Jack finishes his orange and wipes his mouth on his sweatshirt sleeve. He leaves the chair and walks down to the water. He stoops, rinses his hands, scoops some water into his mouth and spits it out. He's always surprised by how salty it is. Earlier, he'd had the urge to strip off and plunge headlong into the breakers, but the water is warmer than he expects. What's the point of diving into tepid water? It isn't all that tepid, he knows, but it puts him off anyway. Maybe it isn't the water at all. He must be getting old, he thinks. Another time, nothing would've kept him from it. He looks south to the pier, then turns north toward the point.

It was always rough surf, and like his memory of it now, a bit gray and foggy around the edges. It rained often. They got wet from the spray splashing fifteen, twenty feet in the air. They crawled across the crusty rocks inspecting the tide pools. The diversity of sea life in just one little pool, no wider than a foot, boggled his mind. Over the years, when they visited other places where the land and sea came together, he was always disappointed that there were no tide-pools to match those in Maine. Maybe that was just in his imagination, or was it his memory? He was never quite sure.

That was before Jack became the full-fledged, dyed-in-the-wool, no-holds-barred freethinker that he was today. They were farther south, near a small fishing village called Jonesport. On a wharf, under the roof of a driftwood and tarpaper baldachino, they ate lobsters fresh off the boat in the company of a tall, faded angel—who, presumably, had been separated from the prow of her ship and lost at sea in some great Nor'easter of the previous century.

Then, one night after dinner, feeling no pain from the wine and still young enough to consider God responsible for all of the shortcomings of the human race, he cursed at the top of his lungs. He hurled rocks at the Great Silent One who, as always, remained hidden among the stars. As they wandered the mudflats, Jack couldn't find the Star of Heaven among the billions raining starlight down on them. In the middle of the night, the ocean deserted the land, like a faithless paramour—promising to return tomorrow.

Jack chuckles, remembering how romantic he thought it was at the time, like something from a J. P. Donleavy novel—railing at God on high, trying to impress Maggie with his sincerity—showing off, basically. Oh, such existential angst he used to have. When did those two young, agile romantics get to be such stodgy, middle-aged gasbags? he wonders. Although Jack could very nearly say where they went and what they did in all the intervening years, he's at a loss to say how. Just living would do that to you, he supposes. He decides that, if for no other reason, man created God in order to have someone else to blame. Jack stops, picks up a couple of stones and heaves them as far out into the sea as he can. He doesn't have the arm that he used to have—or the angst.

Touring the coast from Bar Harbor down to Boston, they ultimately went to visit his high school chum, Cameron, a music major at Boston College. Cameron used to joke that while growing up, he was so effeminate that everyone knew he was gay before he did. The reason he never came out of the closet, he said, was because he was never in one to begin with. He played piano at their wedding. Jack wondered what happened to him, especially in light of the AIDS crisis. He was distant, almost hostile, the last time they spoke and declined an invitation to meet with them for dinner. He would give no reason. Time had a way of diminishing relationships and separating people, and Cameron wasn't the first or the last of their friends to disappear into the past.

Singing Beach near Ipswich—one of John Updike's early haunts north of Boston, as he recalls, where they went with Cameron a week later—was to fascinate him just as much as Thunderhole. The wind blowing in from the cold Atlantic waters through the fine white sand—cylindrically humped like a barrel along the short length of beach—made a sound very much like someone softly singing. The romantic in him liked to think that the beautiful sound at Singing Beach and the booming throat at Thunderhole were the voices of Providence and that the paltry humans that we are just don't know what we're listening to. Jack knew better.

Another one of the prettiest picture-postcard beaches they ever saw was on St. Croix in the Virgin Islands. They visited Maggie's friend, Chris, who worked for a big bauxite-mining corporation on the island. They stayed, three, in her small studio apartment—housed in the huge concrete-block apartment complex owned by the company. It was just a year or so after their trip to Maine.

Jack stops to watch the wind-surfers. They bounce and fly over the foam-crested water. Back and forth they go. From this distance, there seems no point to it, although he knows it must be fun. For him, it's an imaginary thrill. Not that he's so old, but that he has a momentary pang of regret for his lost youth. And it's not just his age; he grows edgy with his memories, especially those that bring back times that were not his best. Jack is anxious with his thoughts about St. Croix.

Jack was not a womanizer or very good at handling his alcohol. He was still awake after a small party—rum and Cokes, chips, dip and a cheese ball coated in chopped walnuts. It was two o'clock in the morning. Jack was the only male. Lying alone in the louvered moonlight, sweating out the rum, sugar and caffeine, he listened in irritation to Maggie and Chris—virtually naked in their sheer pajama tops and panties, completely oblivious to his condition and snoring like a couple of lumberjacks—sawing them off in perfect tandem. He fumed on his pallet in the dark. He was angry that Maggie wouldn't have sex with him after Chris fell asleep. He couldn't get Chris' large breasts, or her coworker, Leila the Queen—the fourth of their party, a ravishing, black-haired coffee-skinned islander with enormous espresso-colored eyes—off his mind.

She'd been flirting with him all evening. He was surprised that Maggie didn't even notice. But it was more than he could stand. He got up, put on his shorts, slipped out of the room, down the verandah, and over three doors to Leila's apartment. He woke her with his soft but insistent knocking. He'd incorrectly assumed that she had been waiting for him. Nevertheless, she invited him in for a nightcap. A short time later, moments before dawn, he slipped back into the studio, and the rest was history.

He wonders if she was really as ravishing as he remembered. Probably not, he thinks. Jack looks back toward the beach chairs to see if Maggie has returned. He doesn't see her and slides reluctantly back into his memory.

Maggie never found out. They'd have been divorced long ago if she had. That's how he knew. Either Leila never told Chris, or Chris never told Maggie. He'd never been able to definitively determine which. However, Chris made one cryptic remark later that week, about not plucking the wild hibiscus on company property, but at the time it didn't strike him as too weird.

They'd been drinking heavily. Maggie seemed strange, distant and aloof for the rest of their time there. He assumed it was because of his drinking—it was all anyone seemed to do at night, the only cure for the symptoms of island fever, "purely medicinal" everyone joked—and his wanting sex with her while he was drunk. In any event, he was lucky. Leila disappeared and wasn't seen again. Jack was not unhappy about that. On the contrary, he was living in constant fear that she'd show up and blow the whistle on him. It would've ended their shaky marriage, right then and there.

"I thought we weren't going to dwell on such stupid nonsense," Jack says aloud, speaking to himself.

He turns north again and ambles along the water's edge, stopping occasionally to examine something he finds in his path. He shudders to think how close he came to losing Maggie then. He certainly wouldn't run that risk today. Why didn't it seem like such a risk at the time? Stupidity? Ignorance? The recklessness of youth? Ah yes, all three. If Chris knew, she must've also known how devastated Maggie would be to hear such news. She must've known how much Maggie loved him and how much he loved her. Though they eventually lost contact with her after her divorce—another relationship lost to history—he thinks that Chris was a better friend to Maggie than she'd ever know.

He regrets his actions—remembering Maggie crossing the beach and climbing the ramp just now. He knows those acts will always be there. Early on, however, he learned that regret is a complete waste of time and energy, like guilt or overblown remorse—something to be noted but not indulged. The regret of not being there for a loved one in a time of need can be ruinously tyrannical, if pampered. There's the regret of being petty—acting badly out of meanness or cruelty toward a parent or a mate, in some snit over an imagined or even a real slight—we all experience one time or another. Being unable to make good for such behavior can be devastating. That type of regret kills the spirit; it roots and festers in the psyche.

Like everyone, Jack has his share of regrets to contemplate—not the least of which are his lack of consideration for Maggie and his selfishness—trapped as he'd been by his monumental ego. He's working on it—will always be working on it—but thinks he's made significant progress over the years, though he knows there's still some distance to go. Like many young people, it has taken Jack some years to acknowledge the simple fact that he wasn't perfect just as he was.

How would he feel, and what would've happened to them, had he not participated in that sordid little indiscretion? Were he and David Rayburn much alike? Does it really take one to know one? Is that why he entertains such negative thoughts about the Rayburns and their social life, though he knows nothing   about them? Did his previous actions color the way he views other people now? Could he even know such things? Would it matter to him, or anyone else, if he did? Could their relationship be any better now if he'd not had sex with Leila that night? After all's said and done, would he not just simply be a better person? On the other hand, is it not the indiscretions and mistakes we make that make us who we are? Either way, he wishes he could take it back.

Jack stops again to look out upon the ocean. A feeling of love for it, and of just how much he enjoys coming here, washes over him in one big swell. He turns and heads back the way he came. He can see that Maggie has not yet returned but feels the need to be there when she does.

It was quite an experience, the first time a woman had ever performed fellatio on him. It wasn't something nice girls did. It certainly wasn't talked about in company, but then most sexual things weren't talked about before the sexual revolution except in locker rooms where it was mostly braggadocio. Ironically, there were no more nice girls. Women today hate that word nice, almost as much as they hate the word girl, or so it seemed.

Chris was right. Leila was a real exotic tropical flower. He never even lost his erection after he came in her mouth. Then—although she wouldn't let him come inside her, coming the second time on her belly—he fucked her with all of the pent-up emotion he'd been repressing the whole evening. Jack's jaw begins clenching, and he feels a strong stirring within his groin as he walks.

But such nasty language still can't be used in certain company, though the language of younger people is rife with it. Is that sensual act so necessary for our survival— giving our minds over to the pleasures and needs of our bodies—always going to be shrouded in the shame of sin? There's no polite way to speak about lust, without sounding like a second-grade schoolteacher trying to explain the birds and the bees. There's no nonclinical language that carries the meaning, without the queasy disdain or a distasteful moralistic baggage that's generally heaped upon the act of procreation. But is there a need to talk about it? And what has the concept of sin to do with anything?

Not much, he thinks. Since Trump's misogynistic pussy-grabbing fiasco, the media has thrust everything into the public's face, and no one escapes the fallout. It isn't the fact of the sexual act itself that's the bother; indeed, humans wouldn't be here to talk about it otherwise. It's about sin, venial and menial—giving up control; humans have learned, and are now forced, to be shamed in the act of surrender. Jack's sin isn't just the sin of sex; it's the sin of

227

adultery and surrender. It's the ego-driven sin of sex out of anger or pique—to punish, or some other even less likely excuse.

Egos are ugly things, indeed. No matter how he looks at it, he can't see himself in a very good light. Jack realizes that he's almost jogging and slows down. Looking up, he pulls himself from his thoughts and notices that Fyodor is working away in earnest. Jack relaxes his shoulders and takes a couple of deep breaths. How can these old memories bother him so much? He never consciously dredges them up. So why today? He doesn't know, and it doesn't matter.

It rained torrents every morning and every evening, like clockwork. The bird of paradise and hibiscus bloomed. Breadfruit, bananas and coconuts grew wild, just ripe for plucking and devouring right from the trees. It was the Virgin Islands, although Leila was no virgin, to be sure. Suppose it never happened. His mind was a powerful and mysterious organ and sometimes played tricks on his memory. It was a constant battle for Jack to keep his focus on reality, to not slip off into some mesmerizing fairy tale.

After a two-week steady diet of rum Cokes and lotus blossom, Jack knew he could never live any length of time on a small island. The island fever would eventually make him violent or mad or both. Going native in his own heart of darkness wasn't his idea of the way to spend the rest of his life, no matter how easy it seemed. He wished it were all a dream of the lush tropical island.

Jack wants to be clear-eyed, to see reality, to know it—unvarnished, raw. He knows also that that's impossible—his mind protects him from the horror and immensity of reality—but he tries. As Jack gets older, his memory is less honest in its dealings with him than when he was younger and more vigilant. There was so much less data in his brain to contend with thirty years ago. And now, there's just a damn sight more to keep up with. Sometimes, it's hard to tell. Maybe it's memory. Maybe it's wishful thinking. Maybe he's making it all up as he goes. Maybe it's fiction.

Back where he started, Jack takes the water from the bag and drinks. He stretches and flops back down in the chair to wait for Maggie. What's taking her so long? He takes an apple from the bag and munches it.

Jack has always been driven by his testosterone. Now, even though his testosterone level is dropping, he's still, most days, at the mercy of it. His interest in sex isn't waning; in fact, in some ways, it seems to be increasing. But his ability to erect and maintain seems diminished, though not entirely thwarted. This bothers him. Who wouldn't be bothered? Isn't that a sign of old age and what comes after? It's true. At the same time, certain other things not so important to him earlier in his life are becoming more important now.

After all, his relationship to Maggie is paramount. Even when they're bickering, something they don't do very often, they're mated to one another for life. Certainly, he didn't plan it this way. Somewhere along the line, he just realized that this was how it was. He doesn't feel emotionally dependent on a woman. But is he? Maybe he isn't totally dependent even now, but he's sure of one thing in his life. He doesn't want to find out just how dependent he is. He isn't sure that he'd be able to survive her loss.

Jack feels his recurring and penetrating love for Maggie. It makes him melancholy because he never entirely trusts his emotions—those slippery mind-states that are illusory, chemically based and, ultimately, not to be relied upon. Emotions come and go; but for the time that they exist, they are palpable entities as real as anything tangible. He wishes he could pluck them from his heart and be completely free of them. But his love for her is as real as it gets, and he knows that as long as he lives that will never happen.

"A penny for your thoughts," Maggie says.

"Oh, hi. I didn't hear you come up," he says, opening his eyes.

Maggie is standing directly in his view of the ocean. With her legs spread, her hands on hips and her pelvis at eye level, thrust out for his close inspection, it's not too blatant a posture—tantalizing as it is—since Maggie is never one to exaggerate a thing.

He imagines that, from a distance, she might look as if she were lecturing him for some defect or imperfection of his character. She always camouflages her sexual antics; as a child, she was taught to hide her desires behind her nice-little-girl façade. Besides, there are now a few more people on the beach, and she doesn't hold the pose for long—too embarrassed at what others might think if they saw her performing such blatant sexual maneuvers. She's been married a long time.

"So," Maggie says. "Are you going to tell me?"

"What?"

"What you're thinking about."

"Oh, I was just thinking that when you got back, I was going to ravish you from nave to chops, like a pirate on a desert island, right here on the sand in front of the pelicans."

"Oh really . . . well, here I am." She smiles broadly.

"I see," he says, dryly.

"Can I have the rest of that apple?"

"Here, help yourself," he says, handing it to her.

"So, what were you really thinking about?" She sits in her chair beside him and eats.

"That beach on St. Croix. Remember how we drove through the rain forest off the highway along the gravel road, and later, through a whole grove of palms down to the water, how excited we were."

"No one was there. We had that wonderful little beach all to ourselves the entire afternoon." She quickly reaches over and gives his penis a squeeze—not something she often does, especially in public.

Taken by surprise, Jack almost jumps out of his seat. "What are you doing?" he yells.

Maggie laughs and covers her mouth. "Just reminding you. Relax. I didn't mean to scare you." She laughs again.

"You didn't scare me. I wasn't expecting that just now."

"Well, I won't do it again, if you continue to make such a big deal out of it. Well? Remember that beach?"

"Yes I do. And what we did there, too. We were totally alone—it was like being the only two people in paradise. The sand was pristine. I felt like Robinson Crusoe stumbling over Friday's footprint for the first time."

"And the water was cold and deep and clear blue," she says, giving herself a hug to soften the shudder of her memory.

"That should've given us a clue right then."

"I suppose, but what did we know?"

"If it hadn't been for that diver at Rocky's Grotto that night, we might have kept going back. No coral barrier. Unprotected waters. Great White Shark feeding grounds. I tell you, Mags, it's a good thing that we didn't have to find that one out the hard way."

"Do you remember how many beaches we've been on together?"

"Well, let's see. I remember two beaches on the Virgin Islands, that one and the public beach, though I don't remember the names. There was North Carolina Beach before we got married, and Galveston Bay when we went to Houston. But that wasn't really a beach, more of a harbor. There was the one in Maine; and then, Singing Beach near Boston; the one in Florence, Oregon, with all those giant driftwood logs laying around like Pick-up Stix when we stopped to visit Rick in Eugene. Then there was Westport, up north, and here. Right?"

"You got them all. I didn't think you could do it."

"I wonder where Rick's at and what he's up to these days."

"Who knows? By the way, I ran into David Rayburn on the way back to the apartment just now. He came in to shower and change his clothes; he's staying all night at the hospital. He told me they found cancer in an advanced stage and were not very hopeful for Ruth's chances of recovery, even with treatment. Her body is riddled with it.

He said there was nothing they could do except to allay the pain and keep her as comfortable as possible—the poor woman. The company's sending someone down to take over for him. He'll be spending all of his time at the hospital."

"What can you do? Death's coming for us all, eventually."

"Yes, well, it's the suffering until then . . . isn't it?"

"I don't know what I'd do in his place."

"Make the best of it. Lend a hand when you can. Try to stay cheerful and not to let it ruin the rest of your life. I know that's easier to say than do. I hope we never have to find out." They stop to watch the ocean and listen to the waves and smell the breeze coming in across the Pacific.

"It really makes you think about what you're doing with your life."

"Seriously."

"When I can't make a decision about something, I just remind myself that I could drop dead as a doornail without a moment's notice. That usually clears up any questions I have about what I should do next. Do you ever get that thought?"

"All the time. That's why it's so hard to think about staying at my job, as much as I like it. There're these other things in my life that I'm unable to find enough time or energy for."

"What are you going to do? I can't even get you to start making plans to do something else. It's not going to happen overnight, whatever you decide. I wish you'd figure it out and get about doing it, whatever it is, so we can get past this—this impasse that we seem forever doomed to suffer." As he utters this last bit of hyperbole, the pitch of his voice rises. He gets out of his chair and waves his arms around in irritation.

"Well, I'm not the only one." She stands to face him, balls her fists and places them on her hips. "You just keep saying that you're going to do more to sell some of those paintings of yours, but you keep sitting on your butt and not doing a whole lot about it that I can see," she says, cool and calm.

"Look, I don't want to argue about this." He backs off. "It's too great a morning to stand here on the sand getting all worked up on our next to last day at the beach. I just want to make a decision of some kind, so I can forget about it."

"Well." She pauses a moment to look closely at Jack before turning away and walking down toward the water.

Jack follows along beside her. Above and behind, the sun crests the tops of the buildings on the cliff, warming the beach and eliminating the shade.

"I've been thinking about what you said the other day," she says, "you know, doing something together. Is there anything specific you have in mind?"

"Not really, but ever since I was a kid, I had this dream to write a book, a novel—one of those things on my list of things that I'd like to accomplish before I die."

"You never told me that before."

"I guess there are some things you don't know about me, huh?—and after all this time, just imagine. Well, you do know how much I love fiction. Besides, I'm sure I told you. I mean after all these years, and you don't know that?"

"But you're a painter, not a writer."

"So what? Look. It doesn't take a lot of writing to publish a book of paintings and photographs. I would make some black and white etchings or colorful paintings to go in counterpoint to your black and white photos. Not to change the subject, but you'll have to convert over to digital at some point, you know? It's just not practical otherwise."

"I know. But you know how I feel about change."

"I do. But face it, Maggie, you've got to keep up."

"I know."

"You go digital. Then, we could build a website and go commercial on the Internet. There are lots of things to explore together, like this beach." Jack stoops and picks up the empty carapace of a chitin. "The flora and fauna," he says. handing it to her. "I mean, if we were creating and selling some really beautiful books—say about all of the beaches of the United States, for instance—we could go and live on the beaches to get our material, couldn't we? We could sell the house, liquidate the assets, get a camper-rig like Fyodor over there, and hit the road. We've already got the truck. I'll write the great American novel some other time. What do you say?" He takes her by her elbows and pulls her around to face him.

"Yeah, and when we're done with that, we could sell the camper and go do a really fat book on all of the beaches in Greece—write off the expenses." She pushes him back with both hands to his chest.

"Hey, great idea. Here we come—lamb-kabobs and baklava, Ouzo and cigars, dancing in the moonlight." Jack can't resist dancing her around the beach, envisioning himself as Anthony Quinn in Zorba the Greek, murdering the music at the top of his voice. "When do you want to get started?" he asks, grabbing her in a headlock and giving her noogies with his knuckles on her head.

"How about first thing in the morning?" she says, wiggling out of his grasp.

Jack tries to catch her, but Maggie's on to his tricks.

She turns, screams "Bonsai!" as loud as she can, and jumps on him. They sprawl in the sand. She straddles his torso, pins him down with her thighs and bounces up and down on his stomach.

He's out of breath and laughing so hard at her antics that he's unable to push her off—until she makes the one fatal mistake that gives him superhuman strength; she reaches around and grabs him by his penis—again.

Tuesday

Chapter Twelve

The first light of day came through the skylight into
Alex's   studio as a soft glow, defining the space with
an ethereal ambient illumination that changed throughout
the year. The sun rose earlier every day as the season
advanced into summer. In winter, the light took longer to
appear—entering the space at an oblique angle. It was
cooler in the spring but warmer in the fall and hotter, of
course, when the sun was at its zenith overhead. True or
not, that was his reasoning about the beautiful cool light
that revealed his studio this fine May morning as he
watched the still sleeping Emma.

Looking about, Alex realized that Emma, and indeed
everything in his studio, was without color. As the theory
goes, it was his own human perception of photonic energy
that lent the blush to Emma's cheek and not any tangible
color that she, herself, possessed. Like all matter, she was
colorless. It was through the medium of light that the rods
and cones of his eye painted her with warm and vibrant
shades of color as he watched her. Unable to take those
same eyes off her as the light sculpted the planes and
hollows of Emma's features from the darkness, Alex was
reminded of the translucent color of the skin in one of Da
Vinci's virgins.

Alex understood that it was useless to try to paint this
particular interaction of light and form. Capturing such
awe-inspiring beauty was doomed to failure from the start;

it was impossible. She had infiltrated his domain and taken command of his attentions in a way that no other woman could have. In his present state—and unsure exactly what that state might be—he could never paint her. She was already too close for him to discern the lines between them, where he left off and she began. He was content, for the moment, to simply watch the enigma unfold. But maybe one day it would be fun to try.

The world had a way of dissolving, moment to moment. Where he went today, he'd leave tomorrow. Truth was a chameleonic phenomenon. Today's gospel became tomorrow's heresy. His understanding of reality metamorphosed, transformed itself, was in doubt simply because the position from which he observed it continually shifted, giving him a whole new perspective on the matter. And often, things were changed so quickly that he couldn't say with absolute certainty just what, exactly, he was seeing. But now, this morning, it was her shape that he saw, and he trusted his eyes in this instance. She was here with him. He wouldn't like to think that this was just an illusion and considered pinching her to make sure he wasn't dreaming.

Alex couldn't stop marveling over how intense his life had become. He was overjoyed at the circumstance— waking from the most restful night he'd spent in a week. His night of rest had come after an incredible day of love-making. They had shared their most private thoughts. Emma no longer wore her wedding rings. Could this be love?—so soon?

Ah, there was the rub. Falling in love was dangerous business. He'd done it once before, and look how that had turned out. Granted, he and his ex-wife were still friends, but might it have been better to have worked out their differences and stayed together—if not for them, then for Josh? He'll never know. Even so, it wasn't an easy thing to have worked it out as well as they did. Deciding to enter such a close relationship again, after failing the first time, gave Alex reasonable trepidation.

Anyone would be nervous. One day his life was going along a perfectly ordinary path. He was enthusiastic with his work—making money, not as much as he'd like, but certainly nothing to complain about. No longer fighting with Jennifer and developing a strong relationship with his son, he never thought of himself as lonely. It was just that life seemed somehow enhanced with Emma around— sharper, more coherent and purposeful in her presence. Things he took little or no notice of previously, now came quickly into focus. Yesterday, his ideas and thoughts had seemed uninspired, but now they were compellingly laden with mystery and unlooked for potential; he loved sharing them with her. The very fact that she listened to him was thrilling.

He looked down at her face. What was she dreaming about? Him? She had been enormously hungry for his body. Their lovemaking was wild and passionate, quiet and tender. Her enthusiasm surprised him. She had shone none of the casualness of more experienced women that he'd known. She fumbled and was embarrassed and explained that she'd only been with her husband. Being with a different man, after all these years, made her self-conscious. She confessed that her sex life had been dull, unimaginative and perfunctory. Alex wondered how they could've lived that long together without some sort of satisfying, ungrudgingly pleasurable sex.

Though his marriage was a failure, sex had never been an issue. Not every time was a rocket to the moon, even in the best of relationships. But to never experience complete surrender or true intimacy was, as he could well imagine, a painful jaunt on the back of a camel over the sands of the Sahara with no oasis in sight. What he couldn't imagine was a man being that selfish. On second thought, he was that selfish and knew that Jennifer wasn't the only one to blame for their break up.

Emma brought him something he'd forgotten—the wonder and magic of discovery, in that early time in a relationship when everything is new territory. He had not realized how he missed the enthusiasm that love engenders. The years he'd spent alone had given him the time he needed to mature. Would he be who he was today without that seasoning? Stronger, more open, understanding and tolerant, he knew that wisdom often came with failure, if not with age. And without that behind him, painful as it was, he might not appreciate now what Emma represented. He'd forgotten how compelling it could be to have his whole attention wrapped up in something as frivolous as sharing his food. He casually swiped at some crumbs on the sheets from the pizza they'd eaten in bed last night. Such lighthearted feeling might have gone unnoticed previously. He would have been the poorer for it.

He also realized that they were not Romeo and Juliet and hoped that their relationship didn't become a tragedy of Shakespearean proportions. Nor could he ignore the fact that they had come from different backgrounds. What she planned to do about Bob was something they needed to discuss. As great as his studio was, it was still a studio; skylight and loft notwithstanding, by definition, it was rough when gauged by almost any standard—one bathroom with no tub, just a plastic shower-stall—with no amenities to speak of. He owned little more than the clothes on his back and the tools of his trade, aside from his truck and camper. It was all very well for him. He'd been happy to be free of the encumbrance of material things. In fact, he had grown to prefer it. It kept his life uncomplicated.

On the other hand, Emma lived in an elegant house with many beautiful objects and was not used to living the simple life that he favored. She was accustomed to finer things, certainly more than he could ever hope to provide— things she could probably continue to provide for herself, if she didn't give up her job at the gallery to become a painter. That could prove to be her financial doom. Would she walk away from Bob to live in this place? Not likely. Why move to Tucson when everything important to her— work, family and home—was in L.A.?

He fancied that he was now an important element in her life, and certainly he could pull up stakes and move his tent to California; he was always on the road to one commission or another anyway. Could he afford to live there? It was questionable. And there was another important factor to consider. How was Josh going to feel about her? And what about her girls? They had no idea that their lives were going to be disrupted and complicated. Would she want children by him?

He was old enough to know that such questions could be answered, but he was also no longer blind to the possibilities of failure. Just maybe, it was not knowing what was ahead that gave him the capability to work things through, or did it? Wisdom was a double-edged sword, cutting both ways. He didn't want to think about it now. It was enough to be here enjoying this incredible vision of loveliness, with her big pale blue eyes wide open, staring up at him.

"Oh, I didn't know you were awake," he said.

"And where were you? You looked like you were in another world."

"Well, I was thinking what a great day we had yesterday."

"Were you? I was thinking that we smell like a couple of hound dogs, and I need a bath. But you don't have a bathtub, so I'll take a shower instead. Would you like to join me?" She got out of bed like a shot and was at the shower, turning on water.

Alex watched, entranced by the swaying of her breasts and the sensuousness of her lines as she reached through the shower curtain to fiddle with the knobs.

"Are you coming in or not?" she asked, testing the water with her hand before slipping behind the curtain.

"Are you sure there's room in there for both of us?"

"Oh it's pretty small, but I think we'll fit if we get intimate with each other."

When he slipped into the shower with her, she was already lathering her hair with his bargain brand shampoo.

"Here, let me," he said. His fingers massaged her scalp. "Mighty tight fit in here." He hit the side of the stall with an elbow, so vigorous in his enthusiasm.

"My God," she said, eyes closed, mouth hanging open. "I'll give you three hours to stop that," she moaned.

When he finished, he turned her around and pulled her closer to him so he could rinse the lather from the hair, plastered about her face. He washed her down with Ivory soap and a faded wash cloth. "Okay, rinse," he said and slowly turned her under the spray of the nozzle. "You know, we're going to have to talk about all of this, eventually."

"Yes, I know, but not now. I'm limp as this rag, and it's my turn to wash you."

They switched places so he could be under the water. She bobbled the soap and dropped it to the floor of the shower.

"Oops, I'll get it." She pressed her breasts against him and shimmied down his body to retrieve it. "Oh, look what I found," she said, settling on her knees and taking his penis into her hand. She picked up the soap, lathered him up and rinsed him down, wrapped her arms around his legs, and ran her tongue in random circles across his belly—and below.

"Well, that was very bold of you," he said afterwards as he helped her to her feet.

"One of my fantasies has always been to make love under a waterfall. You think we could try it under a real one some time?"

"Why not? Say, what are those?" he asked, pointing out the bruises that were beginning to form on her arms and legs, testaments to the vigorousness of their passion and unfamiliarity with each other. "The police might arrest me for assault and battery if they spot those."

"If they put you in jail, they'd have to put me in jail with you. It wouldn't matter."

Alex reached over, turned the water off, slid back the curtain, and stepped out into a pool of water that had puddled on the floor while they showered. He took a towel from the rack and mopped it up. Unable to find another clean towel, he stripped the cover sheet off his bed and wrapped it around her. "I know this isn't exactly fresh as new mown hay, but . . ."

"It'll do," she finished as he rubbed her down.

"Things have gotten very complicated all of a sudden, haven't they?"

"We've gotten so swept up in this, I'm not sure we know what we're doing."

"Life's a big gamble. Stick your neck out, and someone might lop your head off."

"And now, there's no going back—so much to think about, so much to decide and we have so little time. This is going to hurt people close to us, at least some of those close to me. I don't know your people. You don't know mine. We don't really know a whole lot about each other when you think about it. So many things could go wrong."

"My people are gone except for Josh."

"Oh. I'm sorry."

"It's all right. I have friends, and they'll be happy for me. And you're right. No doubt that things will go wrong, but as long as you're with me, it'll work out—one way or another. No sense in worrying about it. It's worth the risk. Trust me."

As she dried him off, he took her into his arms and kissed her. "You know," he said, "a willingness to take the risk is the best we can hope for. But it's enough. What do you say?"

Emma held him close, unwilling to let the moment go. A sense of peace unfurled her brows and settled upon her face. When she pulled away to look up at him, her eyes shown with a beautiful light.

"Okay, so what're we going to do first?" he asked. "There are things I need to do here, and I guess you'll want to get back to the B & B for fresh clothes."

"I don't know about you, but I'm famished. Could we go down to that little café where we ate the other day and eat something before I go? Maybe we could come up with a plan of action from there?"

"Café Arles? Sure. It'll be nice to get out for some air and a bite to eat. Marti and Pris are going to be so surprised at my good news."

"You're not going to tell anyone yet—are you?"

"Why not?"

"Well, I don't know. It's just that it's so new. I mean—I don't know what I mean. What are you going to tell them?

"That we love each other."

Emma blushed at the thought of telling anyone how she felt about Alex. "Okay," she said. "Tell anyone you want to. Tell everyone that I love Alex Cowrie."

"Koury," he said and laughed. "K-O-U-R-Y. A Cowrie is a seashell."

"I knew that, Alex Koury—tell everyone that I love Alex Koury, and he loves me." She laughed. "God, how juvenile—I sound just like a love-struck teenager." She shook her head and laughed again.

Marti was opening the blinds at the front door of the Café Arles when they arrived. Alex and Emma made their way to a table in the back, along the wall, where they could talk. Marti gave them each a big hug when she came to take their orders. She was in a good mood, having just received a five-hundred dollar check in the mail and the best of show award from a photo competition.

"You know," she said, "I sent that photograph off a couple of months ago and completely forgot about it. I was just hoping to be accepted into the show; I never thought I'd win."

"The best things can happen to you," Alex said, "especially when you're not expecting them. You're going along one day, without a thought in the world, and then boom—your life's completely changed."

Emma smiled as he spoke.

Smiling back, he reached across the table and squeezed her hand.

"Well, I wouldn't say my life is changed all that much. The money's good, of course. Pris and I can certainly find a use for it, but I'm still waiting these tables . . . say, what is it with you two? You look like the cats that caught the canary." Marti's eyes squinted as she moved closer to peer at them.

They looked at each other—a couple of complete and utter innocents.

"Hmmm, I see what's going on here." Marti stepped back and crossed her arms beneath her bosom. "So, when's the   wedding?"

"Wedding?" Alex said. "Don't rush it. We haven't talked about anything like that yet."

She scrutinized Emma, who was wide-eyed— attempting to appear non-committal. Marti gave Emma a look that warned if she were to hurt Alex, she'd probably be tarred, feathered and run out of the Old Pueblo on a rail.

"That's all right, but I can tell by looking at you two that something's up. I've known you for a long time now Alex, and this is different. I know when you're on to something."

"You're absolutely right, Marti," Emma said. "We are on to something. We're not exactly sure what that is just yet, but we're working on it. Alex and I have de-cided—

well, not really decided, I guess . . . certain things somehow decide themselves—that we just want to be together and see where it goes."

For a moment, Marti just stared at her. Then she turned her head over her shoulder and yelled so Pris could hear in the kitchen. "Hey Pris, Alex has finally gone and done it. He's got himself a keeper."

Pris, a tall blue-eyed blonde who obviously spent time in a gym, came out of the kitchen behind the counter. "Oh yeah? And who's that? Oh, you. You were here with Alex the other day, weren't you? I remember—you're the one he took on that picnic. You rascal," she said to Alex, pulling him out of his chair to hug him. "And good for you, too," she said to Emma. "You better take care of this man, you hear. If you don't, you'll have to deal with me." Then laughing aloud she said, "I'm Pris by the way," and leaned across the table, sticking out her hand for Emma to shake.

"I'll do my best," Emma said, shaking Pris' hand that, to her dismay, gripped like a vise and was as hard as a rock.

"I have to get back to my stove, but it's nice to meet you," she said, looking Emma right in the eye.

Emma returned the gaze. "You, too," she said. After a moment of mutual appraisal, Pris nodded her head, turned and strode back to her kitchen.

"Me too," Marti said. She started to leave then turned back. "Oh, I forgot. What do you guys want for breakfast?"

"We'll eat whatever you bring us," Alex said, then quickly to Emma, "if that's all right with you?"

"That'll be just fine, as long as there's a big cup of coffee to go with it."

After the coffee arrived, they took time to savor it and the silence and all of the delicious aromas emanating from the kitchen. When the fruit bowl and buckwheat pancakes with real maple syrup arrived, they fell to it with the hunger of lovers who had previously been too enthralled to eat.

"So, where do we go from here?" Alex asked. "When do you absolutely have to be back in L.A.?" He finished the last of his pancakes.

"I've lost all track of time," Emma said. "So much has happened. What day is this, Tuesday? I can't believe it. Yesterday was so intense. It's going by so fast. I was scheduled to be at the B & B until Thursday. Then I was going to move downtown to be with Bob. We were supposed to spend this week together at the Mountain Shadows. Little did I know that all this was going to happen. Now, here I am with you. Who would believe it?"

She paused, put her fork down and wiped her lips. She looked at Alex who also stopped eating. "I don't think I can face Bob right now, here in Tucson. I should go home.

It'll be easier there. Which means, I have to get on my cell phone right away and get my ticket changed, or I might not be able to get a flight. I've put it off all week." She laughed. "And now I know why—so I could be with you. Oh my God, it's hard to believe that this is happening. It'll be a terrible shock for Beth. I'll have to pick her up and take her with me. She'll be upset to leave early. Heather won't like it either. She's her daddy's girl. What are we doing, Alex?"

"Just what we have to, that's all. Alex reached across the table and took Emma's hands. "Now that we've found each other, there's nothing else we can do, is there? I don't want to make light of it, but things'll work out, even for Bob and the girls. You'll see. Are you having second thoughts? Let me know now." He released her hands.

"Oh no, no second thoughts, no doubts about us, at least not yet." She took his hands into hers and kissed them, then blushed furiously when she realized she was in a public place. "But, it's frightening, nerve-wracking and exciting all at the same time—embarking on a new life."

"It's great, isn't it? What do you say we finish breakfast then go back to the studio and get things organized? I've got to make arrangements with Josh. If you leave tomorrow, so will I."

Emma kissed Alex's hand again, but this time she looked around defiantly to see if anyone was watching.

"Take whatever time you need. I'll be with Josh for at least the next week. While we're apart, we can stay in touch by phone."

"That works. Now, that just leaves the rest of the day."

"Aside from my laundry, there's nothing else I can think of except that I want to be with you as much as I can before tomorrow. Since you have to go back to the Mountain Shadows at some point today, why don't we plan on staying out there tonight? You can leave for Phoenix from there. It'll save you forty-five minutes driving time. Besides, I'd love to stay one night with you in the Hacienda; I may never get another chance."

Back at the studio, Emma called the airline and made the ticket exchange for her and Beth's departure from Phoenix at 3:25 P.M. the next day. Nervous, but thrilled and determined, she also called Bob:

"Look Sweets, I'm really swamped right now," he said.

"Can't we talk when I get there on Friday?"

"No, Bob. I'm coming home tomorrow, and I'm bringing Beth with me. I want you to pick us up at the airport."

"Cool your jets, Emma. Stay there, and we'll talk about whatever it is when I get there. Okay?"

"You're not listening. I said, We'll be there tomorrow."

"I told you, I'm over my head with these Collins accounts. I don't have the time just now."

"Then make time. We're arriving at 4:35 P.M., and you'd better be there."

"I don't see why you can't get a cab. You do it all the time."

"I told you, I have to talk to you."

"Why can't we talk later, after the conference?"

"Because we'll be talking when I get there tomorrow."

"What in the hell is the goddamn rush?"

"I'm not doing this over the phone. You're so damned hardheaded sometimes. Now meet us at the airport because, starting tomorrow, there are some things that need to change in our relationship."

"Well, fuck, Emma, this is pretty damned sudden!" The cell phone crackled with emotion. He struggled to reign in his anger and, after a moment, finally exhaled a long sigh—his breath settled into an even rhythm before he spoke. "Okay, okay. Now that you insist," he said, "I've known that you weren't exactly happy. Yeah, things have changed. I guess that I've been trying to ignore it."

"Look, Bob. We need to sit down and talk about this. I know you haven't been very happy either. I mean, now that I look back over the past couple of years, I can see that our lives have grown apart. But I don't want things to be ugly, and there are the girls to consider."

"Now that it's come to this, you're right. Our relationship hasn't been so hunky-dory for me either. I've had to make adjustments, certain accommodations. And I don't want to hurt the girls either."

The thought that he might have been unfaithful to her had never crossed her mind until just this moment—and because of the girls, she knew that he was going to be in her life for a good many years to come.

Meanwhile, Alex was busy putting his studio back into some semblance of order, having ignored the place to spend all of his time with Emma. He hated returning from a trip to chaos. His calls to Randy Whetstone and Josh went through without a hitch. An hour later, with everything done, Alex and Emma went for lunch at El Cocinero where he formally introduced Rosa, the little waitress who'd waited on Emma before. She was surprised that Rosa was a big admirer of Alex's work, until he explained that she was an art student at the University and had painted all the murals at the restaurant.

Back in the studio, Alex could overhear snatches of Emma's conversation with Beth who was too busy having fun to spend time speaking with her mother. They were on their way to the mall, and Emma's call was a true imposition. So Emma quickly told her they were leaving tomorrow and to be ready and packed to go, said her good-byes, and let her go before they could get in an argument over it all. She spoke with Colleen, instead.

"I hope you don't mind," Alex said as he came down from the loft. Emma had just hung up the phone. "It's kind of hard to not overhear with the acoustics in this place."

"Not a bit. I don't want any secrets between us. May as well start off with an open book."

"You didn't tell her about us."

"No sense going into all of that with them at this point. Apparently Bob had called, asking about Beth and wondering if they'd heard from me."

Alex and Emma looked at each other.

"What do you say we take off for the afternoon?" he said.

"Why not? I guess we're done here. I can't think; I'm so excited about everything."

"Let's do some drawing—take some sketchpads and charcoal down to the Mission. Have you ever seen it?"

"No, but maybe you could give me a lesson while we're there."

"You could probably give me one. I've been so busy with the murals that it's been some time since I did any real sketching. You have to keep in practice, just like scales on the piano, if you're going to be any good—you know, the old eye-hand coordination. Besides, they've recently finished a seven-year restoration on the Mission interior, and it's magnificent. You'll see."

"Are all your friends as easygoing as those I've already met?" Emma wanted to know later—apropos of nothing—as they were climbing into the truck for their trip to San Xavier.

"Now that you mention it, I guess so."

"You have other friends that I don't know about, I'm sure."

"Well, let's see. You know Mary and Steve, Marti and Pris, and I mentioned Randy Whetstone. Paul and Holly Ledbetter, artist-friends of mine, are nice people. You'll like them. Then, there's Broadway Jim who used to be a damn good painter, but drinks too much now and lives in a dumpster alcove in the alley behind the studio. Of course, there are all my girlfriends, but I didn't think you wanted to know about them."

"Ha! Aren't you the funny one? Never mind; we'll have that discussion another time. But everyone I've met, so far, seems so open and friendly."

"They're all just people, just my friends."

"Everyone needs friends." She smiled as she slid across the seat to sit closer to him, putting her hand on the inside of his thigh. "Are you my new best friend?" she asked in a sexy, deep-throated whisper in his ear.

"Always," he whispered back. "So buckle in there," he said aloud in his cowboy drawl. "I don't want to lose my new best friend, after I just found her."

They rode this way down I-19, all the way to San Xavier, whispering things to each other and laughing, with his arm around her shoulder and her hand squeezing his leg, feeling close and in love, as new lovers invariably do.

"Just leave the pads and things. We'll come back for them later. I want to show you inside," Alex said as they climbed out of the truck and headed across the dusty parking lot in front of the Mission.

"I didn't bring anything to cover my head."

"That's all right. It's not a problem."

"I don't want to insult anyone. You think it's okay for a couple of adulterers, like us, to grace the house of God with our sinful presence? According to some beliefs, we've been living in a dire state of sin since we met each other."

"If there were a Supreme Being, I don't think it would ever object to people showing their love for one another. What about you?"

"I think how one believes is a personal matter."

"Okay, hold it right here." He stopped directly in front of the church, twenty feet from the doors. "Now, look up there."

She looked where he pointed, first to one side of the façade and then to the opposite side.

"What do you see?"

"Well that, over there," she said, pointing, "looks like a mouse. And that, over there, is most definitely a cat, although it's a bit eroded."

"Right, nobody today knows why they're up there. The legend has it that when the cat finally catches the mouse all of creation will come to an end."

"I wouldn't be surprised if it did—especially for the mouse."

"Maybe life's just a deadly game of cat and mouse, since we're all doomed to die right from the start. One day, you're the cat; one day, you're the mouse. On the other hand, given enough time, this mud façade will eventually crumble into ruin, and the mouse will escape the cat; time could, theoretically, continue forever. They say time is a circle. If that's true, we could all end up back where we started. Just thoughts to consider as you pass through these portals. Come on," he said. They headed inside.

An hour later, Alex and Emma passed out of those same wooden portals into that special afternoon light that falls only in the Sonoran desert. They grabbed their pads and charcoal from the truck and climbed the hill to visit the Grotto of Our Lady, cut into the north face. They took a few moments to discuss the murals and artwork of the church as they climbed, passing between a couple of imperial bronze lions—snarling emblems of the Spanish crown—sitting on their dilapidated masonry pedestals at the top of the slope. Alex pointed north to the fields once irrigated year-round by the running water of the Santa Cruz River. "Today, the river runs only sporadically during the time of monsoon. Which is our rainy season, if you can call it that," he said. "We only get eleven inches a year, on the average."

Alex pointed to the northeast. "Tucson's the major reason for the drop in our water table, of course. It just sits there, sucking up the groundwater at a phenomenal rate. Subsidence of the basin is cracking up the buildings in the center of town. It got so bad they had to shut the central wells down. Now, our water comes all the way from the

261

Colorado River in a big concrete ditch. In the desert, who controls the water controls the power. I hate to see that unchecked growth sprawling all over the valley, especially in the foothills. But it's almost inevitable. Big money dictates—land developers, mines and agriculture decide who gets the precious resources and how they're used. In the fight, this fragile environ-ment gets the shaft. Sorry about that; I didn't mean to get so serious. You may as well know that I'm a bit of a saguaro hugger."

"Me too," Emma said and put her arm around his waist, pulling him close.

"I feel guilty for not taking a more active role, trying to save what we have left." He put his free arm around her shoulder. "The world has gotten considerably smaller in the past fifty years. Some of the most delicate areas are being destroyed—lost at a fantastic rate. There are way too many people; and that's the real problem, the one that underlies all the rest of our problems—and here I am sitting on my thumbs."

"Aren't we all?"

They stood, arms around each other, contemplating their past failures to act on their beliefs, and looked at Tucson pulsating under the sun.

He leaned down and kissed her, and they turned away from the city.

Along the road to the west of the Mission, the mortuary chapel, school, playground and graveyard bathed in the late afternoon sun. Across the valley, the adobe dwellings of the Tohono O'odham faded into the dusky haze amid the foothills of the Tucson Mountains. Following their shadows down the dusty gravel path, Emma and Alex circumnavigated the hill, arriving back where they started with the lions. Alex led Emma up to the rocky outcrop on top. For the next hour as the sun set they quietly sketched the scene before them. Once in a while, Emma asked for help, and Alex offered suggestions but no criticism about her progress. Occasionally, a curious tourist climbed up to look at their work.

"I don't know about you, but I'm getting parched," Alex said. "Have you had enough yet?"

"Can't we stay just a few minutes more? It's so beautiful here. The sun's almost gone, and this is the most incredible light. I know it's not very good,"—she was indicating her pad—"but it's been so long since I've done this. I'd forgotten what peace there is in just sitting and

Alex put his pad down and moved over to look at her drawing.

"You don't want to wear it out your first day, do you? You've got the rest of your life. Besides, that's done. Don't overwork it. You have talent."

"You think so?" she asked, smudging charcoal across her forehead while pushing a few stray curls out of her eye.

"Oh yes, I do. If your color sense is as mature as your eye for relationships, and if you give it the time it takes, you can become very accomplished."

Emma beamed. "Then, let's go. I'm thirsty and hungry too, now that I think about it." She gathered her stuff.

On the drive back, they stopped at a small Mexican café in South Tucson that served the best menudo in the Santa Cruz Valley. They had it with limes, chilies, cold beer and paper-thin flour tortillas. Back in the studio parking lot, just before Emma got into the Crown Vic and left for the Mountain Shadows, they kissed affectionately and agreed that Alex would join her as soon as he could.

He arrived at the B & B around eight with a big grin on his face, clean clothes on his body, and his toiletry bag under one arm. Emma greeted him at the door as if she hadn't seen him in years. He was thrilled to be with her. It was only his natural modesty in front of others that kept him from grabbing her up and flinging her around in a big embrace. When they told Mary their good news, she insisted that they all toast the new couple and had Steve open a bottle of champagne.

Later, Emma asked Alex to use the bathroom first so she could turn down the bed and make the room more comfortable for him. The Hacienda was glowing in the soft rich color of the murals when he returned. He'd painted them in another existence; a whole life had passed beyond him. His world had changed so radically since he had last been here that it could only be explained by the machinations of the stars. Studying the figures in the mural, he felt like he'd returned home from a long and arduous trip to be among friends that he missed.

Perhaps he was the one they've been waiting for, the one for whom they were making all of their preparations of welcome. He took off his clothes and lay across the bed to wait for Emma. Emma came back, several minutes later, dressed in her silk nightgown, the one he first saw her in. What she found was a thoroughly exhausted Alex, sleeping peace-fully, curled up with his head propped on his arm

"Well, some lover you are," she whispered as she crossed to the bed; she wanted a better look at his features. Standing there gazing down at him, she followed the sensual lines of his form across the muscles of his arm and shoulder, along his back and down the flank of his hip, thighs and ankles. She was compelled to pick up her sketchpad and charcoal. Turning away and looking behind her, she pulled the settee from the wall and sat down; she needed to see him more clearly. She rose to tilt the shade on the table lamp next to him. Moments later, she began drawing him with the soft black charcoal. "Oh yes," she whispered. "Some lover you are, Alex Koury. K-O-U-R-Y. You really are."

Chapter Thirteen

For the first time since Maggie can remember, she doesn't feel the customary happiness of being on the beach. Collaborating on their new project since an hour after dawn, she and Jack split up, having collected as many interesting samples as they can find. Jack takes them back to the truck while she continues to shoot. She works all the way up to the north end of the beach where the land juts into the water. She can only walk there when the tide is out, leaving the rocks exposed. Even then, she soaks her feet as the surf rolls in beneath the cliffs that stand crumbling like a broken wall against the sea.

Farther up on the rock and out of reach of the surf, Maggie sits down to remove her wet shoes and socks and change out her roll of film. As she rewinds her camera, she looks back the way she came to where she's been and what she's done. Jack has returned to the beach. He's working at his drawing board, perched upon a ledge of the cliff about six feet above the sand. Tying her laces together and stuffing her socks in her shoes, she slings them around her neck, recognizing that her unhappiness this morning—a morning that she should be ecstatic with their new beach book collaboration—stems from her recollection of their trip to the Virgin Islands.

Maggie had successfully tucked that little episode away into some deep recess in her mind until yesterday when Jack had dragged it, and its attendant pain, out into the open all over again. It was not a pleasant memory for her, even though her memory was not as sharp as it used to be. Jack had slipped out at two or three in the morning and didn't return for a couple of hours. She didn't know where he went, or what he did. She didn't want to know. She didn't want to speculate, though she had her suspicions. She knew it had something to do with Leila, that friend of Chris who had so blatantly flirted with Jack, but it was too painful to contemplate. His leaving like that, so surreptitiously in the dark of night, crushed and angered her. Maggie thought of it as the first of several occasions, over the years, when she fell out of love with Jack.

It was the very day that they were driving across the steamy interior of the island in search of a new beach to swim. They had stopped at a crossroads, right next to the carcass of a dead horse bloated and decomposing in the tropical heat. A thick carpet of flies, a buzzing, seething mass that crawled all over the rotting animal, had exploded into a billowing black cloud above it. The wave of stench that enveloped her was so putrid and the sound so ominous, Maggie thought she was going to puke in the car before Jack could drive away. All her memories of that trip were tainted and mingled in the odor of that decomposing animal, leaving a bitter taste in her mouth and a painful twinge in her heart.

Later that week, down at the Hotel Raleigh for an evening of frivolity, Jack, Maggie and Chris were drinking Rum Collins and eating the peanuts and chips off the bar, unable to afford dinner in such a swank dive. Although Maggie still harbored bad feelings over Jack's behavior, she was trying to get past the sordid affair. They were dancing with him, in turn, to the music of the steel drum band that played by the pool. Then suddenly, as if a squall had blown

267

up in rough seas, the Captain of the US submarine, Sea Wolf, and eight members of his crew showed up, having docked just that day after six months at sea. They were on liberty till one in the morning. Jack was outnumbered and escorted the only two young, good-looking women in the place. The men descended upon them like a flock of starving frigate birds. Jack didn't stand a chance.

Serves him right, she thought, as he sat there and watched them taking turns twirling her around the floor. Dancing close, she was not surprised when one of the sailors pulled her even closer and pushed his knee between her legs, wanting the feel of her crotch pressing on him as he twirled her round and round. She enjoyed the thrill of feeling attractive to these strange men. They were so drunk and boisterous that they threw everyone in the bar— except the members of the band and two older couples who had seen trouble brewing early and hurriedly escaped—into the pool.

The one other exception was the Captain. Apparently he ran a tight ship because no one dared risk his displeasure by tossing him into the pool. Not one to be slighted or left out of the fun, however, the Captain pretended that he was attempting to save Maggie from drowning and jumped into the pool beside her. He held her close, crushing her breasts against him. Turning her around, he placed his hand between her legs and lifted her up, by her bottom, above his head into Jack's arms. When Jack gave him a hand up, he let the good ol' Capt'n fall back in. He pretended it was a slip of wet hands, all in good fun. It wasn't so much fun later.

While dropping off one of the crew who had joined Chris for the evening, out at the end of the wharf where the ship was docked, Jack had to smack a drunken sailor in the face. The man was pushing in through the VW window, kissing Maggie and pawing her breasts as she unsuccessfully fought him off. After, when busy locking doors and rolling up windows, other returning sailors— drunk and excited by the fray, one of their own being so unceremoniously knocked to the deck—began to rock and bounce the little car. They threatened to topple it over the edge of the dock if the women didn't get out where they could be a little more sociable.

Jack put the car in reverse and backed over some-thing. Maggie thought she felt a bump. Fearful of the growing ugliness of the mob, he put it in first and drove quickly down the wharf. She felt no bump going forward. To this day, she didn't know what they ran over, if anything. They could still hear the men calling for them to come back when they rolled down the windows and cleared the gates at the end of the dock. They wanted to show Chris and Maggie a real good time. They also wanted to teach Jack some manners.

Back home, it was a difficult period for the young couple. Now that Maggie was married, she envied Chris her freedom, her own apartment, and living alone in such an exotic place. Harboring unrealistic expectations of marriage, having moved away from family and friends and feeling isolated, Maggie wondered if she hadn't made a mistake. Disillusioned and doubtful of Jack, she consulted an attorney about leaving him. She never told him how perilously close he came to divorce court. Maybe the only thing that saved him was the fact that Maggie hated, more than anything, to admit that she'd made a mistake. Failure was not acceptable when she was committed. And besides, it didn't help to have her mother waiting in the wings practicing her one line walk-on part in this little drama: "I told you so."

Rather than admit defeat, Maggie took the advice of her counsel and waited a couple of weeks to see if the situation would offer more hope. She'd maintained that position ever since; she was ready to walk out the door at a moment's notice if things weren't copacetic. It was the only way Maggie knew to keep from feeling trapped, her way to maintain independence and self-reliance. It was one reason she had continued to work most of her married life; she didn't want to be dependent on anyone, not even Jack.

Now, as she sat on the lichen-covered rock, she regretted her actions that night. She knew she must have hurt Jack deeply. There was no excuse for what she had done—that little fiasco with Leila notwithstanding. The sailors kept buying drinks, but the alcohol was no excuse. She'd wanted revenge straight out, to hurt him, punish him for what he did that night—not that she could've said so at the time. Only now, in retrospect, could she see how angry and hurt she had been, and how badly she had wanted to hurt him back. Maybe that's why, after the fact, when things were going sour at home and she realized that she'd fallen out of love, she couldn't bring herself to confront him about that night or leave him later on.

Her memories of their trip to St. Croix were full of mixed emotions. Until Jack had stirred them up, she had not remembered the anger and humiliation she'd felt—only the good things about their trip: the white sandy beaches, the smell of the rain forest, the laughter, the rhythms of steel drum music, Chris's friendship and the island with its fascinating history of slaves, sugar cane, rum and pirates.

Looking out upon the swelling waters, Maggie feels the weight of her thoughts and memories as they swim in and out of her consciousness. A morning mist shrouds the distant horizon, although the day is clear otherwise. The smell of life along the intertidal zone is redolent with rotting kelp and bladder wrack. Below, in between the rocks at her feet, in the small pools left by the errant tide are the periwinkles, acorn barnacles, limpets, anemones and mussels that she reads about in her field guide.

She wonders what it's like to be one of them—she can't imagine. It's all she can do to recognize the existence of her own improbable awareness. And yet, sensing that in some fundamental way she is one of them, she welcomes the strong affinity of this relationship. Aside from the obvious, just what are the true differences between them? For the moment, sitting on a rock at the edge of a little pool in the backwaters of the Milky Way galaxy, Maggie experiences a profound love for this place and its life, for the world, for Jack and even herself. It pushes hydraulically through her, like the blood in her arteries. The pressure heats her body clear down to the tips of its extremities. She may never again be as clear about anything in her life as she is right at this moment: Love is common to all things, no matter what form or shape they assume.

But it wasn't enough for Jack to unsettle her by uncorking her memories of the Virgin Islands yesterday, he also stirred her memories of their trip to Eugene, Oregon, where she came close to changing both of their lives forever. It was less than a year later that Jack was invited to interview for a position at the university. It was largely due to the ministrations of Rick Chapin, his best friend through grad school who did his Ph.D. work in Philosophy and Comparative Religion. Rick's main interest was Buddhism. Maggie found his lifestyle intriguing. He was soft-spoken while Jack was loud; reserved when Jack was forward; and as slow to burn as Jack was quick to anger.

Rick had convinced Jack that he'd like teaching there. It was a noted progressive school in the arts and offered Jack a chance for an interim appointment until he could find something better. It'd be great fun for the two friends to be reunited, even if it only lasted the year. Though he never liked to show emotion in the presence of another male, Jack was just as excited as Rick about the prospect of the two friends being together again.

At the time, Maggie found herself extremely attracted to Rick. Seeing him again after a year or so, she was surprised that she felt so close to him, never having considered him in that way before. She'd always felt comfortable with Rick; but there in Eugene, she saw him in a new and different light. The contrast was remarkable. Jack had always overshadowed him because Rick was so quiet.

But Rick seemed more grounded, more solid than Jack. He was so serious where Jack was always joking around. He seemed at peace with himself in a way Jack never did. He was a vegetarian and sat in meditation twice a day, every day. Jack couldn't sit still if his life depended on it. That type of discipline was never Jack's forte. Back then, he was always so rowdy—smoking, drinking, overeating, staying up all night—generally living life by throwing himself into it full steam ahead.

It was a quality that had attracted her before they were married; now she thinks differently about it. His courage and willingness to give himself over to new experiences are still qualities she admires, especially now that she's growing older and it's even harder to make changes in her own life. Although he's given up the rowdiness of his younger days, Jack still seems willing to take up new challenges and strike out for lands unknown. She is not so brave, she thinks, and sometimes feels a sense of shame at being so timid.

Having found herself out of love with Jack and alone with Rick several hours each day while Jack attended meetings, Maggie seriously considered testing the waters to see which way Rick would go if she nudged him a little bit. She fantasized going to bed with him—what it would be like to kiss, undress, and make love to him. She and Jack had sex often, but at that stage in their marriage, they were simply satisfying the needs of their bodies; there just didn't seem to be a lot of love involved. Maybe it would be different with Rick, with his slow deliberate manner and reticence, his sense of caring and understanding.

She watches the line of ships in the distance move slowly by, like the targets in a carnival shooting gallery, and remembers how much she had wanted Rick at the time.

Oregon was a dream. Shrouded in mist and rain, the sun never shined the whole time they were there. During their one sojourn over to the coast, in a little town called Florence, they ate an early-afternoon dinner of sausages, sauerkraut and beer in an old, German restaurant, a heavily weathered Swiss-style chalet perched high among the fir trees, facing the sea above the coastal highway.

Rick, with those sultry dark eyes, pale skin and black hair, had never overtly made a pass at her, although she felt sure he found her attractive and could fall in love with her, given half a chance. In fact, if anything, it was this possibility that was so exciting to her. His spiritual pursuits had made an impression on her, and Maggie found herself drawn to everything about him. Standing outside, beneath the dark green and white weathered awning, out of the cold drizzle, waiting while Jack used the bathroom and paid the bill, Maggie didn't know why she took such a risk. She stepped up close and kissed Rick a full, deep kiss, pressing her body against his with a passion that she'd not felt for Jack since before St. Croix.

Surprised, at first, Rick foundered before returning her kiss with equal ardor. She knew that he felt a strong attraction to her, having been alone together so much over the week. The last two days of their visit, there had been several times that Jack was away at the University when they could have set upon a whole new course in their lives. He was always ready and attentive to her. But Maggie, for one reason or another, chose not to turn away from Jack. She decided to stay with him, without any assurances that they could make it.

Rick had been mystified by her behavior—first hot, then cold. But he was understanding and listened while she talked about matters that weighed on her. She still had not come to terms with Jack's probable betrayal of her in the Virgin Islands. Rick advised her truthfully that he'd never known Jack to act that way before. With that little bit of hope, she turned back into a life that was uncertain at best. She could say now, with some pride, that it was a better life than she could've hoped for on that day as she stood there at the edge of the Pacific, between the two men, getting soaked in the cold rain as it blew down off the Bering Sea.

Sometimes she suffers a real stab of regret, but most days she's glad of her decision. The minor guilt she occasionally feels for desiring Rick is burdensome enough, and she doesn't like to consider how she'd be feeling if she'd slept with him. Still, she's never been with another man, sexually, and sometimes wonders what she's missed. Fyodor, for instance, is an attractive man, and she's sure that he finds her the same by the way he smiles at her. She can see it in his eyes. She wonders why she's drawn to these strange, dreamy artistic types.

For a few short moments, Maggie drifts off, day-dreaming a passionate sexual encounter with Fyodor in the back of his camper. She laughs at her mental picture of Jack, standing on the balcony of the apartment across Eden View, looking down and wondering what's going on inside as it creaks and squeaks, bouncing up and down like it's being buffeted and blown about by a gale-force wind.

Looking down into the pool between her feet, she notices, or rather her consciousness—that part of her mind not currently involved in fantasizing about sex with

Fyodor—notices what appears to be, strangely enough, a brain. Momentarily startled by such a ludicrous image of a brain sitting at the bottom of a tide pool, Maggie slides out of her daydream and hesitantly reaches down into the water and picks the thing up. She wonders how it got there. Its weight is astounding—not a brain, of course, but a rock that has the size, shape and appearance of one, or rather what, she thinks, a real one must look like. She's never before seen one, except in pictures. This rock looks very much like those pictures. Pleased by the thought that she's found a gift for Nick—a brain no less—she suddenly has the urge to show it to Jack.

An hour later, standing on the sand just below the ledge where he's drawing, she says, "Look at what I found," and holds the rock up for his inspection. "I finished off my film. Why don't we call it a day, go back to the room, eat something, and then come back down to hang out for the rest of the afternoon?"

"Sounds great to me," he groans as he gets up and stretches. "I'm tired anyway. I can't believe we're doing this—you know, actually working on our own book. You're going to like these sketches. I think we've got enough varieties and sample shells to work on back home. With your shots, we can probably call it quits. Let's figure it out in the room. Guess what?"

"What?"

"Working on these sketches has given me a great idea for a whole new series of paintings."

"Oh, yeah? And what would that be?"

"Just wait. You'll see."

"You're not going to tell me?"

"In due time, my love, in due time. I don't want to talk about it—yet. You know how things can get talked out, and lost, before they become reality."

"Then why did you bring it up?"

"To get you excited, why else? So, what is that? Looks like a brain."

Looking exasperated, Maggie pauses before speaking, "I found it for Nick. We didn't think to get him something for watching the house while we were gone, and we're leaving in the morning."

"We gave him some money before we left," Jack says as he hands down his board. He jumps from the ledge onto the sand next to her.

"I know, that was for groceries," she says, handing it to him. "I was thinking about getting him one of those big T-shirts from the surf-shop, but he'll like this, especially with his interest in consciousness studies and all the reading he's been doing about brains lately. I can't believe how much it looks like the real thing."

"Yeah, and now we can tell him that there's no excuse for his thoughtless behavior with a brain like this." He chuckles at his own stupid joke.

At the top of the ramp, they stop to speak with Mike and his parrot companion, Barnacle Bill—acquaintances they met at the pier on one of their previous trips. Mike seems pleased that Maggie remembers their names. He can't remember theirs, of course, meeting so many people as he does, with all of the attention Barnacle Bill draws. Barney got his name when he and Mike lived aboard a small sailing craft covered with barnacles. "It ultimately sank," Mike says, "not because of the barnacles, but because it was riddled with dry rot." Barney, as Maggie recalls, is a Yellow-crested Amazon.

As his species' name implies, Barney's head is covered by a cap of brilliant yellow feathers that taper off into iridescent, shimmering green plumage, the same color as the rain forest from which he comes. Short, fan-tailed and an intelligent bird as far as parrots go, Barney's perched on Mike's shoulder and, as usual, he holds forth on the nature of reality, reciting snatches of Shakespeare and the Beatles for which Mike rewards him with sunflower seeds. Barney would do anything within his power to earn those seeds. Although Barney has no idea of what he's talking about, he continues to expound vociferously at great length.

When Barney spies Maggie, he raises a leg—his command for Mike to put him on her shoulder. Bobbing his brilliant crown and dancing back-and-forth along her shoulder in a little two-step—some type of parrot protocol or mating ritual—Barney recites his profundities. Maggie can't make out most of what he's saying as the bird's speech is not very clear, except for one phrase—"All you need is love"—that he keeps repeating. When he tires of this and runs out of poetry, Barney cusses like a sailor and has, on occasion, been known to make unkind remarks about one's mother. Mike says that Barney generally prefers the company of men, something that Maggie can understand. He seems surprised, at a loss to explain Barney's attraction to Maggie. He chalks it up to the "birdbrain."

The interesting thing about their encounter with Barney and Mike is that, just the night before, Maggie dreamed that a wild African Grey flew down out of the trees, landed on her shoulder and whispered a secret message into her ear—a secret she wishes she could recollect.

In the dream, she was in a jungle in deepest Africa and dressed in a leopard skin, like Jane in the old blackand-white Tarzan movies with Johnny Weismuller. In fact, she had completely forgotten that she even had the dream, until just this moment when Barney hopped onto her shoulder and began to dance. What a coincidence, she thinks—life is definitely stranger than fiction.

Later, they stroll down to Mama-San's Noodle Emporium to pick up lunch. Back at the room, on the balcony, they can't stop looking out at the sea; they never

279

get enough of it. Her encounter that morning with Barnacle Bill, she recognizes, is something out of the ordinary. Aside from the fact that he's a marvelous creature and exhibits such odd, fascinating behavior, it's a change from her routine. It's not every day that she gets to touch a bird all the way from the rain forests of Brazil. Nevertheless, just this morning, there he was striding her shoulder, resplendent in his full array of yellow, green and gold feathers and his piercing gold eyes. Even though Maggie knows that Barnacle Bill was probably bred and raised in a bird factory in the United States and that such beauty could, with time and exposure, grow mundane and contemptuous with familiarity, she sees her struggle to stay alive in these terms. Without such beauty or the mysteries of existence to ponder, her life would be as dry as a mouthful of dust.

"Yeah and what are you so quiet about?" Jack says. "I thought you were hungry."

"I am. I was just thinking about Barnacle Bill."

"What about him?"

"You know, we take so many things for granted."

"Haven't we had this conversation already?"

"I suppose. Maybe it's one of those conversations we need to continue having."

"Maybe. Say, come on. Eat up. We've got to get out of here. I want to get back to the beach. This is our last day, and I don't want to spend it in this little room thinking about taking you for granted."

"Oh, slow down. I'm going to finish lunch. Have you had your, uh . . . you know?" She nods toward the bathroom.

"Do you mind? Let me finish lunch for God's sake. Besides, that's not something I'd ever take for granted. I might take you for granted, but I'd never take a good dump for granted."

"Jesus, Jack. Do you have to be so crude?"

"Hey! You brought it up. Besides, life is crude, my dear. Here we are, stuffing ourselves, shoveling it in one end and praying for it to come out easy on the other. Life's not passing us by; it's passing right through us. Don't eat those hot red peppers. You'll be sorry, tomorrow, if you do. Not even sixty yet and here we are, discussing all of our gross bodily functions just like we vowed that we'd never do. I guess . . . because that's just what old farts do, huh?—when they've taken everything else for granted. I hate to say this, but we, my dear little woman, have become our parents. A thorough but deadly discussion about your fibroids and my prostate is forthcoming. What can I say?—except, eat hearty, mate, for tomorrow we shall all be eaten."

"Well, what set you off? That's a terrible image."

"Not really. What that is is the mystery of life, my dear, the mystery of life."

Ten minutes later, they're crossing the parking lot headed for the beach.

"You know, I have a feeling things aren't going so well for Ruth Rayburn," Jack says. "David's car has been here all morning. Maybe she's already dead."

"Don't say that. You don't know, and you shouldn't say those kinds of things until you know something about it—one way or another."

For the moment, they speak no more about Ruth as they go on to the beach.

"I wonder what's happened to Fyodor?" Jack says.

"That camper of his looked vaguely forlorn when I saw it earlier this morning. It looked downright abandoned."

"You're right. I haven't seen him since the morning we discovered that he's a writer."

When they find a spot on the sand that they both like and can agree upon, they set their chairs in place and lay out their towels for the afternoon. Jack surprises Maggie by telling her that he feels the need to go for a walk. He usually invites her to go with him; this time, he asks her if she'd mind watching their stuff while he's gone. They always talk about things when they walk together; it's how they solve problems. It's a way they have of deepening and renewing their relationship that is, in part, what these trips to the beach are about. But sometimes he has a need to be alone, and Maggie understands.

Just moments after Jack leaves, the constant sound of water turning over on sand filters into her consciousness so completely as to become non-existent. The gulls crying overhead and the pelicans fishing out in the distance catch her attention for a moment. But then, like the light, the smells and the people, they slide—along with everything else—into the background of Maggie's mental landscape. And, as Jack becomes just a speck down the beach, she once again turns inward, to that little grain of irritation that has been chafing her mantle the whole time they've been here.

You can't take life's recriminations, worries and hassles too seriously. Ironically, she does, sometimes, take her life and all of its best things for granted—precisely at the very moment she's telling herself that she's not. It's all, she realizes, stuff and nonsense, an insidious diversion from the reality of her life. Jack and Nick and her grandson, Mark, are her life. Her photography is her passion, but her job and her friends at work are also important to her. Getting up in the morning and breathing fresh air. Feeling the warm sun on her back as she waters her garden before she goes to work. Reading a good book for a few stolen hours when she has the house to herself. Playing basketball with Mark at the park. Eating exotic fruit, sushi or chocolate eclairs. Listening to Live from the Met; singing with the soprano as she cleans house on Saturdays. And this trip, too, so full in so many ways that she couldn't begin to describe its complexity and richness, even if she had a hundred years, is her life. All of these things and so much more are her life. It's just a matter of seeing it—of keeping that fact in focus.

What may have been with Rick or Fyodor, or with any one of a dozen other men that she's found attractive over the years, is living some other life. It's some other multi-dimensional past or future that she's never really been a part of, except through these fantasies she indulges when she's dissatisfied or angry with Jack. It is, she understands, a waste of her energy—energy better spent on what really matters to her.

What is it about the ocean that makes her so reflective and brings her to this clear picture of herself and her reality? What is it that's always so clear over here, but then daily, little by little, is lost to the grind of her routine at home? Maybe she'll never know, maybe she doesn't need to. She turns away from the water to look down the beach. Jack is singularly emerging from the crowds of small figures that stand about or walk the shingle. He always appears so clearly in her vision—her future and her past coming toward her.

At that instant, with her eyes burning from the salt-spray breeze blowing gently in from the sea, she feels her love for him swell up in her chest. Catching a breath—as if for the moment her body had forgotten to breathe for her—she knows that she loves Jack more than she can say.

Without him, she wouldn't wish to go on with her life—not that she couldn't, but that she doesn't care to imagine it. She's so close to him, so much a part of him, she can feel his heart beating clear down the beach. She turns back to look at the ocean coming toward her and retreating, forward and back, in the rhythm of oceans and tides as it flows forward and back. She recognizes the rhythms of her own life in it. The mysterious and the commonplace coming forward and retreating, constantly changing places. The miraculous and the banal, first one, then the other, always changing, never still, always finding another position, another place to rest, another viewpoint, but momentary, just momentary, like time itself.

As Jack walks up, Maggie has the strange sensation that she's transparent to the world—invisible to everyone except Jack whose presence, sometimes, has this liberating effect on her. He says nothing and just stands there serenely looking, not at her, but out at the ocean, emulating her. After a time that could have been an eternity, and as if for no other reason but wishing to add his own voice to the resonance of the world around them, he says, "You know Mags, I love you."

"I know," she says. "I love you, too."

He sits down in the stumpy little beach chair next to her, reaches over and gently squeezes her shoulder; runs his hand down over her breast, across her belly and pubis to her thigh and lets it rest there. Silently, they watch a couple of herring gulls fight over an empty plastic sandwich bag that has floated by on the breeze.

They watch the pelicans and pipers, the kids and surfers as the sun burns the water into mist. Evaporating off the sea, columns of cloud roil up and dissipate into nothing as they float inland, overhead, bathing everything in beads of sweat as they go. The smell of coconut oil wafts across them mingled in the odors of burgers and beer and something sweeter. As the afternoon fades, they drift together in and out of time. They read, eat, sleep; and later, as the sun settles on the horizon and the day begins to cool, Maggie and Jack rouse themselves out of their sleepy afternoon lethargy. Their bodies bend and stretch, converting energy to matter and matter back into energy. Moving among the people all around, they are free, immersed in the moment, in this harmonious effervescence, true lovers and initiates to these happy rites of re-creation.

"Say, look over there," Jack says to Maggie sometime later, returning to their chairs. "Remember him? Remember the first time we saw him?"

"No, but I remember seeing him the last time we were over here. I wonder how old he is. The man looks so fragile, like he can hardly walk." Maggie rearranges their possessions on the sand between them.

"Yeah, I remember seeing him the first time we came. He's got to be eighty, if he's a day." Jack watches the man enter the water.

"I know. Look how long it takes him to get past the first small breakers. They almost knock him down. That water's got to be icy cold. I'm not going in." Maggie shivers just thinking about it.

"I think it's amazing that he's even out there at all. I wonder if that hump on his back, that stoop he has, is swimmer's hump or if it's scoleosis? Seems I read somewhere that some professional butterfly strokers get that from the long hours of practice."

"Sounds to me like something you would make up," she tells him, cocking an eyebrow in his direction.

"No, really, I'm serious," Jack swears, raising his palms out. "Look, there he goes. He dove right in. He looks like a sea lion out there. He sure can swim."

For several minutes, they watch him swimming the overhand crawl and then a breaststroke.

"He certainly looks different than when he's walking around out here on the beach," Maggie says. "He's so graceful and strong in the water, like a seal, the way he bobs in the surf with the sun reflecting off his skull like that." They just watch the man in silent admiration, until he returns.

"That was fast. He's already done. He used to swim longer and farther out beyond the surfers. At his age, I guess it's more dangerous than it used to be."

The man stands up in the surf and walks up onto the beach. He's moving slowly and appears tired.

"He's coming our way," Maggie says. "Why don't you say something to him? Ask him how cold the water is."

"I'm not going to do that."

"Go ahead, say something; he's coming right past us."

They watch as the old man approaches. Jack notices that the man's Adam's apple is bobbing furiously, and that his face lights up in sheer delight when he looks in Maggie's direction. Of course, Jack thinks, no wonder the guy's smiling so broadly. She's beaming at him, like she's just found her long-lost father.

"Hi. My name is Maggie, and this is my husband, Jack," she says as she steps up close, offering one hand and pointing at Jack with the other. "How's the water?"

"Well, the water's pretty cold today," he says. "I'm Clarence, by the way." He shakes their hands in turn. Though stoop-shouldered, he's still taller than Jack's six-foot two.

"You looked like you were having some fun out there," Maggie says.

"Oh yes, I enjoy swimming." He runs his large fingers around the top of his balding skull, wiping the water from the closely cropped fringe of hair at the sides and nape of his oddly shaped head.

"You've been coming to swim here a long time. We've noticed you before."

"Let's see. It's been about fifty, fifty-five years, I guess. I don't come every day like I used to—maybe one day out of every three now. I'm retired you know." He laughs, showing his big yellow teeth.

"If you don't mind our asking, would you tell us how old you are?"

"Not at all. I'm rather proud to say, actually. I'm eighty-four next fall."

"Well, you sure are a marvelous swimmer."

"Thank you, but I don't swim as well as I did years back. I get a little winded, and my old muscles tire out faster than they used to; but I have to keep going, you know?"

"Oh, don't I know it."

"There's no alternative that I can think of. Sit down too long and you can't get back up. Can't get up and you're a dead man is what I say. Do you folks live nearby?"

"Oh no, we're over from Tucson on a little vacation."

"Well, it's nice to make your acquaintance. Enjoy the beach and take care now. See you again, sometime." He nods his round head, makes a little wave with his hand and leaves them to watch as he makes his way back up the beach for his towel.

"Well, that was interesting," Maggie says to Jack. "How come you didn't say anything? I like the name Clarence."

"It's a great name. I've often thought I should've been named Clarence."

"You're not a Clarence. You're Jack."

"I know, but haven't you ever wanted to be someone else?"

"Since being married to you . . . on many occasions."

"Well, thanks a lot."

"You asked for it."

"Yeah, well anyway, I hope I'm still going that strong when I'm his age, if I live that long." And with that, he turns and walks quickly down toward the water.

"Are you going in?" Maggie yells at him.

"Just watch!" Jack runs toward the water. He doesn't stop running, until he's deep enough to plunge headfirst into the biggest wave of all and disappear from sight. When she sees him popping up at the surface, he begins to swim an incredible overhand crawl with correct breathing posture elevating his mouth out of the water, his arms moving in a fluid motion, executing each stroke flawlessly.

He'd started swimming a mile every other day at the spa when he went to work out, but she had no idea that he'd gotten this good. Just then, he stands straight up, and the water is only knee-deep, not deep enough for swimming. He's just pretending to swim. She can hear his laughter all the way back here—a real comedian, she thinks. He's waving and calling her to come out, and she can't resist joining him, even though the water's so cold.

Later, when the sun has finally slipped into the sea, they dry off, pack up and head back. Dropping their gear at the truck, they notice David's car still parked in the same place.

"Here, hold this, I won't be a minute." She gives Jack her purse and heads for David and Ruth's apartment.

"What are you going to do?" he calls after her.

"I'm going to find out how Ruth is and see if there's something I can do for the poor man."

"Wait!"

Maggie pauses and turns back to stare at Jack who just shrugs his shoulders and holds out his hands. "Okay, okay," he says.

She turns and continues to the door where she rings the bell. Jack and Maggie stare at one another, then at the cars around the lot, back out at the ocean and finally to the ground until there's a sound of shuffling feet coming from inside the apartment. Maggie lifts her shoulders, straightens the towel around her waist, and clasps her hands tight in front of her.

David Rayburn opens the door in his slippers and bathrobe. He scratches the stubble on his chin and looks at Maggie as if he'd never seen her before. "Yes, may I help you?"

"Well, Mr. Rayburn, I'm sorry to bother you, but I was just wondering how Ruth is doing."

"Oh yes—what time is it—did you say?"

"It's around seven, I think. I don't have a watch," she says, looking down at her wrist, although she's never owned one.

"Ruth died yesterday," he says rather matter-of-factly. "The cancer took her." He adjusts the oxygen ring where it fits into his nostrils.

"Oh, I'm so sorry to hear that," she says, indicating Jack who's standing out in the lot, looking off in the direction of the ocean. David doesn't seem to even register Jack's presence. "Is there anything we can do?"

"Oh no. No, thank you. Ruth's daughter, Nancy, by her first marriage is going to be here sometime tonight. They were never very close, you know . . . but that's very kind of you. Are you folks enjoying your stay at the beach?" He's looking right through Maggie as though she's transparent.

"Oh yes, we love it here . . . the beach and all."

He continues to stare at her, vacantly.

"We really love our apartment and hope to stay here again real soon . . . but I'm so sorry about Ruth. Are you sure there's nothing we can do?"

He looks on the verge of comprehension.

"We'd be more than happy to help anyway we can."

"Yes, thank you, but everything's being taken care of. I saw to the arrangements yesterday. I think my water's boiling on the stove. I'm making tea, you see. Will you excuse me?" He closes the door quickly but softly in Maggie's face.

"Poor man," Maggie says again as she rejoins Jack in the parking lot.

"Well, that was gruesome," Jack says as he returns Maggie's purse. "What did he say about Ruth again?"

"She's gone."

They leave the parking lot and cross the courtyard to their apartment. "I should've reminded him that we're leaving tomorrow," Maggie says. "I wonder if he'll be taking our keys, or if there'll be someone else. Didn't he tell us the company was sending someone down to help him with this place?"

"I think so."

"Well, it doesn't matter. Someone'll take care of it."

In their room, Maggie's in a strange mood and feeling chilled as she slips out of her wet suit. The events of the day and the news about Ruth have affected her; she feels the need to be closer to Jack. She crosses the room to where he's standing with his back to her, looking through the sliding glass door at the ocean that's disappearing from view, incrementally, under nightfall. He, too, seems unnaturally subdued. Naked and vulnerable, she puts her arms around him, fiercely hugging his back to her face. The warmth emanating from his body comforts her.

Surprised, but lightened at Maggie's touch, he puts his hands along her arms at his waist, acknowledging her need for him. He senses that she will be reassured he's there, that he exists. He continues to watch as the elements outside fade into the dark, like these shared tender moments of consciousness.

Standing silent, front to back, she feels his heart through his clothes, beating counterpoint to her own. She holds tight until their hearts are beating in sync. Turning away, she takes his hand and brings him to bed. She lies across the unmade sheets, one knee bent along the surface, the other pointing to the ceiling. She waits for him to remove his clothes. Though emotional, she appears unmoved as she, in turn, watches, first the shirt then his suit fall to the floor. Her hand presses down, rubbing twice across the cradle and then the saddle of her pelvis. She sits up and slides to the edge of the bed where she sucks him urgently, lustily into full tumescence—stopping only to say that he's salty.

He caresses her hair, releasing all of his anxiety, and slowly shifts synchronously into her rhythm. They touch each other as only long-time lovers can. He joins her on the bed. They're oblivious to the world, but for the surf, and listen only to the intimate sounds of desire. Her body arches like a bow as he pushes into her, coming over her in waves. They kiss—arced in the beautifully ludicrous pose of coitus—melding into each other, sharing in giving this pleasure, slow and joyous and intense.

They've learned each other over the years, inside-out, merging just like this. Holding on, they slip simply, inevitably—with his elbows above her shoulders—into the efflorescent climax that continues as long as they possess the power to sustain it. They hold it in abeyance, savoring it, improvising on the theme, until they've resolved every prickly issue between them and discovered by what true light they may come to know themselves, deep within the other's loving eye.

Wednesday

Chapter Fourteen

Alex woke peacefully with the remnants of a dream fading from his memory. Among the surreal and disjointed fragments, he remembered that he was alone, climbing among the rocks and sand at the edge of the sea, looking for something that was lost to his memory.

He was standing on a beach, in that sparse and seemingly lifeless intertidal zone where the desert slipped beneath the ocean, and there was nothing as far inland as his eyes could see except boojum trees. He was aware of a great swell spanning the horizon, but he didn't feel threatened by its size or the speed with which it grew. He simply thought it unusual that the waves at the beach were silent—that they didn't crash upon the rocks, but rather rushed in and about, filling the space around them. Inevitably, the swell washed over the land and pulled him deep into the sea.

He thought he would drown, so he held his breath and struggled against the force of the water, trying to reach the surface. But as he willed himself to swim with the swirling water and not against it, he was reassured that he belonged there. The salt didn't burn his eyes. Bubbles rose about him through the pale green water, and a beautiful blue light flickered down from above as in a Gothic cathedral.

He felt no discomfort in not breathing and left off worrying. He relished that he could stay under water without the necessity of breath for an eternity. In that half-waking state, before he completely emerged from the dream, it occurred to him that by some stupendous intervention of fate, magic or metamorphosis, he was transformed into a Great Blue Whale. He often dreamed of animals and reveled in this newfound sense of wildness— free to cruise the seven seas and plumb the blue depths. He woke up in the room with Emma gone.

He stretched, arching his back full-length in the bed, remembering as his dream faded away how Emma had cuddled close in the night, needing him to kiss and hold her and speak of his love for her. They whispered in the dark; their words penetrated each other's hearts. They made love slow and easy as if borne along on the swell of the deep. Her softness made him want to hold her; the taste of her skin was the taste of life itself. He could no longer live without the touch of her, like the oxygen in his lungs, or the sweet compelling fragrance of her presence.

Looking over at the clock on the table, he saw that it was ten past eight. Where was Emma? She'd have to leave by half-past eleven to make her plane in Phoenix, and he even earlier if he was going to make any distance before he slept that night, somewhere between there and Houston. She was not even gone yet, and he was already missing her.

He heard the music of her laughter in the other room where the two women were talking. Outside, the irritating noise of a car starting up, idling for a moment then pulling out over the noisy gravel of the drive, drowned out her sweet voice. Steve was leaving for the university, he thought. As he got out of bed, Alex noticed Emma's sketch pad lying on the settee that had been moved away from the wall. Thinking to look again at her rendering of the Mission, he opened it and discovered the portrait of a man sleeping. For an instant, he didn't know what to think; it didn't register as a picture of him. Then, just as abruptly, he recognized that she had sketched him while he slept.

His mouth fell open; he was amazed at what she'd captured of him. She had caught him—slack-jawed, clearly taken by his slumber—with a resolute faithfulness to his form, a veracity that even he, as a professional, would be hard pressed to accomplish in such simple, straightforward and economic strokes. The most compelling thing about it was what it revealed of her. In her quest to capture the light as it   washed across his form, she had revealed the complexity of her own emotions by drawing from herself an expression of the reality that she saw as Alex. Within the urgency of the line, the smudging, erasures and tone, her love so thoroughly suffused the page that the work could be seen, in some ways, as a self-portrait. Again, he heard the tintinnabulation of her laughter and decided to join the women in the dining room.

Emma was sitting in her robe, and Mary was in her corral clothes.

"Oh, there you are, sleepy head," Emma said.

"Morning. Alex," Mary said and smiled.

"And a very good morning to you two lovely ladies," he said. "You still keep that good mocha java in that thermos, Mary?" He walked around the table and proceeded to kiss Emma on the top of her head; she hugged him by the waist. He helped himself to coffee and sat next to Emma facing the Catalinas—stunning as always, beyond the French doors. The room was cozy with morning light and the tantalizing smells that Alex associated with women at ease around a dining room table.

"Is that my sketchpad?" Emma asked.

"I thought you might like to show your drawings to Mary."

"They're not that good, but I don't care if she wants to see them." She was somewhat embarrassed at being put on the spot, but pleased he felt they were good enough to show.

"I'd love to," Mary said.

Alex flipped open the cover and pushed the pad over to her. She took several moments to appreciate them before telling Emma how fine they were.

"They are exceptional, aren't they, especially since she hasn't done any drawing for some time," Alex said. "What do you think of that portrait? Looks just like me, wouldn't you say?"

"Not bad. But I think she's made you appear a little more handsome than you really are."

"Really," Alex said and grinned.

"Oh, not that you aren't handsome, mind. But we really can't blame her, now can we? Love is blind, is it not?"

Emma remained quiet through this little exchange, unspeakably happy to be sitting next to Alex, enjoying Mary's company on what was shaping up to be a miraculous day. She felt reborn.

"Look Emma," Mary said, turning to look at her. "I really like this drawing of the Mission. Do you think you could part with it for a small sum?"

"You're not serious. It's not that good."

"I want it," Mary said simply and smiled. Then, after a moment in which Emma didn't know what to say, Mary fixed her with a fierce stare. "I shall have it, if I have to steal it," she said.

"Well, okay . . . if you want it that bad," Emma said and laughed. "I can't take anything for it; I'm just flattered that you want it."

"Perfect. Now that that's settled, and since this is such a special occasion, how about if I make us all some of my fancy crepes with blueberries for breakfast?" She turned to Emma. "Could you eat some of those in lieu of payment?"

"Sounds good to me," Alex piped up before Emma could speak, knowing a good thing when he heard it.

When Mary left for the kitchen, Emma turned to Alex and took one of his hands in both of hers.

"Well, today's the day," he said.

"Yes, I know."

"We start our new lives—you going one way, me going another. Funny, huh? Going off in opposite directions, hoping to arrive at the same place at the same time, at some point in the future." They fell silent for several moments. Morning shadows were rapidly disappearing in the burgeoning sunlight. They could hear Mary rattling pans in the kitchen.

"A week ago, I could never have dreamed this. And now here we are. It boggles my mind."

"Love will do that to you. I haven't been myself since I first saw you, standing right over there in that nightgown. Your eyes were about this big." He drew a large circle in the air with his free hand.

"Oh? And when did you get the chance to notice my eyes?" She squeezed his hand and smiled. "I'm afraid I'll wake up tomorrow, and it'll all be a dream."

"Well, it's no dream and will get very real soon enough, when you see Bob."

"But my mind is settled about Bob; I'm more concerned about the girls."

"Are you sure? You have no way to know just how he's going to take this. It could get nasty. Divorce is never easy."

There it was, the word divorce. An idea, something ever dreaded that Emma never thought would be part of her life. She felt herself hardening to the fact that the life as she knew it was in for considerable change. "True, but whatever his reaction, I'll deal with it."

"I suppose. But now is not the time to be worrying about that either. You and I have so little time before you have to go." He took her by the hand and led her over to the French doors, so they could look out the windows. She put an arm around his waist. He put an arm over her shoulder. They stood this way for a long moment watching a couple of male Inca doves heatedly displaying for a seemingly disinterested female out in the dust beyond the patio.

"When are we going to see each other? I have my commission so soon," he says.

"If you spend time with Josh, then I'll spend time with Beth. I don't know if I can bear to be away from you that long, but Bob and I will have surely come to some basic agreement about who's living where by then. I'm pretty sure we'll be selling the house, unless he has an uncommon stroke of generosity and allows us to stay there. I just don't know how this will all play out. Perhaps it's time for me to get my own place. Maybe I should get a place where I can have my own studio." Again their conversation lapsed as they held each other near the windows and basked in the beauty of Sonora.

"In any case," Emma resumed, pulling away from him to see his face, "you have my cell number and can keep in touch with me, directly. If things change, and you can't reach me there or at the gallery, I'll leave word with Mary, here, and you can reach me through her. She knows everything from our discussions last night and this morning. You know, she told me the night before you were supposed to leave for Texas that she thought I was letting you slip through my fingers."

"Well, Mary"—who just came back from the kitchen, carrying a tray with bowls of blueberries, butter, whipped cream, honey and maple syrup—"knows what she's talking about—most of the time."

"Let us give you a hand," Emma said as she pulled Alex away from the view at the window.

After breakfast, they cleared away the dishes, and Mary excused herself to do some chores in the corrals, leaving them to themselves and the emotion that inevitably came with impending separation.

Emma took her things and went to the bathroom. She showered while Alex sat on the toilet lid in the steamy bathroom and told her about his upcoming mural project in Seattle. He described his dream of becoming a whale and how he thought it might, in some useful way, help him create the new work for the Aquarium. She told him about her favorite painting, Dream of the Great Blue, and they laughed at such a coincidence, wondering what it might mean for the future, if anything at all.

When she got out of the shower, he toweled her dry and kissed her neck just below the ear, only once, almost as though it were an inappropriate thing to do until they could get past the next few weeks of separation. He sat back down and watched, totally fascinated, as she put on her panties, bra and bathrobe. "Okay, enough," she said. "You've had your fun. Now, let me finish with my face and hair. You've seen the worst." She got him up, ushered him out and closed the door behind him.

"But I love watching you."

When she returned to the bedroom, with her hair fluffy dry and a pale blush on her cheeks, she found Alex standing at the window, looking out on the scrub desert. The room was silent for some moments before he spoke.

"Well, Em, I've got to hit the road. By the time I get back to the studio, shower, throw my bags in the truck and gas up, it'll be way past time. Josh is waiting for me. Anyway, I've got something for you in the truck." He turned back to where she'd begun to dress in her travel clothes.

She couldn't keep the tears from coming and just stood there as they fell. There had been something unbearably sad about the slope of his shoulder as he waited with his back turned at the window when she'd come into the room. Taking a tissue from the box on the night table, he crossed the room and handed it to her.

"We can do this with our hands tied behind our backs." He had a quaver in his voice.

She dabbed at the tears on her cheek and tried, nearly unsuccessfully, to slip into her shoes while leaning on his arm. "You bet," she whispered, her voice failing her as she moved into his arms where he held her tightly and kissed the top of her head.

"Nothing to it, you'll see. Then we'll be together."

"I know, but I just found you—now I'm going to miss you terribly."

"Look, they're not crying," he said, smiling and tilting his head, indicating the figures on the walls.

She pushed his arm and tried to smile.

"It's okay, Em. I'll be missing you too, even more. But it'll only be for a little while. When I finish the mural, we'll do whatever it takes to be together from then on. I love you, Emma. Don't ever forget it—promise?"

"Promise."

"Okay. It's time then."

She pulled him to her and kissed him fiercely, abandoning herself totally. He kissed her face then her mouth. She could taste the salt from her tears on his lips and, for an instant so brief that it hardly registered in her consciousness, she could taste the ocean. Finally, he stood back to look at her.

"Oh God, I must look a fright," she said, dabbing at her makeup.

"No. You're the most beautiful thing I've ever seen," he said, took his bag and led her from the room.

Mary was vigorously brushing one of the horses as Alex and Emma came out of the house and walked along the short path. She watched them cross the gravel drive to the truck where Alex reached in, took his golden bronze Buddha from the seat and gave it to Emma. They stood looking at each other for a long moment. Mary stopped brushing the horse and moved over to the corral gate. Alex hugged Emma, turned and waved to Mary, then climbed into the truck and started the motor. When Emma stepped back, Mary put her brushes down and joined her in the drive. Alex backed out slowly, changed gears and drove off.

Emma and Mary stood waving goodbye, watching the truck raise a cloud of dust in its wake as it gathered speed. Mary moved closer and put her arm around Emma's shoulder. Gripping each other tightly, they watched until the dust obscured their view. It billowed and blossomed up behind the truck, but not before they saw Alex raise his arm out of the window and make one grand, loving sweep towards Emma with his hand, the image of which would remain with Mary for years to come.

Chapter Fifteen

"Well, I can't believe it's really time to leave," Maggie says. "It seems like we just arrived. Did you ever tell me what time you have?"

More out of habit than having forgotten that he just did so, Jack looks again at his wrist and remembers, then tells her, what he already told her not two minutes before, that he left his watch on the table in the apartment. After a short walk along the beach, they stand elbow to elbow, leaning on the rail at the end of Crystal Pier, getting a last look at the ocean before they finally have to turn their backs to it and leave.

"And I can't believe this weather either," she says.

Unfortunately, he thinks, she's right about the weather. Mist mingled with rain blows steadily in from the sea and condenses into droplets on their faces; they occasionally wipe them away with a sleeve. Wearing their sweats and jackets against the unseasonable cold, they can't see any real distance—can hardly see the water directly below—much less the ocean or the ships passing with foghorns occasionally sounding out their invisible presence through the wall of fog that surrounds them— solid and white as Carrera marble. But that, of course, is simply an optical illusion of the sun, of the atmosphere and clouds, which play tricks on their senses. At times, in fact, depending on the changing density of the fog and the speed with which the wind is blowing, they can just barely make out their fingertips when holding them at arm's length.

With the weather as it is, Jack's not surprised that they have no company on the pier—except for an old raven that stands stoically on the corner rail, and periodically sticks out its neck to croak hoarsely in their direction.

"What do you make of that?" Maggie asks.

"I don't know. Caustic comments on our conversation, maybe. Complaints about hunger or just a general, disgruntled doomsday mongering, I can't say. But for some strange reason, it puts me in mind of the Old Testament prophets." Jack was astonished earlier in the week to discover ravens perched in crannies at the top of cliffs at the north end of the beach when he and Maggie began working on their picture book. "You know," he says, "in some Native American cultures of the northwest, ravens were worshipped as gods. In others, they were considered omens of evil tidings and lost time. They're predatory scavengers like us. I've never seen them here at the ocean before. I don't know why."

"Well, now that you mention time, I believe that that old bird over there is loitering here to make us think about just how well we've been spending our time."

"You could be right." They both fall silent in the mist.

Safely enclosed in this little pocket of otherworldly insulation, they feel distinctly absurd facing the prospect of returning to the hot glare of the desert sun and their humdrum routines in Tucson. Time, that true gold, that somehow during the week came to a complete halt and virtually ceased to exist for them, is now running out all too rapidly.

Jack catches a glimpse below, now and again, of what he tells Maggie is a sea lion that's popping in-and-out of the waves, hunting fish. At times, it turns out to be just a surfer trying to catch a wave in the fog instead.

"There it is," Jack yells as he jumps back from the rail and points off to his right. Maggie is too slow to see it before the fog again obscures her view.

"You're just kidding me, right?" she says and settles back into her place at the rail.

"No, really. It's a sea lion or something like that. Would I lie to you?"

From out of the blue, Maggie thinks about asking Jack if he slept with that girl in the Virgin Islands the night he slipped out in the dark, all those years ago. She knows he'd be unable to lie to her. But in that moment before uttering the words, she realizes that she already knows the answer to that question and, for whatever reason, it doesn't matter to her one stinking iota, not one jot, not any more.

"Look, there it is again," Jack yells and points as before. And this time, Maggie sees it too. Indeed, big as life, bobbing up and down in the water, looking up at them with its large moon-shaped eyes, it watches them just as closely as they watch it. For an instant, it looks human and Maggie feels an affinity for it that even if she were to think about it, she'd be unable to express. But then, just as silently as it appeared, it disappeared beneath the water without a ripple. Gone.

"See, I told you, didn't I? Wasn't that something?"

Maggie realizes her heart rate has climbed. The sea lion's presence has quickened her imagination. She's never before seen a sea lion in the wild, so close in its natural habitat, swimming free on its own. The experience has made her unreasonably happy. She wonders what it would be like to be a whale or to encounter a group of whales at sea and makes a mental note to go whale watching with Jack when they come back.

They went to Sea World and watched the Killer Whale show when they first started coming to San Diego. In fact, they'd stayed right where they sat the first time in order to keep their good seats—just beyond splash range—and watched the show three times in a row. Jack just couldn't get over the sight of Shamu, beached on a platform with his full length and girth out of the water. It was an amazing sight to behold, but Maggie thought that it would be even more incredible to see one of them, or better yet a whole pod of them, out in the open waters where they roamed the ocean freely. Yes, that would be the real thing. They never returned to Sea World. It made Maggie sad and Jack grouchy to see such lovely animals in captivity, doing tricks, the cruelty of it all.

"You know Mags, I dread leaving. Every time I come here, it gets harder to go home. Now, I go home and I'm ready to return in a week. I feel like I already need another vacation."

"It's just our age," she says. "It's hard to get up the steam to go in the first place. Then, it's hard to get up the steam to return. And when you do, you just don't want to move again. Who knows, maybe feeling like you need a vacation will eventually become permanent, something you can't alleviate, no matter how far or how often you go."

"I'd hate to think that. Anyway, this time we're taking something back with us—our beach book. I've got all kinds of ideas about what to do when I get back in the studio. It makes going home more exciting." He stands away from the rail and squares his shoulders.

"I guess, but we've got to make plans to come back here sooner. I shot eight rolls of film. Considering that I only get one or two good prints per roll, I need to shoot a lot more."

"The sooner you go over to digital, the better. Be so much easier."

"Yeah, I know. I have to, eventually, can't get the film and chemicals anymore anyway. I just really love the old black and white process. . . . Want to buy me a new camera?"

"I think it's clearing a bit," he says, looking up at the sky. "I saw a patch of blue through the clouds for just a moment. Actually, it was the most beautiful shade of ultramarine violet. Yeah . . . so do the research and buy it yourself."

"I will. . . . Just watch me."

"Listen to you, getting all feisty and taking charge."

". . . It stopped raining. Must be about time we started   back." She steps away from the rail.

Jack faces inland, which is just barely discernible as a dim silhouette through the fog.

"You know," he says, "looking at the land with all of those houses and palm trees sticking up with the people in the patchy fog, it seems as though we're going back to a far different world than the one we came from just a week ago."

"It does, doesn't it? Who knows? Maybe it will be different this time, especially if we decide to think about it that way. I know I feel different for some reason. What about you?"

"Me too. Strange, isn't it?"

"I hate to say it, but we better get started. We don't want them charging us for overstaying our time."

"You're right. Time is running out. Ruth Rayburn's time ran out. You know, I really didn't mean to imply to her that I wanted her job." He leans back against the rail on his elbows.

"I know that."

"I don't think she knew it."

"Oh, I'd say she did." Maggie turns to look at him. "She was just sick and tired of people, like us, coming in all excited about being on the beach—the very same beach that she could no longer enjoy because of her age or her illness or her job or maybe even because of her marriage. Maybe it was just something she took for granted. Who knows?"

"I suppose if we live long enough, we'll reach that stage sooner or later, you know, when we're better off dead." He stands away from the rail and looks south where the fog is still obscuring the view.

"There you go again, being negative. You really shouldn't talk that way."

"I'm not being negative. It's the truth." He turns back to her. "You might not like to face it, but there it is, and you can't keep ignoring it. Sooner or later, we all get it in the end."

"Well, the way you go on about it, one would think you were afraid of dying," she says, crossing her arms as she smiles up at him.

"I'm not afraid of dying. Under the right circumstances, I'd welcome it. There are some things in life it would be better to bypass, like living with Alzheimer's, maybe; or puking my guts out because of chemo treatments; not being able to feed or bathe myself, not to mention the unbearable pain that comes with it." He crosses his arms and smiles right back down at her. Just like that they lapse into a momentary silence. "Then again, who really knows until you're actually on your death bed?"

Abruptly, Maggie turns and walks back down the pier towards the shore. "Are you coming?" she calls over her shoulder as she goes.

"Well, I've got to tell you, the weather's clearing," he says after her. "I just saw another patch of blue sky, and I think the sun's trying to burst through those clouds above us to the east." He catches up to her.

"None too soon for me. I hate to leave the ocean in such a gloomy mood."

"Well, don't. Besides, thirty minutes from now and twenty miles inland, there won't be a cloud in the sky; it'll be ninety-five degrees. Just think, Mags, we're like new creatures crawling out of the sea, headed inland beyond the shore; within a day, we'll evolve into desert rats. Imagine, from the ocean to the desert in seven short hours—more like four billion years give or take a hundred mil or so. We're evolving, Mags. Can't you feel it? Time passes so fast. Before you know it, we're going to be entirely new beings. It just occurs to me that we could talk about our beach book while we're on the road. We could work out the whole structure. I still can't believe that we're going to do it."

"I don't know why. We are doing it. We're going to keep on doing it as long as we need to."

"I don't know either. For some reason, I always thought that book of mine would be fiction."

Below them, the water is slapping itself on the beach in waves beneath the pier. Maggie moves to the rail to look north along the waterline, reluctant to leave so soon. Jack, who has walked a few steps past, comes back and joins her there. The fog has lifted sufficiently to make out the cliff line where it curves into the water and turns north to La Jolla. They stand for several minutes, once again, looking silently along the beach.

"There aren't many people out today," Jack says. "You can count them on two hands."

"What do you expect in this weather? C'mon, let's go," Maggie says, unable to put it off any longer.

They walk slowly to admire the pier's white clapboard cottages with their blue shutters, flower boxes, and shingled hip roofs stained white by the guano of perching gulls, huddled there against the weather. Maggie always says she wants to stay in one, to be lulled to sleep by the sound of waves gently washing the beach. Jack always says it would probably keep her up all night peeing with that water crashing so relentlessly on the beach, directly beneath them. They always say they're going to stay in one of them, some day, but they never do. Maybe next time.

Back on the boardwalk, Maggie's tempted to buy a fresh hot cinnamon roll at the shop that makes them all day long. Ever since they started coming to the beach, she has thought about eating one. She always declines for fear the anticipation she enjoys will be destroyed by the reality. Although the fresh baked smell of the cinnamon, caramel and butter makes her mouth water, she recognizes that it would probably never be as good as her idea of it.

Farther down the boardwalk, they spy a couple of young lovers. The teenage girl is sitting on the top rail of the sea wall with her back to the sea and her arms around his neck. The boy stands between her legs with his hands about her waist. Kissing languidly, they occasionally part to laugh at something whispered between them, reminding Maggie of another couple they passed that first afternoon they arrived.

Totally oblivious, this young couple shares the same indifference to the world experienced by all true lovers. Their attentions are completely focused upon the only objects of their devotion and on nothing else but each other. Maggie senses something broader than such single-minded clarity—something deeper than knowing that nothing else in all of existence is more important than her lover. At present, however, nothing she can think of is more illuminating, compelling or revealing than the light of love focused through the lens of desire. And maybe there's no other time in life as right, as necessary or as simple as that time of being the one and only object of someone's total devotion.

Leaving the boardwalk and trailing back north along the sand, they pass directly in front of a young dark-haired woman who's looking out to sea so intensely that she doesn't notice them as they go by. She wears a shawl wrapped firmly beneath her chin. Maggie wants to stop and look at her more closely, but doesn't wish to intrude on her reveries.

"That's the woman I told you about, the one with eyes like mine," Maggie whispers as if the woman might overhear them speaking about her. "Remember? It was that day the weather was so bad. I can tell just by the way she's standing. I've got this same sad feeling that I had the first time I saw her."

"How do you know she's sad?" Jack whispers to Maggie, even though they're beyond earshot. "What if she just likes to look at the ocean in the fog, like us?"

"I don't know. Call it women's intuition, but I just know. She's waiting for someone. Maybe she's in love with someone lost at sea."

"You sure are a romantic. Sounds like you've been reading one of those Gothic bodice rippers with the square-jawed heroes and fainting heroines."

"You know I don't read that fluff."

"I didn't say you did. But you're right, she does look mournful."

"Yes, mournful maybe, but I sense she has more strength than we think. There's a mystery about her. I want to empathize with her, but I can't."

Jack doesn't know what to say. Back on top of the cliff where Eden View dead-ends at the sidewalk, they cross the street, heading for the apartment. Maggie's the first to notice that Fyodor's truck is gone.

"Well, I wondered how long he was going to stay," Jack says. "I really am surprised he didn't get towed away. They would've hauled me in for sure."

"How do you know he didn't get towed away?"

Chapter Sixteen

Later that morning, with the sun bearing down, Emma left for Phoenix, hugging and kissing Steve and Mary, waving goodbye through a torrent of tears as she drove off in the big Crown Vic, leaving her own whirlwind of dust behind her. She had not expected this rain of emotion. Collecting a surly Beth from Aunt Colleen's, they headed for Sky Harbor airport. For Emma, the hour-long flight from Phoenix was tense and fraught with apprehension about getting home and facing Bob.

On the approach to landing at LAX, their plane experienced some minor turbulence from a somewhat unusual storm passing through the L.A. basin. She recalled that it had been an unusual stormy, misty day when she and Beth left for the B & B just a week earlier, and noted that the sunny days of Arizona were already gone, fading into the past, just memories. Would she ever see the sun again?

Bob had originally agreed to pick them up at the airport, but was not there when they arrived; they were forced to take a cab home. It wasn't the first time he'd stood her up. She remembered how he had skipped out on the week at the Mountain Shadows before the coming conference. He'd been showing a definite lack of consideration for her for some time. When she called his cell number from the airport to find out where he was and why he wasn't there, he didn't respond. Alex had warned her that Bob might not be as willing to accept things as Emma had hoped.

When they arrived at home, there was a note in Bob's scrawl on the dining room table. It was just like Bob to write: "Sorry, something came up and I couldn't make it. I'll be late." She tried his cellphone again and was this time sent directly to his message service. Beth had already stomped off upstairs to her room. "Get busy, Emma, before you have a seizure," she told herself, livid with Bob. "Beth, unpack all the dirty clothes from your trip and drop them down the chute. I'll start a wash," she yelled up to Beth.

"Come and do it yourself. I'm too tired," Beth whined.

"You come down here right now, young lady. . . . And don't make me come up there.". . . "Well. . . . Come on. Where are you?"

"Okay. Okay." Beth tromped half-way down the stairs and stopped, refusing to completely relinquish her newly acquired sense of autonomy.

Emma moved closer to Beth in order to speak without having to raise her voice. "Do you want to spend the rest of your life grounded in your bedroom?"

". . . No."

"If you're going to grow up to be your own woman, then you and I are going to have to be better friends for the time being. And we certainly don't need to inflict any more grief on each other than we already have . . . Don't you agree?"

". . . Yes."

"Okay, then. Now go on up there and do as I say."

Beth paused and looked at Emma. She'd felt something in her mother's voice, something she hadn't felt or heard since she was just a young girl. Though it puzzled her, it was also reassuring and she accepted this new resolve that vibrated between them bringing a sense of peace in its wake.

Emma watched Beth climb the stairs until she'd gone from view. She knew Beth was probably exhausted, but she was worn-out as well; and if anything, she was going to get a lot more worn-out before her life returned to anything like normal. But now, here she was back in her old life; the familiar, the rut, the daily grind, the stress and difficulty with Bob—almost as if she had never left it in the first place. But was she back, really? There has been nothing normal about her world for the past week. Alex had come into her life and if she had any say in the matter, he was never leaving. But . . . .

Emma could hear Beth's clothes dropping down the laundry chute. She went into the laundry room, separated the clothes and started her wash. She returned to her bags, sitting just inside the front door, and took them upstairs to her bedroom. She changed out of her linen travel suit and put on something comfortable. She unpacked the soiled clothes from her trip, dropped them down the chute and went into the bathroom to freshen up. Who was this woman staring back at her from the mirror? She had the same eyes, tired though they were, the same hair, the same cheekbones. She ran a warm wash cloth around her face and began to have thoughts around the idea of moving into her own place where she could have her own studio.

But first things first, she thought, and turned back to her bedroom to unpack the rest of her clothes. This loss, this failure with Bob was going to be a lot harder than she had imagined while being with Alex. It was not just the money. And it had not all been for the girls. She had loved this house; they had struggled to acquire it, and here she was harboring the idea of calmly walking away, moving out into a place where she could have a studio of her own. What had once been at or near the center of her life had become in some ways a prison. As much as she had loved this house, it was now just a reminder of the life unlived, of the life she lost and what might have been had she followed her heart into painting. How indulgent could she be? Be a painter? Count your blessings, her mother would say, Thank God, Bob had come along to save you from such a fate. "Oh, Mom."

She hung the Johhny Was and the Fitigues back on hangers and put them in the closet where they belonged; and they did belong here, Emma felt, even more than she did, she could argue. This room, what had once been her domain was like the satin box where she kept her jewelry. Baubles, fine things and she appreciated, maybe even loved them, but they no longer felt necessary to her life. On the other hand, what was necessary was authenticity; such a funny word, she thought, authenticity and a sense of purpose. What purpose? Purpose in painting? Were there not goals to accomplish? Was there no new life to be found and lived?—to recapture that which she had lost? Come on, Emma, get real. It all seemed so real when she talked to Alex. She could feel the day catching up to her, surpassing her, overwhelming her. What's with all the tears, she thought.

Stunned, Emma took several Kleenex from the box on her bedside table, turned and went downstairs into the living room. Finally stopping the tears, she poured herself two fingers of her favorite Scotch at the liquor cabinet and sat down to look at her most recent painting purchase, the one she and Bob previously fought over, 'Dream of the Great Blue' by Jack Lawrence. It never failed to raise her spirits.

Of course, nobody needs an $18,000 painting. It can't save your life. You can't eat it or breathe it or drink it and it costs a lot of money, while there are people going hungry around the world. The fact of her privilege, of her good fortune in a world populated with people just getting by day to day, with virtually nothing, does not go unconsidered. It's not fair, never will be; so she gave to her charities, not as much, maybe, but considerable. At least Bob never quibbled over that. But it was just the irritating fact that Bob would've bought that painting himself if he had wanted it, and not batted an eye over it, that gets her. Paintings, like music or books, symbolized to her all the finer elements that life offered to elevate one's spirit, one's mind and one's intention to be a better human being. To Emma, it was the difference between living and existing; it was nothing to Bob.

But without Bob none of this would've ever been possible. Can she do this to him? Can she just cast reason aside and jump off a metaphorical cliff in the belief that doing so will bring her a more meaningful authentic, and therefore a better, existence? Would being a painter be a better existence? Would setting up her own studio where she could get on with the discoveries that awaited her in her quest to become a painter, make her life more meaningful, more authentic? She realizes that she doesn't know the answer to those questions. Maybe she needs to think about things a little longer. Not be so hasty, so ready to toss it all off for a chimera, a possibility, a dream. Could she turn her back on her home, on all the years of struggle it took her and Bob to make it all happen? Nineteen years. Can you just walk away this easy, Emma? Can you live an illusion?

Apparently she had fallen asleep in the chair because she found herself waking up when she heard the key to the front door. It was after ten by the watch on her wrist. She had slept hard and remembered the clothes she'd left in the washer. She wondered if Beth had eaten anything, if she had gone to bed. She stood up as Bob walked into the living room, dropped his case in a chair walked over and poured himself a drink. Neither one spoke until he turned around to face her.

"Well?" he said. "I'm here. You want to talk? What's so urgent that you had to keep calling when you knew I was so tied up?"

"What if one of the girls had been hurt and had to go to the hospital, and I couldn't reach you?"

"That really what you wanted to talk about?"

"Are you still going to your conference tomorrow?"

"My flight's at eleven."

"Will you want breakfast here?"

"No. In fact I'm not staying here tonight. I've got a room at the LAX Hyatt. I just came by for some things I'll need on the trip. It'll just be easier than trying to get out of here in the morning. So where are we?"

"Where do you think, Bob?"

"Up shit's creek?"

"More or less."

"That all you got to say about it?"

"What do you want me to say about it? I'd tell you everything, if I could find the words and knew where to start. Things have not been good between us for some time."

"You think?"

"No need to be flip."

"You're right, things have not been good. Now what's this revelation about changing our relationship that you couldn't talk about over the phone while you were in Tucson?"

"I want to be a painter."

"A what?"

"An artist."

"Go right ahead. What's stopping you? I've never stood in your way, when you really wanted to do something."

"I know."

"Why you'd want to do something like that is beyond me. But if that'll solve your problems go for it." He finished his drink and poured himself another. Emma picked up her glass from the side table where she had left it, and held it out for him to pour. "It's Scotch," he said.

"Good."

"Look Emma, get to the point. I haven't got all night. I have to try and get a little sleep at the Hyatt before tomorrow."

"I met a man and I want to pursue a relationship with him."

"Yeah. I figured it was something like that. Did you fuck him?" He just looked at her. "Yeah, you fucked him alright. So what's next? You want me to move out, I suppose. Doesn't matter, anyway."

"What do you mean it doesn't matter?"

"It just means that I'm really fed up with all this crap, Emma. So do what you need to do, until I get back from the conference. I knew this was coming; I've been thinking about this since we talked, couldn't put it out of my mind. This is really the shits, Emma."

"Yes it is, and it's not something I wanted to happen. But it has, and we have to deal with it." Emma knew right then that there would be no saving their marriage. It was written all over Bob's face. For a second she couldn't find a breath. Until that very moment the possibility they would stay together had always existed, even if it was nothing more than a possibility. . . . "So what should I tell the girls in the meantime?" she finally managed to utter.

"Nothing. At least, not until I get back on Monday."

"Beth has already guessed pretty much everything. She's not stupid. I had to tell her some things; I didn't want to outright lie to her."

"Have you talked to Heather?"

"No and I don't think we should mention anything to her, until she gets back from Europe. No sense spoiling her time over there. What can she do about anything anyway? Besides, Beth is enough to deal with as it is." There was a break in their conversation before Emma continued: "Have you been seeing someone?"

There was a long moment of silence from Bob. "We can talk about all this when I get back from Arizona."

"From what you said the last time we talked on the phone, I got that impression."

Another long moment of silence.

"You're not denying it."

"No. I'm not. As I said before, our relationship hasn't been all that fulfilling for me either. And I've made certain accommodations of my own. I've been seeing someone for the past year. So, we'll talk about it on Monday."

Emma couldn't stop the tears filling her eyes.

"Stop blubbering . . . I suppose you and Beth should remain in the house, until we decide what we're doing."

"That's generous of you."

"Don't get used to it. Fact of the matter is, since you've more or less decided to take us down this rocky road on your own, we'll have all sorts of legal matters to resolve between now and a final divorce decree if and when that comes, including who gets custody of Beth. I don't want this to get nasty, but I'll probably call an attorney tomorrow and he, undoubtedly, won't be as generous or as nice as I am. I suggest you do likewise. I'll see you Monday afternoon." He put his empty glass on the liquor cabinet, grabbed his bag and went upstairs.

Emma poured herself a final Scotch, shut off the lights in the living room and followed Bob upstairs to help him pack for his trip. . . .

"Hi, Em. It's Alex."

"I know, darling. Where are you?"

"Still in Houston, and I'm really missing you.

Here, I want you to say hello to someone."

She hears Alex cupping the receiver and coaxing Josh to take the phone.

"I guess he's a little too shy right at the moment. I think he wants to meet you in person first."

"It's okay. Tell him I'm looking forward to meeting him too. I miss you so much, Alex. When are you coming?"

"We'll be there in another week and a half. We're going to the Gulf. Josh wants to get his fishing line wet, and I want to do a little sailing. I don't get many opportunities for that in Tucson. If things work out with his mom, I'd like to bring Josh with me to L. A. for a short time, before I go on to Seattle.

"Yes, by all means bring him with you. We're excited to meet him. They're only young once. He needs you. Until then, I could use a little more time alone with Beth—we're ironing out some ground rules at this end. But it'll be fun."

"If you're sure?"

"I'm sure. Beth doesn't like to show enthusiasm over anything, but I can tell she's interested to meet you both."

"How has she taken the news?"

"Surprisingly well, I think. As I said, though, she's testing me all the time. I think she and Heather sensed more about what was going on around here in the past year than I did. Apparently, Bob's been seeing another woman. He came right out and admitted as much after I pressed him on it. Actually, I think it's been a relief to get it all off his chest. He isn't really the kind to be sneaking around with another woman. Does that sound silly and naïve on my part?"

"Not at all. So, what's Beth doing?"

"When we returned from Scottsdale and after her father left, we spent time together, and I answered her questions as truthfully as I could. She went into a funk, and has been working me over with the silent treatment for the best part of a week. Then it was acting out, the occasional outburst, one drama after another, always taking up for her father. I know things always take longer to straighten out than you might imagine. I'm not taking it personally."

"He is her father after all, and you've been together for some years. It'll take time for the wounds to heal."

"Yes. Beth is resilient and, I think, accepts that we're doing what we have to do. With time to adjust, I doubt we'll do her much damage in the long run. If she's terribly unhappy, she's hiding it extremely well. I know she's accomplished at hiding her feelings, but without forcing the issue, I'll keep an eye on her. We'll see. I love my girls. I'll do what I have to, to make it right with them."

"What about Heather?"

"We've decided not to tell her anything until she returns. We all agreed, even Bob. There's no reason to spoil her trip. Asking Beth to keep this secret has made her feel very grown up about it all."

"Sounds like things are progressing better than they might have."

"Not really. Bob and I have both retained lawyers and are fighting over what to do about the house, among other things, like alimony and who owns what. But I don't want to talk about that now."

He paused a moment and listened for her breath along the line. "Well, Josh is jumping around like a frog, itching to hit the road. I guess, I have to go. I'll call you tomorrow. I love you."

"I love you, too. Bye. Call soon."

When they could finally bring themselves to hang up the phone, Emma called Gen and asked for an extended time off to make her final decision about becoming a partner. Gen said to take whatever time she needed.

Emma could hardly wait to find her own place and set up her studio. She spent several days looking and found a small two bedroom L.A. cottage with a garage in back that with a little work would make a brilliant studio, closer to the art community downtown and made an offer on it. They refused her offer, she countered and they finally accepted after two days more. Everything went into Escrow for the next two months, an eternity to Emma.

Meanwhile, for Emma undeterred, the small, unused bedroom on the north side of the house with the soft light was perfect. She spent hundreds of dollars on materials and dove right in, like a kid with new toys. She hung a large mirror and began her personal odyssey with a self-portrait. "Who is this plucky woman of the whirlwind?" She laughed at herself. "Wherefore that smile, that confident countenance?" Such silliness, she thought, to be this overwhelmed by joy and circumstance.

She shamelessly bribed a reluctant Beth to pose for her, until she would sit no longer. Emma was possessed and lost herself for hours, working on sketches and drawings of everything around her, tacking them to the wall beside her first sketch of Alex, to study. With each, she saw growth and accomplishment, and her life seemed to open out before her, thrilling her with its promise.

The Buddha sat on a small table in the corner, next to her easel, where she set fresh cut sprays of gardenia and scarlet crepe myrtle from her garden—to paint still life from them. In a short time, she was more serene there than in any other place she could think of. For the first time in her life, she could see how she might begin to grow a little strange. Enraptured by the process of creativity and self-discovery, she became silent, hermetic and oblivious to the happenings of the outside world. There was so much more to do, and so much less to talk about. The essence of studio life was a heady thing. And Bob always found a way to mess it up, to intrude on her solitude and work, with his demands for her attention to some detail or other in a legal document. But she missed Alex.

After his sojourn to the Texas coast with Josh, Alex called Emma to let her know that the Aquarium had changed the schedule for the mural dates and had moved Alex's time forward; he had to drop Josh in Houston with his mother and immediately go straight to Seattle from Houston. They would not be able to visit as planned.

Instead, Josh's mom promised Josh a trip to Seattle for his dad's opening.

During his first month in Seattle, Alex wouldn't allow Emma to visit, explaining that the project had expanded in scope, that he was consumed by it and needed to remain focused, at least until it resettled itself into final form. He asked that Emma not visit during the second month as well. It was just that the project was nearing completion and, as badly as he wanted to be with her, he needed to keep at it—alone.

"You, of all people, should understand that," he said. "I know you've been working in your own studio. You don't like interruption, do you? Right now, I'm up to my neck in this work, and I'm just not my own man."

"I do understand. But don't you want me to come?"

"Oh yes. I do. I do. That's the funny part; I do want you to come, but then I would never finish and leave here, and we would never be together in L.A. Besides, I want to keep this work a surprise for you . . . until it's done."

So until close to the end of the second month, they talked every night on the phone, like a couple of teenagers. Sometimes, when they were too fatigued, they only spoke several minutes—those words all lovers need to hear, savoring the sound of the other's voice.

One night, Alex didn't call as arranged. When he didn't call the next evening or the following morning, she began to worry about him. He had never failed to do anything that he'd told her he would. Later that morning when she'd very nearly decided to telephone him, she received a call from Mary O'Brien. Emma had spoken to her just the week before, thanking her for her note and the invitation to the open house at the Mountain Shadows. Emma knew the moment she heard Mary's voice that something was terribly wrong.

"What is it, Mary? Tell me."

"Emma, I'm so sorry."

Feeling her legs grow weak, Emma sank to the arm of an old wing-backed chair in her studio. "What is it Mary? Is it Steve? Alex?"

"He went sailing. I talked with Dr. Williams . . ."

"What are you saying?"

"Alex went sailing; there was a storm, and he didn't return."

"No, that's not right."

"They're still searching for him."

"That can't be right," she said.

"I'm so stunned, Emma, I don't know what else to say. You know how he loved to sail. He used to tell me how much he looked forward to this trip and the sailing he was going to do. I can't believe that he's gone."

An icy calm took possession of Emma. "There must be some mistake," she said. "This can't be true. Tell me again, Mary—who did you speak to?"

"I spoke with Dr. Williams, the Director at the Aquarium. Is there anything I can do?"

Shaking in disbelief, she thanked Mary as best she could and hung up. Fumbling through her cellphone contacts, she found the number and called her travel agent. Within ten minutes, she had confirmed a seat on a plane bound for Seattle before dinnertime. She called Bob on his cell phone and arranged to leave Beth with him. She called Beth at a friend's house and told her that her father was picking her up in an hour, to stay with him for the next day or so. When Beth wanted to know what was happening, Emma said that she'd explain it all when she returned.

Googling the number from the internet, she called the Aquarium and, unable to discuss Alex over the phone, made arrangements to meet Dr. Williams there later in the evening. She went to the liquor cabinet in the living room and poured herself a large Canadian whiskey. Sitting across from her painting, Dream of the Great Blue, she tried to regain control of her shaking body. Time had a painfully slow way of dragging, dissipating and dissolving into the ether; it was two hours later when Emma returned the glass to the bar, went upstairs to the bedroom and packed a small carry-on bag.

She arrived after dark, called Dr. Williams and grabbed a cab straight from the airport to the Aquarium—closed to the public after hours. It was raining. Dr. Williams, a trim, fit older man with a weathered leathery complexion and white hair waited for her inside the lobby and let her in. He was solicitous and empathetic of her situation. He led her past the mural, but in her state of shock, Emma was too numb to notice.

In his office, they spoke of Alex for half an hour. Emma gave Dr. Williams all of the information he needed to contact Josh and his mother. She also learned the facts of Alex's disappearance as far as they were known. Two days earlier, in the morning, Alex had told Dr. Ford, the Aquarium's Curator of Marine Mammals with whom he'd become friendly, that he was having a hard time completing several passages in the mural and felt that he needed a little time off to clear his head. He decided to take the day and go sailing.

Later that afternoon, an unexpected squall blew up, bringing strong winds and rain. There had been no previous warning; coming out of nowhere, it was one of those unpredictable aberrations of the capricious weather. Dr. Ford remembered that Alex was out alone and gave the alarm.

When it became apparent that Alex was lost, they went through his rooms and personal belongings for information about his family, found the packet of invitations to the Mountain Shadows open house, and called Mary. Search and Rescue were still searching, although after this much time the chance of finding Alex alive was virtually non-existent. As customary, they would continue to search for a week.

Sensing that Emma was not only emotionally devastated but exhausted as well, Dr. Williams asked about her plans for staying in Seattle. When she told him that she hadn't thought about it, he graciously offered to let her stay in one of the Aquarium's guest apartments. Impulsively, Emma asked to stay in Alex's quarters instead. He gave her the key, took her bags and escorted her there.

Walking about the rooms, touching his things, picking them up and putting them down in different places, gathering his clothes together—for what she didn't know—she couldn't cry, not even when she picked up his sketch book and found his drawings of her. Emma hadn't cried for Alex—not from the moment she first talked with Mary, in the airport, on the plane or throughout the time she was with Dr. Williams.

It was not until she slipped into her nightgown and dropped across the bed, putting her head on his pillow where she could smell the faint animal odor of him, that his total and incontrovertible absence enveloped her like a cloud. She wept for him with deep body-wracking sobs, and lamented throughout the night, crying herself out—finally accepting the harsh truth. Alex was gone, had been taken from her without reprieve.

The next day, Emma stood alone on the beach, not far from the Aquarium, looking out at the sea, like a ghost in the mist. For three days, fog and intermittent rain blew inland over her; but in her grief, cloaked around her like the shawl wrapped tightly about her shoulders, Emma didn't feel it. When she was too tired to stand and watch the ceaseless waves, she sat on the wet shingle, oblivious to the damp cold, and waited. She didn't think to eat or drink while she waited, or, if she did, she didn't bother. She kept to her lonely vigil every day. When it was too dark to see her hand beyond her nose, she reluctantly returned to his rooms where on the last night she slept peacefully—a sleep as deep as the ocean itself.

Early the next morning, the Coast Guard called off the search, and there was nothing left for her to do but pack her bag and return home. Meeting one final time with Dr. Williams—who had kept a vigil of his own throughout the previous days, watching her from his office window—she thanked him for his kindness. As he escorted her out through the lobby, they stopped to look at the mural.

They looked unhurriedly at the unfinished work.

"What's to become of it? Now, it will never be complete," Emma said.

"Well, the committee has not yet convened. Undoubtedly, they'll get around to it very soon," he said. "I'm thinking, though, since the mural is so far along, we should leave it as it is. It's quite beautiful. I'll be making some strong recommendations to keep it as a memorial to Alex. I have my reasons for this, not all of which are altruistic, and not the least of which is that it's already a favorite with our visitors. There's a faction on the committee who'll fight it, of course, but, not to be immodest, I do wield some authority, not only with the committee, but with our board of directors as well. So, I'm confident that we shall prevail in the end."

"That would be wonderful, Dr. Williams. It is incomplete in places, I know; but you're right, it's very far along and not in the least indecipherable. It shows an incredible strength, love and energy." She began to look more carefully at the mural and saw, over to the right, a small figure—a mermaid. "I didn't know this painting was supposed to have fantasy elements in it." She walked over to get closer to the image.

"Well, that's correct; the original plan was for this mural to be a straightforward depiction of the creatures of the oceans. But Alex convinced us to enlarge the scope of the work. He wanted to explore the mythologies that have grown up around the sea, to capture that sense of awe that the marine world has always evoked. Of course, that meant using images from books like the Odyssey, Moby Dick and the Bible. Oddly enough, being stodgy old bureaucrats and adverse to change as we are, the committee embraced these ideas. It was a complete surprise to me that he was able to convince such hard-shelled old sea turtles to expand their visions. Our group, as you may imagine, is very conservative."

"Alex could be very persuasive," she said.

"Somehow, he did it; and I'm very sorry that this painting won't be finished as Alex had envisioned, not only because it's so fine, but also because I had grown very fond of him. Would you like to sit for a moment?" He led her to a long bench in the middle of the lobby where they could view the entire mural.

"I know what you mean. I grew very fond of him as well."

"I'm a scientist, Ms. Brighton," he said as he sat beside her. "I work with the ocean and its creatures every day. But old as I am, I'd begun to take it all for granted. Listening to Alex talk about his love for the ocean and watching him create this painting has re-ignited in me the feelings I'd lost and helped me to see it fresh again."

"Alex had that way about him. He had such depth of perception and love for the sea. We had spoken of it, and of what he wanted to accomplish here, before he left L.A. He was thrilled and honored to be chosen to paint this mural." Emma took a handkerchief from her purse just to hold; she felt the need to touch something. "He wanted to help educate all those who saw it, especially the children who he hoped to inspire toward a life of environmental consciousness and preservation—something he felt guilty not pursuing himself."

"I know. We had spoken of it also." As he said this, something in the mural caught his eye. "Well, well, what's this?" He stood and walked over to get a closer look. He removed his glasses, cleaned them with a tissue that he took from his pocket and put them back on. "Well, I'll be . . . now that I look closer, I can see why you were so familiar to me at first. The mermaid—" he looked at Emma, then the mural, then back again—"that's either a portrait of you, or I'm a Tridacna Gigas."

Emma had recognized the likeness, herself, but for some reason had not wanted to draw attention to it. Finding nothing to contribute further to his statement, she stood, thanked him again, shook his hand firmly, said goodbye and walked out of the lobby. She passed through the short line of people waiting anxiously to get inside, out of the rain. At the street, the cab that she'd called earlier was waiting for her.

Looking out the car window, through the mid-morning drizzle, at a city she was unfamiliar with, Emma felt as if she'd been transported to another dimension, to a world beyond her comprehension—a sad, lonely place without love. But in her mind's eye, she could still see the mural, and she knew that as long as the mural existed, Alex wouldn't be forgotten. He would always be with her.

The thought that he'd changed her life, that without him she would never have known what it meant to love so passionately, lifted her spirit as she rode along through this alien landscape. Then, too, there was her studio and work waiting for her—just the thought of it raised her spirit even more. The reality of her short experience of him, of his love and help in her self-discovery, made her grateful. She felt herself a new self, traveling forward into a whole new and undetermined existence. There were butterflies in her stomach, and she had an urge to bite her nails. She looked out at the rain, instead.

There's no going back, Emma, she thought. Looking down at the paint stains on the hands in her lap and listening to the rain, she remembered the first image that she had sketched of Alex, still pinned to her studio wall. She felt the charcoal on her fingers and saw her brushes next to the easel by the paints where she'd left them ready for her to take them up again. His bronze Buddha, too, sat on the table in the corner next to the wilted iris—her still life, what the French call nature morte—this flower taken before its time, cut prematurely from its stem in the fullness of its bloom.

. . . And going

Heading east, out of town, past turnoffs for Julian and Jacumba, they crest the divide, going down once again through boulder, rock and pebble into the Mojave. The road straightens out as they pass between worlds from mountains to shifting sands at seventy miles per hour into Imperial Valley. Giant corporate farms, stretching for miles across the land of agribusiness, pump millions of acre-feet of ground water over plowed desert soil that sits just below sea level. This was once the bottom of an ocean. Jack doesn't believe in agribusiness—especially farm subsidies for the big conglomerates that are wiping out the family farmers—although he does love cheap produce prices when he shops for groceries.

"You know," Maggie says to Jack who has been quiet for some time. "I was just thinking."

"Me too," he says, putting aside his negative thoughts on corporate farming perks and practices. "You want to know what I was thinking about?"

"Oh, I know what you were thinking about," she says and grins. You were thinking you wanted me to move over there next to you and rub your leg." True to the script, it's not as if they haven't done this before.

"Well, yeah, that too," he says as she slides across the seat and buckles herself in the center, next to him, "but I was thinking that when we finish this coffee-table book, I'm going to use those images and maybe some of your photographs to do that series of paintings that I was telling you about. I can already see the first piece in my head. I'll call it, The Big Blue Dream or The Great Big Blue Dream, you know, something catchy like that."

"Dream of the Great Blue? You like that?"

"You got it. That's it; I like it."

"Sounds like you have your work cut out for you. Think you'll live that long?"

"Doesn't matter; I'll die trying. This trip has got me all fired up. I feel a certain . . . something I haven't felt for a while. But, never mind, I don't want to talk it to death. What were you thinking about? You were just about to rub my leg. I didn't mean to interrupt you."

Maggie looked puzzled. "Oh, well—I was just recalling that young woman we saw at the beach. I can't get her out of my mind. Just imagine, what's the worst thing that could happen to you? What if she lost her one true love to the sea? How does she go on? How would we do it?" She looks at him, waiting for an answer. "Well?"

He just smiles at her.

"Answer me, and quit that," she says, pushing his hand off her thigh, where he was sliding up the hem of her dress.

"C'mon, forget about her. We've got this beautiful road all to ourselves, a long way to go and the whole afternoon in front of us. Might as well sneak in a little fun— here, just feel this," he says, sitting up taller behind the wheel, loosening the bind at his crotch.

"Jack Lawrence, you dog—it's so big . . . ."

acknowledgements

It's a cliché, certainly, though nonetheless true—no one writes a good novel alone. This is especially so with this one. Thank you Ian, my son, for always encouraging me. You are a beautiful soul with a gentle tongue, sharp pencils and even sharper eyes. Tim Trithart, you were steadfast and challenging, those nights over cake and coffee, as you showed me the many errors of my iniquitous literary ways.

Special thanks also to Anne Tyler for Muriel; to Richard Russo for Sully—who always knows the exact and deadliest point of insertion as well as the required degree of twist; to Richard Ford for Frank, Rock Springs, and the ducks—elsewhere on a Mississippi lake in the mist at dusk; and to Barbara Kingsolver for that voice (shudder) that calls me back to my old Kentucky home and grates me raw with memory.

To the rest of you—and you know who you are—I will thank you as I can, when I see you next.

Don West—Tucson, AZ 8/22/19